ZERO MARGINAL VALUE

JASON COLE

Today is About...

Second Edition

This edition published in 2024 by Today is About

ISBN 978-1-7398384-6-1

Printed in England

Today is About, 3rd floor, 86-90 Paul Street, London, EC2A 4NE

today-is-about.co.uk

To my mother, Nancy, who taught me the value of art.
To my father, Jeff, who taught me to dream.
To my partner, Jeanne, who taught me love.

ZERO MARGINAL VALUE

CONTENTS

1

THE JOB

LIAM LEANED back against the cool cement block wall as the sun crept over the top of the building. A bead of sweat ran down his forehead and crept to his eye. He blinked it away, as he shoved a silver shopping back behind one of the dumpsters. He wished again that the gray narrow alley filled with garbage but no active cameras, wasn't the only place they could find to start the job.

"Keema, we need to get started or I'm going to look like a wet cat," he whispered. "And, ironically, the coffee is getting cold."

"Almost time. We should get peak traffic flow in a few minutes," she said. Their tactical communication system picked up the slightest whisper, and transducers embedded behind his ears fed her voice directly into his skull. No one could overhear their conversations.

Squinting into the harsh morning light, he could just make out their little quadcopter drone high over the office park across the street. He knew she was watching through its eyes. Keema was his second brain, one he readily admitted was smarter than his first. She had an incredible ability to integrate the fire hose of incoming data from the drone, local communications, and network traffic. Having her along freed him to focus on the physical mission.

"Looks good. Get started now," she said.

"Starting my checklist," Liam replied. He stretched his arms out. The thin silver wires tattooed into his skin to form his bodynet tingled slightly as they reached full power. As the sensors in his fingers pulsed their test patterns, he did a quick scan. The stream of automated system checks flowed across his specs, a set of smart contact lenses that functioned as his heads-up display. As the messages scrolled by, he rolled his neck, flexed his jaw and blew out a few deep breaths, trying to ease the tension creeping up the side of his head.

He pushed himself off the wall and glanced down the alley. The stink of rotting garbage from the battered green dumpsters burned his nostrils.

"Come on… Let's go. The smell is going to kill me," he said.

"Oh no, you must endure a mildly unpleasant smell before making a boatload of money. You poor thing."

Liam pressed his lips together, trying not to laugh out loud. "Touché," he whispered. He refocused on system checks and re-running the plan in his mind.

"Dammit!" An error message flashed in the upper right side of his vision. "Hey, Keema, the dragonfly control module isn't loading," he hissed. If Denver hadn't gone so badly, he could have afforded the latest upgrade.

"You don't need the dragonflies today. They aren't in the mission brief," Keema said.

"The mission brief is never perfect. I'm always better when I have all my tools," he countered. "What if the map isn't completely accurate, or they have more security patrols than we think?"

He flexed his jaw again, trying to fight the tension creeping through his body. They had spent weeks building contacts, analyzing networks and understanding the security. Now they were ready. One mistake and he would miss his payday and dent his reputation. A surge of acid burned the back of his throat.

"You need to calm down, Liam."

"I *need* to nail this. If I can't bring this home, I'm out on the streets. You better hit me so I can focus."

"If you think so."

The medi-patch implanted under his armpit clicked, releasing a dose of beta-blocker. Cool relief surged through his body. His throat finally relaxed. He rubbed his hands as the blood flowed back into his fingers.

"Thanks. Much better. Better living through chemistry," he said.

"I worry about you," Keema sighed.

"I know. That's why I gave you control of the kit. I'd probably dope myself into a stupor. Then neither of us would get paid."

"That's exactly why I worry. We'll talk about it later. It's time to go."

Liam picked up two takeout coffee cups off the lid of the dumpster, then made his way down the alley.

"Watch the puddles, you can't smell like you've been hanging out in a garbage filled alley," Keema said.

Liam grunted his response and carefully picked his way to the street.

He came to the corner and scanned the road. A little after peak morning rush hour on a weekday in an office complex outside of San Jose. The sidewalks were empty.

"Five seconds, then go," Keema told him. Two G-Cabs rolled by, then the street was empty.

Liam shuffled down the street to avoid sloshing the coffee. Then he crossed the deserted parking lot of the three story NewReal, Inc research park. Four years ago, the parking lot would have been full. Now, everyone commuted in self-driving G-Cabs, rented by the mile. Liam would have taken one himself, but G-Cabs were hard to fool. To defeat the cab's facial recognition, he would need a complete fake identity. He had burned his last one in Denver and building that kind of ID cost more than this job was going to pay.

So, he trudged across the empty asphalt, his khakis sticking to his legs. His fake NewReal employee badge slapped against his thigh as he approached the front door. "Slow down about twenty percent," Keema whispered to him. She put up a cadence meter in his left contact and he slowed to match it.

His change in pace allowed two G-Cabs to pull up between him and the lobby door. They rolled to a stop. When his cadence meter quickened. Liam scurried behind the cars as the passenger doors opened. An overweight, balding man in his fifties got out of the second car. He waved his badge at the lobby door card reader. It opened with a click and swung open. With hands full of coffee cups, Liam scurried behind him into the chilled air of the glass lobby. The lobby was a security air lock, an empty space between two bulletproof glass walls. Employees needed to badge in and out at both sets of doors. His fake badge wasn't in the internal database. So, he brought coffee.

A woman in her late twenties, with thick dark hair and fashionable octagonal glasses, sat at the receptionist desk in the middle of the lobby. She narrowed her eyes at him. Liam thrust his hip out to show her his badge, lifting one of the cups to his mouth as if he were going to hold it with his teeth. The fingerprint prosthetics he wore were slippery. He had to double clutch to avoid dropping the cup.

"Hold on, sir," the receptionist said, walking toward him. Liam stopped. He lowered the cup, squeezing it to spill a little on the front of his T-shirt.

"Aw damn," he said.

"Don't worry, no one will notice," she said. "I don't recognize you. Are you new?"

"I'm from the San Francisco office. I'm supposed to meet Jim Cornwall to interview for his team. I'm really hoping to transfer over," he said with a weak smile. "I even stopped to get him coffee."

She gave him a little sympathetic smile. Liam shrugged and raised his eyebrows. Her phone rang. "Well, good luck," she said, turning to her desk to answer it.

"Thanks!" Liam said. He hesitated. The employees he had been hoping to tailgate had gone through.

"Thirty seconds until the next arrival," Keema said. A countdown timer floated off to one side. He walked over to the receptionist's desk.

"Yes, Mrs. Killian. I'll make sure lunch is ready for you and your team next week," she said. Liam put one of the coffees on her desk. He pointed at the box of tissues on her desk. She nodded at him. He grabbed one.

"Sure thing, Mrs. Killian. I can look for a time the following week as well," said the receptionist.

He watched the final seconds tick away as he carefully dabbed at the spot on his shirt. He tried to hide his impatience.

A G-Cab pulled up outside, unloading another employee. Liam mouthed a thank you to the receptionist. She nodded and gave him a wave without looking. He could hear the shrill voice in her headset and winced. Picking up the coffee, he turned to follow the man who had just entered the lobby. Seeing Liam, he held the door open for him. He nodded his thanks and walked into the building.

"Mrs. Killian is a hard ass," he muttered.

"I know... but if I didn't demand the best, we wouldn't be the best, would we?" Keema said. "Okay. That was the easy part. You have ten minutes max before the building realizes you don't belong."

"Yes, ma'am," he muttered. The building AI looked for patterns of behavior in its occupants. He had to engage in an approved activity it recognized, otherwise it would trigger an alert and security would investigate.

He walked through the small entrance lobby with stairs up to the second floor on both sides. In front of Liam was a large food court. There was a long line at the stimulants counter, and a few people eating breakfast as they began their workday. Liam headed up the stairway to the landing connecting the two wings of the building. He closed in behind a skinny man in his thirties as he swiped his badge to the office suite beyond. The man walked through, and Liam caught the door with his foot before it closed. He shouldered the door open and slid into the corridor. The door sighed closed behind him.

He walked down the hallway, scanning the nameplates on the office doors. The carpeted hallway was quiet and peaceful. The suite was almost empty as most of the developers were in their morning meetings.

He followed the map in his display to Simon Williams' office. Simon was the team lead developing New Real's augmented reality overlay technology. According to the rumors, they had finally achieved full-motion, three-dimensional objects so detailed they looked real. It would change the way people would see the world and create billions for whoever owned it.

He glanced through the narrow window next to the door. Simon was inside, gesturing at something only he could see. Liam stepped to the side and shifted both coffee cups into the same hand. With a quick swipe, he tacked a small sticker onto the wall next to the door. It blended into the wall, matching company branding color guidelines. "Sticker is in place," he muttered as he walked away.

"Good work. Five minutes until we are detected," she said.

He turned and walked back toward the entrance of the office suite. He ducked into a small, shared kitchen by the door and threw out the cups.

Liam headed back across the landing into the other wing of the building. Conference rooms lined both sides of the hall. Most of them were full of developers in their morning meetings, their attention firmly fixed on the screens as the project AI's marched through schedules, progress reports, and issues. The machines watched their progress, constantly adjusting plans to meet corporate deadlines. Liam felt the unblinking AI presence in the network, but their focus was so narrow they couldn't see him yet. He moved faster down the hall as he scanned the meeting schedules on screens next to the doors.

Finally, he found an empty room and opened the door. He took out a marble sized watchdog and placed it on the floor against the wall. Then he ducked inside and closed the door behind him.

"I'm in," he said. He drew a work deck the size of a pack of cards out of his pocket and placed it on the table in front of him. Everyone at NewReal had one to augment their bodynet's processing power. The work deck connected with his specs and started sifting through the local network traffic, looking for a way in.

A few moments later, the deck sent him passwords from one of the marketing managers. "Word to the wise. Don't use your dog's name and your birthday if you like to share pictures of your dog on your birthday," he muttered.

He hunted for the augmented reality project code. There was an urge to grab everything he could find but the people who bought his services didn't like big smash and grabs. He passed over several promising targets and finally located the file he needed. He quickly copied it to his onboard bodynet storage.

He sighed as he scanned the data. "They've encrypted the database," he whispered. Without the encryption keys, it was worthless.

"We planned for this. He's still scheduled for his regular meeting with marketing," Keema said. She had spent the last week making meeting requests to Simon's automated scheduler. His regular meeting pattern had emerged like a pencil rubbing of a gravestone.

"I'm ready," he said, flexing his fingers.

"He just left his office." she said. "The sticker sensor cloned his key, so we are good to go. Move it. Three minutes until the building knows you are there."

2

THREE MINUTES

"I'M MOVING," he said. He picked up the deck and left the room. On the way out, he stopped to tie his shoelace, and palmed the watchdog, dropping the small bot into his pocket. As he approached, the door to the office suite opened from the other side. Liam grabbed it and held it open. He smiled at Simon as he entered, exchanging a small nod. Liam watched him head for the conference rooms and slipped through the door.

He walked over to Simon's office and dropped the watchdog. He touched the lock panel and the antenna embedded in Liam's finger sent the access code. It gave a happy chirp and popped open. With a quick check of the hallway, Liam stepped into the small office. A silver workstation was neatly aligned with the corner of the table. Liam took a snapshot of the space with his specs.

"You need the physical unit," Keema said. "The keys are specific to the machine. We can reverse engineer the hardware encryption to unlock the database, but it will take a while."

“Yeah, yeah,” he grumbled. He had hoped to avoid this. In the best operations, he simply copied the data he needed and walked out. It was hard to think of it as stealing. But today, he couldn't pretend he wasn't a thief.

He pocketed Simon's work deck and then took his own deck and put it on the desk. Visual guides in his specs helped him put it in the same place. Connecting to it through his bodynet, he sent a special packet of code he had developed. The machine emitted a small whine. Then there was a pop and a thin curl of smoke floated out of the back. Anyone inspecting the deck would assume the power supply had failed and destroyed the machine.

"I've got it," he said.

"Good... let's get out... oh, shit. Liam, Simon just used his ID to buy a snack. The building noticed he can't be in two places at once. There's a security alert. Get out now!" Keema said.

"Dammit!" Liam hissed. He looked around, letting his system compare the office to the snapshot he had taken. Everything lined up. He backed out and closed the door. He ran through the narrow hallway toward the door to the landing.

"Liam, the watchdog," Keema said.

"Shit," he murmured. He spun around and ran back to the office. He picked the drone off the floor without breaking stride.

"They're in the office suite," Keema said.

"A dragonfly would be useful right now," he whispered.

"And I'd like a pony! Keep moving, we'll get you out."

He circled the quad of offices and headed for the small kitchen area. He pulled a disposable cup off the stack and hit the button on the drink machine. Leaning against the counter facing away from the hall, he hoped he looked relaxed. He heard two guards run past behind him. They would circle the office quad, letting the AI scan faces through their specs.

Liam exited, turned into the corridor behind them and hurried out of the office suite. He scurried down the stairway, and into the cafeteria. In the lobby, two security guards checked everyone leaving the building.

"Dammit. They've blocked the exit already," he said. He moved into the cafeteria, looking for a route out. The glass back wall opened onto a grassy courtyard. But there was no way out of the courtyard except back through another part of the building.

"Cops picked up the alert. Drone inbound. I have about a minute before they get here," she said.

He winced. Keema would have to move their drone coverage out well before the police unit arrived. "I have an idea. Hold on," he replied.

He moved as quickly as he dared to the VietPhong stand. Like the other food counters, it was completely automated, owned by a local chain. They were marketed as robot food trucks, but without the wheels and engine. "I'd like a tofu pho."

He stood to one side of the camera, letting the sunlight from the courtyard backlight him.

"How hot would you like it?" the kiosk replied.

"Hot," Liam replied, tapping his foot in impatience. "Damn helpful machines. C'mon, let me pay." he muttered to himself.

"Thank you. That will be twenty dollars. I am unable to process your image. Please use your ID card to pay."

Liam touched the card reader and transmitted Simon's ID code to pay for the meal. He hurried away from the kiosk, positioning himself by the stairs. He could see the lobby and the front door. He knelt as if to tie his shoelaces.

"The building sent an alert about Simon in the cafeteria," Keema said.

The two guards from the lobby jogged into the cafeteria, stun guns at the ready. The NewReal employees gave them a wide berth. Liam now had a clear path to the door.

Liam stood and walked to the lobby. As he opened the internal door, the receptionist's phone rang. As she looked down he walked through the lobby, head turned away from the cameras. He pushed through the front door into the blast of hot air outside. He turned to get out of her line of sight as quickly as possible. Once he was clear, he walked as quickly as he dared across the parking lot.

"Get back to the mall ASAP. I've got to bug out. I'm going to lose coverage in a few minutes. Stick to the plan and I'll pick you up on the other side," Keema said.

"Got it. Talk to you soon," Liam said. In the distance, he heard the low growl of a larger police drone. His neck tensed as he waited for the prickling of the police's forced network recognition signal. Every bodynet had a built-in ID that had to respond to the police signal. There was no way to hide from it. He had to get out of the drone's range. He began to run.

3

SHOPPING

LIAM WAS BACK in the alley he had left less than an hour earlier. He retrieved the shopping bag he had hidden behind the dumpster and stripped off his sweat-soaked T-shirt. His silver bodynet tattoos glistened in the sunlight as he put on a clean shirt.

He then pulled out a large, dark gray overcoat and slid it on. He relaxed as it wrapped itself around him. It was the most expensive thing he owned. Made of bullet resistant, reactive cloth, it had a range of sensors and extra power supplies. Wearing it had saved his life more than once. The tension eased from his jaw and shoulders as the coat reintegrated with his systems and its' cooling system kicked on.

He slid his dirty T-shirt into the bag under a shirt he had purchased earlier that morning. Buying the shirt created an electronic trail and an excuse to be in the mall. He checked himself over and blew out a sharp breath.

At the service door his hands tingled with the frenetic electromagnetic chatter of the mall network. He reached out and found the quiet area next to the door. The security cameras were still offline, their wireless chatter silenced. Sharp pulses spiked around them as the mall tried to reclaim its eyes.

With a deep breath, he pushed open the door and ducked inside. The white walls were marked with grease and streaks of black rubber, and it smelled like cleaning products and food. But it was quiet and empty. He trotted down the hall, listening for the squeaking tires of a garbage bot.

He approached the door leading back into the mall. He cracked it open, checking for passersby. He had nearly blown a job in Seattle when a man taking his small child to the bathroom happened to see him step through the wrong door. "Doors and corners," he repeated to himself. There was no one in the little corridor leading to the bathrooms. He stepped through and walked down the hall. Liam re-entered the mall, joining the stream of people. Away from the food court, he twitched his hand. As his bodynet released its hold on the outside cameras the mall's presence rushed in like blood into an arm released from a tourniquet. He severed the connection.

Using the pace indicator in the corner of his vision, he moved at the statistical average speed of the crowd. The indicator varied his pace, keeping him within the norms for the mall at this hour. He spent one standard deviation less than the average amount of time browsing. Then he wandered to Brown and Yakushima, a shoe store where he fit the customer profile. Turning off the guidance system, he stepped over the store threshold. A small shiver spread up his back as his bodynet transferred his preferred style and a model of his feet to the shop. The clerk looked up from his screen, alerted by the burst of data and smiled. "Good morning, Mr. Baron," he said. The store overlay displayed the clerk's name in Liam's specs.

"Good morning Victor," he said. "I need a new pair of boots."

"Excellent. We have a few new styles, fresh in this morning. I can have a pair assembled for you here in under an hour," Victor said. Liam noticed the fine scrollwork on Victor's hands as he reached below the counter and pulled out two plastic insoles.

"Nice elaboration," Liam said, gesturing at his hands.

Victor inspected the back of his hands. "Thank you. I think it's nice to have some decoration."

He waved Liam over to a short platform set in front of three screens. Then he set the insoles down and stepped back. Liam took off his shoes and stepped onto the plastic templates. In the mirror, the boots were overlaid on his feet.

"You don't find the decoration interferes with your transfer rates?" Liam asked.

"It's a small price to pay, I find. It's not like I'm in the military," he said, nodding at Liam's blocky, hard-edged tattoos.

"That was a while ago," Liam replied, curling his hands back into the coat.

"Of course, I meant no offence. Just like our footwear, we must choose the fit, fabric and sole to match the application. We have a wide range of choices. There are a great number here in the store. Any unusual requests can be shipped in a day." A menu appeared in the screen in front of him, with the fabric and color options available in the store.

"I'm pretty straight forward. I'll take the black, with the electrical generator in the sole. Oh good, you have ballistic nylon uppers. I'll take those." He shuddered as the cost of the boots appeared in his specs. He had told himself he needed them this morning. The power output from his current pair was decreasing and they were starting to hurt his knees.

"Excellent. Those will be ready for you in twenty minutes. Can I interest you in a pair of loafers as well?" Victor said, smiling. His eyes flittered back and forth as he read something in his specs. Liam checked the mall feed and found a security alert about the door he had used, but they didn't have a picture of his face.

"No, thanks. I'll be back to pick up my boots in a little while," Liam replied. He walked out in what he hoped was a casual manner and merged back into the crowd. He resisted the urge to hurry as he made for the mall door.

4

ESCROW

OUTSIDE HE CROSSED another empty expanse of black asphalt to the Apollo coffee shop and walked into the small building. The smell of coffee was thick in the air and he immediately perked up. He knew it was artificial, but it had the desired effect. He shook his head and found a table. Then he signaled the system for his usual soy and stim. It tasted surprisingly close to a latte for something produced by engineered yeasts. "Or what you think you remember it tasted like," he muttered to himself.

A young, attractive brunette in a too-tight Apollo t-shirt, picked up the mug from the burbling dispenser. She walked it over to his table. He smiled and nodded at her. Her smile in response failed to reach her eyes.

"Thanks, Arya," he said, reading her name off the overlay in his specs.

"You're welcome, Liam," she said, obviously reading a script from the store customer relationship system. With the right access she could learn more from the store database than he'd ever tell her in a month of dating. He knew because he had stolen that data for a job two months ago.

He watched her pick up another drink out of the machine and walk over to a middle-aged man with grey graphene tattoos overlaid on the scars from the removal of an older system. The man stared at Arya's chest as she approached and her butt as she walked away. Liam looked away in disgust.

Liam wondered how long he could do a job like Arya's. The machines timed every order. Scripted her interactions with customers to ensure optimal emotional response. And docked her pay if she deviated from their plan. He added a generous tip to the coffee order.

Adding a wireless connection to his tab, he accepted the terms of service, although he had no intention of following them. His bodynet made an anonymous, encrypted private connection to his personal server. He pulled out the small silver box he had stolen from NewReal and connected it to his network.

"I'm on-line and connected to the work station."

"Great. I've got the connection. I'm running the encryption key generator now," Keema said.

He turned his attention back to the combinations of numbers, letters and symbols streaming through his vision. Keema's systems searched for the right combination of hardware keys to unlock the database.

Experience told him this might take a while, so he pulled up the latest news feeds. The first story caught his eye. "Lung fever growing rapidly in North America! Lung fever, an antibiotic-resistant form of pneumonia, was first reported in India last year. Half the people who contract it die within a week, and another third within a month. Will the US be next? Is this the one?"

Liam couldn't decide if the threat was real or the latest in a long string of disease scares. Every new bug sparked a huge inflammatory wave of press. But then they disappeared with the next mass shooting or pandemic du jour. Liam hoped this would disappear as well. It was likely something was going to break out and put a dent in humanity's teeming billions, but after so many false alarms, it seemed more distant than ever.

The next story was closer to home. "The Worm's latest hack reveals payments to top senators, including majority leader Shelton to approve the American Restoration Act that privatizes disaster response. They also released the following statement.

"*The capitalist turns the natural world into money, they turn the built world into money, they turn our relationships into money, they turn us into money. If, as capital, we do not provide a return to them, we are liquidated. Our children are taken from us. We are cast out, made to wander the concrete wilderness they have created.*

But the capitalist machine is ever hungry. It must constantly be fed and its output consumed to pay its masters. Everything that is not-capital must be turned into money by the manipulation of a colonized human race. Now they will turn our tragedy into money for the sake of the few."

Senator Shelton could not be reached for comment.

Liam pushed away the news in disgust. Of course, they were paid. He didn't expect anything different anymore. The Worm made him nervous. They dug up scandal after scandal, but over time their rhetoric was getting more radical. He worried they would start causing real damage soon.

The deck chimed, bringing him back to the job. He opened the NewReal project and scanned the data. The list of thousands of training cases and output results told him he had what he needed. NewReal had trained a machine learning system to render virtual content mapped to the real world. He looked over the output graphics, impressed with the way they had captured the variations in light and reflections.

He had dreamed of becoming a software engineer in his teens. He wanted to create something out of nothing using only imagination and logic. He had lasted three months as an intern after the army. But there was too much sitting, too much grunt work. And that was before the AI's had taken over writing the code.

Liam closed the database and encrypted it with his own keys. With a sigh, he uploaded the file to his own private server, which then forwarded it on to an escrow server in Manilla. He sent the encryption key to another escrow server in Switzerland. Whoever the client was would pick it up in exchange for his payment.

The upload completed, he finished his drink and left the Apollo. He walked back across the parking lot and into the mall. As he re-entered the cool, soft air of the Mall, he heard the hourly fountain show begin. He re-engaged his guidance system, making sure he didn't hurry.

Victor at Brown and Yakushima was putting his new boots in a box. There was no need to try them on. The boots would fit perfectly, built from a 3D scan of his foot. So he accepted the box and gestured at the payment terminal to complete the transaction.

With the box tucked under his arm, he walked out of the mall and summoned a G-Cab for the ride home. As he sat down, the car connected to his bodynet to confirm his identity and then drove itself out of the parking lot. Across the street, the NewReal offices were quiet. It was as though he had never been there at all.

5

HOME

An hour later, the G-Cab pulled in front of his apartment building. He unfolded himself from the back seat. The front door of the building unlocked with a clunk and swung open once his bodynet and the building sensors exchanged codes. The building also recognized his face and opened the inner door to the lobby. The potted plants, tasteful modern furniture, and stylish carpet were bland and inoffensive.

The cute attendant from the neighborhood Apollo down the block popped up on one of the many screens in the lobby. Liam gritted his teeth.

"Hi, Liam," she said. "You haven't been in to see us for a few days. We'd love to have you back. I'll link a free extra shot of stims to your loyalty card. See you soon!"

She gave a smile and a little wink as the video cut to displaying the coffee shop logo.

Liam flinched at his own flutter of interest. The machines made his coffee, pizza, burger, and almost anything else exactly as he liked it, every time. The employee's job was to create an emotional connection to the brand.

The store systems required employees to record personal ads based on their attractiveness to a customer. Social Loyalty Marketing (TM) was the industry term. It made Liam's skin crawl, even as he thought about heading out to the Apollo. He'd never know if Emily liked him. She was being paid to create the hope. Whether that was genuine was irrelevant.

Liam tried to shake it off as he walked through the lobby. The elevator anticipated his arrival and opened as he walked to its door. He stepped in and it automatically took him to the seventh floor. Liam walked down the hall to his small apartment and went in and hung his coat on the charging rack. He checked the readouts to make sure the super capacitors in the coat were topping up. He kicked off his old boots and put them in the closet. The new boots went below the coat, and he enabled their access to his home network.

"I'm home. Logging off, Keema."

"Nice work today. I'll ping you as soon as the money clears escrow," she replied.

He rolled his shoulders. The adrenaline had gone and the beta-blockers had worn off, leaving his limbs tight and heavy. He wandered over to his kitchen display, and listlessly flipped through the options. After staring at the contents for a few moments, he decided he wasn't hungry.

"I need a shower and a drink," he said aloud.

Behind him, the apartment shifted. The couch moved itself against the wall, and a shower stall rolled out into the space. The shower spent most of the day tucked into the wall, ready to service the apartments on either side. It saved him square footage and it was less expensive than a unit with a dedicated shower.

The shower started up, and Liam stripped off his clothes and stepped in. He inspected his bodynet tattoos. He linked his specs to the camera in the shower, enabling him to inspect his back. The GPS antenna at the base of his skull was showing a little wear. He resolved again to stop rubbing the back of his neck when he was nervous.

The timer buzzed, indicating he had used his allotted time. The building would charge him if he stayed longer. He sighed and turned off the water. Throwing his toiletries into a locked cubby in the stall, he grabbed his towel off the rack. As soon as he stepped out, the shower rolled itself back into the wall and hissed through its cleaning cycle as he toweled himself off.

He found his robe crumpled in the corner of the room where he had thrown it that morning. He shook it out and put it on. In the kitchen, his automated bar unit burbled. As he approached, it dumped a measure of synthetic euphorics into a glass of soy milk. He took the glass and sat down on the couch as it rolled back into the living area. He stared out at the Bay Bridge, the cables of the western span illuminated by an array of lights.

A message from Keema flashed in his vision. The client had released the payment from escrow. Liam's shell company in the Caymans automatically generated his paycheck. He brought up his account balances and his bill payment interface. Switching on the news feeds, he decided which bills to pay.

He stopped as he recognized the voice on the feed. The host was interviewing Senator Shelton from the great state of Texas. The Senator shook his finger at the host. "The Economic Terrorism Act of 2035 will protect intellectual property, our most important national asset. The greatest creator of wealth is our knowledge and inventions. Those who would steal these are terrorists. They threaten the livelihood and economic freedom of millions of Americans.

Foreigners who benefit from the theft compete with Americans. Those who steal intellectual property are terrorists."

"Shit," Liam muttered. He never knew whether he was working for a foreign power. His contracts were anonymous, obscured through many layers of cryptography and misdirection.

The talking head on the feed continued. "The young today romanticize this sort of theft. They think it's harmless. They believe the rantings of terrorists who hide behind their ridiculous screen names, like 'The Worm'. Who would call themselves that?"

He pushed a payment into the ever-hungry maw of his student loan. It would cover the penalty fees and bring him up-to-date. But the balance didn't move. He grabbed another payment from his bank account and pushed it into his credit card. The negative number on the card moved closer to zero, but didn't quite make it there. Making a living was hard enough without worrying about terrorism charges.

"Intellectual property is as American as free speech and guns," said the congressman. "It's in the constitution, granted to us by the Founding Fathers. It's what this country was built on. I'll be damned if I'm going to let those who would tear down this great country pretend IP theft is any different than blowing up a church."

With the last of the money, he decided to upgrade his drone controller to make the dragonfly work again. Every six months the manufacturer made a small change to the system. making the old versions obsolete. He'd stay on the older versions as long as possible, but the drones forced upgrades every month.

If he was going to be an economic terrorist, he should have the best functioning equipment. The new version of the software downloaded and he checked to make sure everything worked.

As he finished up the installation process a reminder popped into his field of view. He had completely forgotten his dinner date. He jumped up, pulled on some clean clothes and grabbed his coat off the rack.

6

PROTEST

LIAM GROANED as the G-Cab stopped to avoid another young man with a placard complaining about the lack of jobs. Crowds filled the sidewalks, holding signs, chanting, and singing. Most of the protesters avoided stepping into the street. Interrupting traffic would result in a fine assessed by the facial recognition cameras lining the streets. Too many fines and they issued an arrest warrant.

Some of the protesters disrupted traffic flows by half-stepping off the curb. The G-cab's automatic safety systems would expect a collision and stop. It would then take a moment to make sure the route was clear before starting forward again. The protesters would time their half-step to stop the car again as soon as it started.

The city-wide traffic routing algorithms would notice the slowdown. They would then try to shift traffic onto nearby streets. The protesters would then spread out to those areas, causing cascading reroutes. A few people willing to risk arrest by stepping off the sidewalks could gridlock the entire city. The police couldn't patrol the entire length of the protest, making it an effective strategy and magnifying the impact of the protest. Scenes of gridlocked streets made good fodder for the social media feed.

But most stood on the sidewalks, shouting their fury and impotence. Liam had seen them before, time and time again. He shook his head. Nothing had changed in the two years since the New America protest movement had started. They disrupted traffic, government meetings, and public parks. The programmers, drivers, accountants, and fast-food cooks who made up the movement had little common ground - their old class and educational divisions were too great. But they all wanted the old world restored, so they banded together in these protests. Liam knew in his bones that their jobs weren't coming back, ever.

Liam's cab moved forward a few feet and stopped again with a jerk, interrupting his musing. He was getting nauseous from the constant starting and stopping.

Up ahead, he saw another small group run across the street, standing in front of the cars for as long as they dared. Liam sighed and pulled up the car hailing interface in his specs. He was going to have to walk the rest of the way, through the protest to have a chance of making it to dinner with Julie on time. He canceled the rest of the ride, agreeing to pay a penalty for abandoning the car. It irritated him that he needed to pay the penalty. But it was in the terms of service, and he didn't have much choice.

Opening the door, he clenched his teeth as the noise surged. The protesters nearest him whistled and jeered as they celebrated forcing him out of the car. Liam tensed, fighting down his irritation and discomfort. The crowd was thick on the sidewalk, taking up every available space. Pushing his way through that crowd was going to take forever. He started walking down the gutter next to the sidewalk.

The evening was turning breezy and cold as the fog rolled into the bay and funneled down the street toward him. Liam shivered. The size of the crowd threatened to overwhelm his bodynet sensors. He felt exposed to both attack and disease. He wondered how there were this many people in one place with the threat of lung fever hanging in the air. He couldn't decide whether ignorance or denial was the more likely cause.

Liam pulled the collar of his coat around his neck and turned on its active sensors. The crowd was too large to track but the millimeter wave radar systems embedded in the fabric would warn him if someone came at him. He walked as fast as he could down the street, ignoring the calls for him to stop and join the protest.

A platoon of G-Cabs were trying to nose their way down the block in the opposite direction. A group of protesters danced off the sidewalk and into the street. They were young and were wearing masks to avoid the facial recognition cameras on the street. Several wore shoes with uneven soles to fool the gait and body shape recognition systems. Others wore elaborate costumes with colored patterns to confuse the unblinking electronic eyes. The effect was just as disconcerting to the human eye. They seemed to him like alien jesters and the protest itself seemed just as foolish. Liam knew they weren't going to achieve a damn thing in the street. Real change happened behind closed doors in board rooms and conference rooms. Those doors weren't going to open because a few thousand people chanted in the cold.

His specs flashed an alert. The police systems had pinged his bodynet for ID. He flinched and ducked back onto the sidewalk. His heart raced as he tried to push through the crowd, trying to find room to run.

A notice appeared in his specs. The police systems had tagged him and fined him for blocking the street. They had deducted the amount from his credit card, adding a small convenience fee on top of the fine.

He let out a sharp breath, feeling the panic drain away. He cursed his carelessness and turned on his camera detection and denial system. His coat activated a set of small infrared lasers embedded in the shoulders of his coat. They scanned the surrounding light posts and buildings. It watched for the telltale glare from the lens, like a wild animal at night. The lasers would then dazzle the cameras, making facial recognition almost impossible.

He scurried along the edge of the crowd, trying to make up for lost time. He gradually became aware of another group within the larger demonstration. There were small groups dressed in black, with lower face coverings and active systems like his own. They were standing together in twos and threes, observing the crowd. Most of them had a silver worm emblem on their sleeve. The Worms were here. There was plenty of police footage of them smashing G-Cabs and assaulting police. He felt a small twist of fear in his gut. Their presence meant the protest could turn violent. He needed to get off the street. His livelihood depended on him staying out of the legal system.

Lost in his growing anxiety, he jumped when his coat stiffened its left arm and ballooned out. He caught movement out of the corner of his eye. Someone from the crowd stumbled forward and reached out for him. Liam stepped back with his left foot, pivoting to face his assailant with his hands raised. The coat read his movement. It relaxed the left arm. The front panels stiffened into a ballistic vest.

The man reached forward and fell at his feet. Liam grimaced, thinking the man had missed as he tried to grab him and fallen. The man rolled over, a fevered, panicked look on his face. He started coughing uncontrollably, gasping for breath. Liam stumbled back. His collar wrapped around his mouth and nose, forming an antimicrobial filter. He and his coat recognized what was happening at the same time.

The crowd on the sidewalk tried to get away, a wave of pushing bodies radiating out from where the man lay. The frantic pushing finally cleared a small semi-circle. Liam realized he was alone on the street with the stricken man.

7

OPEN PARTY

HE BROUGHT up his communication interface in his specs, hoping to call for help. When he couldn't get a signal, he realized the cellular networks were being jammed.

The man curled into the fetal position, struggling for breath. Liam looked around, trying to find help. He saw two policemen at the end of the block, watching the crowd.

He waved at them. "Help. We need help here!" he called.

The policemen turned toward him. They were both wearing full body armor, helmets, goggles and respirators with black rifles strapped across their bodies.

"This man needs medical attention. Can you call an ambulance please?" he yelled.

Neither of the policemen moved. Liam started walking towards them, with his hands up. "Hey. Can you hear me? This man needs an ambulance," he shouted.

He took a few hurried steps towards them. Then he froze as both officers brought their weapons up, pointing at him. He hadn't had a gun pointed at him since basic training, and that one had been unloaded. The shot detection microphones blanketing the city and drone response units made guns useless in his line of work. His coat shot an alert into his specs. The manufacturer claimed the coat would stop most handguns, but the high-powered police rifles would go through it like tissue paper. He stepped back, hands still visible. The two cops lowered their weapons. One returned to scanning the crowd; the other kept an eye on Liam.

As he debated what to do, the crowd parted next to him. Four people, all wearing green plastic painting suits and face coverings, walked through the gap. They knelt next to the prone man as he gasped for air. One of the figures pulled an oxygen mask out of the backpack he was wearing and placed it on the sick man's face. Another unpacked a small stretcher and unrolled it on the street. They slid the man onto it, then each took a corner, lifted him up and walked back into the crowd.

Liam blinked in surprise as the group made its way up the sidewalk and turned into an alley. Liam jogged after them, curious to see where they were going. As he got to the alley he tried to push his way through the crowd blocking the entrance. As he struggled, several larger members of the protest linked arms in front of him. They stood motionless, each one of them taller and wider than Liam. He caught a brief glimpse of the team, through their linked arms, rounding the corner and disappearing down a small side street.

"We'll take it from here," said a voice next to him. A woman had taken his arm.

She was short, the top of her head just clearing his shoulder. She had a strong grip on his arm, which had started the coat's shock defense system. Her purple streaked, jet black hair, pulled into a ponytail, fell past her shoulders.

She wore an Open Party t-shirt under a brown leather jacket, cargo pants and well-worn combat boots. Liam was transfixed by her, unable to do anything but stare with his mouth open. He swore he could feel the warmth from her hands through his coat. She held his gaze, waiting to make sure he had heard her. He realized his microbial filter was still up and he signaled the coat to relax. The collar softened and wilted away from his face.

"Are you okay?" she asked.

"I'm fine," he said, trying to keep his voice steady. "Where are they taking him?"

"To get whatever help we can provide," she said. She looked down the alley. "I'm not sure what good we can do though, he's pretty far along."

"Wait. Aren't they taking him to a hospital?" he asked.

"Yeah. Yeah, uh, they are. Well, thanks for trying to help," she said, reaching out her hand.

Unthinking, Liam took it. As they touched, he noticed the gray, graphene bodynet tattoos stretching out from under her jacket. He tried to pull back, but she tightened her grip. A tingle of network traffic shot up his arm. His network responded, replying with his bodynet ID. He closed his eyes, trying to shut off access to his router before she compromised his core systems.

Then, it was over. She released her grip and the attack stopped. She took half a step back, squinting at him. "Well. Have a nice rest of your evening. Remember to vote for the Open Party!" she said. She turned and pushed her way into the crowd.

"Wait. Who are you? What's going on?" As he turned, two men in their twenties happened to step in front of him and block his path.

"Dammit." He sighed. He slid sideways trying to push

past them. Then muttered apologies as he bumped into someone else. Pressed against the bodies around him, he wished he had kept the breathing filter in place. He struggled through a group of chanting and singing college students, his hands up close to his chest. The incessant noise and pressure made his neck tighten. His bodynet noticed the increased stress and went to a higher state of alert. The radar and infrared cameras swept faster, and the coat stiffened. In the corner of his eye, he saw the system lower the reaction thresholds for his active defense systems. The system assumed if he was feeling this much stress, he must be under threat. Liam turned off the automatic reaction system. He wanted to clear a path around himself with a surge of electricity, but that would draw unwanted attention.

He had taken his eyes off the woman. Who was she? He cursed himself for letting his attraction lower his guard. She had forced his system to respond with the root ID, but it hadn't felt like the blunt force police command; this was a razor instead of a club. But that didn't mean she wasn't police, or part of an intelligence agency. Whoever she was, she could now find out more about him than he wanted.

On his tiptoes, he caught a glimpse of the top of her head as she moved through the crowd. She walked quickly, shoulders back, her head upright, even though she was only at most people's shoulder height. People stood aside to let her pass. He pushed forward, hoping to catch up to her before the end of the block. The crowd didn't part for him in the same way, and he lost sight of her.

He grunted in frustration as the five-minute reminder popped up in his field of view. He was going to be late for his dinner with Julie now. A wave of anxiety passed over him. Whoever she was, he wasn't going to find her in this crowd. He uploaded the data from the encounter to his private data store. Then he sent a note to Keema, asking her if she could help trace her. There was nothing more he could do tonight. He pulled up his collar and hunched down into his coat. Liam turned and started pushing through the crowd toward the restaurant.

8

JULIE

It took Liam fifteen minutes to get out of the crowd. He ran up the sidewalk and pulled open the front door of Nos Aladdin. The chanting and drumming echoing up the street spilled into the dining room as he slid inside.

Liam scanned the room. It was a small space, with Middle Eastern rugs hung like tapestries over a southwestern decor. His systems loaded the building plans from the city database. They mapped an escape route through the kitchen to the back alley. He loaded it into his specs.

The smell of slow-cooked spiced meat made his mouth water. With one more breath his systems finally stood down from their alert status. As the hostess approached him, he saw Julie sitting at a table against the back wall of the restaurant. Her long blonde hair hung around her face like a curtain as she read her tablet. Their mother used to work like that, her hair creating a screen against the distractions of the world. He pushed that thought down. It was too early in the evening and he had not yet had enough to drink. Gesturing toward Julie, he walked past the hostess and into the restaurant.

He made his way across the room, smiling at the way she still used a tablet, instead of specs. She claimed specs distracted her. She wanted more control over when and where she interacted with the network. Her long, thin hands flicked the screen to scroll down the page. She was completely absorbed in her reading.

He gently touched her shoulder. "Hey Jules."

She jumped at his touch. "Liam," she said, looking up blinking.

She stood and hugged him. She felt thinner than usual, her ribs hard against her skin. Her cheek was hot against his face. Her hands were usually ice cold, but it was warm in the restaurant.

"How are you?"

She took half a step back to look him over. Dark circles under her eyes were visible through her makeup. "I've been working too hard... I'm glad you made it through the mess out there," she said. She was only four years older than him, but she was already greying at the temples.

"It's a zoo. But I couldn't miss tonight," he said. He moved between her and the chair she had been sitting in. She hesitated. He glanced out the front window. The translucent shades were down, and the street outside was quiet.

Julie patted his shoulder and took the seat facing the back of the room. He sat down and set his bodynet to work probing the restaurant's network.

"Have you been here long?"

Julie settled into her seat and slid her tablet into her bag.

"A few minutes. I walked from the lab," she said. "I took the liberty of ordering drinks - real ones."

"If there's a night to splurge, it's tonight," he said. "Have you talked to Dad recently?"

"I called him a few weeks ago... probably three weeks now? I left him a message and invited him out tonight, but I haven't heard back from him," she said.

"You've done better than me. I haven't tried since last summer," Liam said. "Not that it does any good. If I manage to catch him all I get is five minutes of - *'How's work? What's the weather like*?'"

"I know. I get the same. But the heart attack really took it out of him," she said. Liam nodded slowly. He wanted to get up and pace the room. Their father had pulled through in the end, but he was a shell of his former self.

The waiter arrived and put two small margaritas in tumblers on the table. Condensation formed on the outside of the glass, and the salt was a perfect halo of white.

"To Mom... Happy birthday" Julie said, picking up her drink.

"Happy Birthday, Mom," Liam said. They touched glasses and Liam took a long sip. The salty, citrus, smoky flavor brought a tear to his eye. "She always did love a good margarita."

"Yes, she did," Julie replied, her eyes closed. She put her glass down with a sigh. "Remember that last summer, when she made us virgin margaritas? But she let us believe they were real? You used to stagger around like you were hammered. You believed they were real. Mom and I always got a good laugh out of that."

"I was so disappointed when you two finally told me. I swear they made me dizzy though." They both grinned for a moment. Liam took another sip, savoring the real tequila, and put his glass down.

His network probe reported back. It had accessed the

restaurant security cameras. Whoever installed them hadn't bothered to change the factory default password. He logged in and put the feeds in the corner of his vision. With a glance, he could see outside the front and back doors, the host stand and the kitchen.

When his attention returned, Julie was staring at him. "You done checking the exits?"

"Better safe than sorry," he said. "How's work going? I saw your company is raising money. That's great."

"It's not great. It should be a government grant funding this work, not private investment. But your corporate superheroes convinced everyone that the government was worse than the plague. So now the rich get to own it. And we are so close to having a cure for lung fever. Every sim we've run shows we can cure it in ninety to ninety-five percent of cases. We need to finish the testing, but I'm getting pressure to finish my work as soon as possible to raise the stock price. I know this will work, but I'm afraid we're going to miss something."

"That's great, Jules! Man, that should boost your stock options once Biotron goes public."

Julie let out a sharp breath. "You know that's not why I'm in this," she said.

"I know. But some money wouldn't hurt. You could pay off your student loans, own your house outright," he said. "Making money doesn't make you a bad person."

"That's the problem. In my line of work, making a lot of money does make you a bad person. The more money we make, the fewer people can afford our medicine," she said. She took a large gulp of her drink.

"I don't get it, Jules. You work all these hours, sacrificing your health... for no reward in the end?" Liam said.

"How can you say there's no reward? I get to help out

millions of people, prevent hundreds of thousands of deaths." Her eyes narrowed. He'd seen that look before. It was the one she used when she caught him pretending to be sick, so he could play in an online gaming tournament. Or the time he and his friends almost got arrested for violating a park curfew playing football. He realized he had seen that look a lot. "What is there not to understand?"

"I don't understand how you're happy letting other people take all the reward for your work. It's the game Jules. We don't make the rules." He looked over his shoulder and made eye contact with the waiter. He regretted going down this path with her. He hoped an interruption would allow him to change the subject.

Julie brushed her hair out of her eyes. "Why should the investors get the lions' share of anything? All they contributed was money. That's the least interesting, least creative part of the whole process. They get to decide who lives and dies, because they have money?" she asked, trying to control her voice. She took a deep breath. "I'm sorry. I'm tired. Short tempered."

A small cough brought their attention to the waiter standing next to the table. He pursed his lips in disapproval.

"Good evening," he said. "Have you had a chance to decide?"

Liam glanced at the menu the restaurant pushed to his specs. Tagines with Afro-Caribbean flavors were the house specialty. Lots of vegetables, not a lot of meat. Liam knew he'd be hungry later, but Jules loved this place. "I'll have the lamb tagine and another margarita," Liam said. If they were going to splurge, they were going to do it right.

Julie hesitated. She looked at Liam, looked down at the menu and sighed. "I'll have the vegetable tagine in the Caribbean style."

"Very good. I'll be back in a few moments". He frowned at them and turned toward the kitchen.

"We just got scolded," Liam said and gave her a small smile.

She smiled back. "Yes, we did." She paused, gazing at the ceiling. "I know what's going to happen. We will release as soon as possible for as much as we can. Which means soaking those who can afford it, and everyone else gets to take their chances," she said. Her right hand curled into a fist, and she wrapped her left over the top. "The stupid thing is that this is stuff made from a common soil bacterium from northern India. We just happened to find it while we were doing other research. It's existed for thousands of years. But we stumbled upon it first, so we own it?" she said, her palms pointed to the ceiling in a shrug.

"Without getting to own the intellectual property, why would anyone fund your research in the first place? If they couldn't get a return, they wouldn't put up any money," Liam said. He mentally kicked himself for arguing about this with her again.

"It's human history. If you had enough seashells, you could buy food for your kids to survive. If you had enough silver, you could buy an army and take land. I don't see how we change that, Jules. Not you and me," he said. "We have to play the game that's in front of us."

"I know," she sighed. "It's not like I have the money to strike out on my own. I'd be out on the street in a month without a paycheck."

The waiter returned and placed steaming bowls in front of them, along with their drinks. Liam took a sip of his margarita. The alcohol was beginning to relax him. He picked up his spoon and picked out a piece of lamb from the fragrant yellow stew. He chewed it slowly, savoring the heat and slightly silky texture. He knew it was vat grown, but they had captured the texture and earthy flavor of real lamb. The tension building up in his gut began to release.

"At least you're making a difference where you can. There are days..." he said.

"There are days, what?"

"Nothing. Never mind." He checked the video feeds to avoid making eye contact.

"No, tell me. What's up?"

"I wish I was doing something different," he said. He swallowed hard and reached for his drink to distract himself.

"You can, you know. You're smart, you have military experience, you could do something else. Although I'm not clear on what you do now," she said.

"I'm a freelance corporate intelligence analyst. Companies hire me to do competitive analysis. It's a lot like what I was doing in the service," he said. "Anyway... I'm just tired. It's been a long day."

She pursed her lips and watched him. "That's not all you do, is it?"

He flinched. "What do you mean?"

"You don't just do analysis. It's more… hands on?"

"What makes you think that?" He picked up his glass and carefully poured the last drops of the now diluted margarita down his throat.

"The way you are constantly checking the exits, looking for angles. Hell, even your coat. Why do you need a smart fabric coat if you have desk job?"

He stared past her out the window. He wanted to tell her, but his fear of her reaction stopped him.

She squinted at him again. Then shrugged slightly. "Mom would be happy we still talk."

"Yes, she would," he said, grateful for the change in conversation. They ate in silence for a moment.

"Hey, I've been meaning to ask you. How's it going with what's-his-name at work?" he said with a half-smile and raised eyebrows.

"You mean David? He's my boss, Liam," she said, unable to hide her small smile.

"I know he's your boss, but that doesn't change the way you talk about him. Or the fact you blush every time I bring him up," he laughed.

"I don't know if he sees me that way, he's so involved in his work. But of course, so am I..." she said. "Maybe someday one of us will work up the courage to ask the other out. But not now. So, what about you?"

"I'm not seeing anyone. Hell, I haven't been on a date in months. But there was this woman in the crowd today. I'm not sure who she was, but there was something about her. Of course, she was probably a cop or something," he said.

"A random woman in a crowd? Did you get her contact info?"

"No. It wasn't like that..."

A sharp motion caught his eye. His fingers tingled as his bodynet registered a change in the activity outside. Two figures ran past the front of the restaurant. Then another four, then a larger group. "Uh oh," he said. He signaled the restaurant billing system from his bodynet and paid the bill. "Julie, get your coat on." He stood up and pulled on his own coat and initiated the defensive systems.

9

INTERRUPTION

"WHAT? WHAT'S WRONG?" she asked as she looked around the restaurant. Everyone else was still eating and talking.

"Get your coat on and grab your bag," he said. He stood and put his coat on. Julie hesitated, looking around in confusion.

Outside what had been isolated groups of people walking down the sidewalk had turned into a steady stream of protestors running down the street. Liam guessed they were running from something from the way they kept looking over their shoulders.

A series of sharp bangs shook the windows. Julie yelped in surprise, ducking her head. There was a moment of stunned surprise, then chaos followed as everyone panicked. Some dove for the floor, others grabbed their coats and bags and ran for the door.

A cylinder spewing white tear gas landed outside the door. A man in a black hoodie and a gas mask ran over, picked it up and threw it back up the street. Then he collapsed, the rubber bullet shattering the glass of the door.

Liam's systems went into high alert. He grabbed Julie's coat and bag and shoved them into her hands.

Through the haze, a line of police - gas masks and riot gear hiding their humanity - marched down the street. Another group of protestors, carrying a mix of homemade shields advanced towards them in a line. They met in a confused clash of plastic, metal, and human flesh. The two lines pushed against each other, beating at each other with batons and bats.

As Liam pulled Julie towards the kitchen, the front window of the restaurant shattered. Liam risked a glance back as he pushed Julie through the kitchen door. One of the protestors lay on the floor. He didn't move as two armored police stomped into the restaurant and started to hogtie him.

Liam pushed through the door and grabbed her around the waist. Liam hurried on his programmed route through the kitchen. He found the back door, kicked the crash bar, and dragged Julie into the cool night air. "Come on. We have to get behind the police lines," he said as he hurried her down the alley.

When they reached the corner, he stopped and tried to understand the situation. An armored personnel carrier blocked the end of the street. The cop standing in the turret kept his rifle focused on the crowd further down the block. The drifting gas stung Liam's eyes. His coat pulled itself up around his mouth and nose. Beside him, Julie coughed and wretched. He thought about giving her his coat. But he had to keep himself operational to get them out. He pulled her back, hoping the police couldn't hear her.

He waited until the carrier moved beyond the end of the alley. Then he hurried Julie across the street. He half dragged her down the next few blocks as the sound of the conflict faded behind them. Julie staggered, coughing from the gas.

"Don't rub your eyes, it will only make it worse," he said.

He let go of Julie's waist and took her hand. "A few more blocks and we should be safe," he said. She nodded, mucus flowing freely from her nose.

They walked on, staggering uphill until the noise of the riots faded behind them. He found a small park and sat her on a bench. Gradually her coughing eased.

"Okay," she said, her eyes watering and red. "That gas is awful," she said, regaining her breath.

"Yeah, it can be pretty bad," he replied. "Let's get you home." They walked down the street, hand in hand, like they had done as young children in the woods around Portland. A few G-Cabs rolled by, their windows sealed to the world outside. Liam signaled a car from his bodynet, while Julie wiped her eyes with a tissue from her bag. She coughed again and wiped her mouth.

The G-Cab rolled quietly up to the curb and the door opened. Julie got in and Liam followed her in.

"What are you doing?" she asked.

"I'm making sure you get home ok. I'm sorry those idiots ruined Mom's birthday."

"It wasn't ruined. I got to see you, and you got to rush me out of the restaurant."

He smiled and let his head rest against the seat. "That isn't usually the highlight of my day."

They rode the rest of the way to Julie's small house near the beach in silence. The lingering smell of tear gas made it uncomfortable to breathe deeply.

When they finally rolled up to her house, the cool, damp air was a welcome relief. Liam got out and helped her out of the car. Her eyes were still bloodshot and she fought down a cough.

“Go shower, make sure you keep the water out of your eyes. If you can, keep your clothes outside tonight, then get them in the wash tomorrow.”

“Thanks,” she said. “I don’t feel that great. But I’ll be ok once I get this shit off me and have some tea.”

“I can come in and hang for a while if you want,” he said, putting a hand on her shoulder.

“I’ll be fine. I just need to get clean. Go home and get some rest.”

He hesitated. The G-Cab chimed. He needed to either let it go or get in.

She smiled and gave him a tight hug. "I miss you. Don't be a stranger."

Liam wasn't sure of any such thing. "I know. Love ya, sis. Don't work too hard," he said. He turned and got into the cab. The door closed and he watched her house as long as he could.

10

SERGEI

LIAM SHUFFLED into his apartment and hung his coat on the charging hook. The adrenaline from earlier was wearing off making him feel empty and jittery at the same time. He wasn't used to operating without the beta-blockers. He was becoming too dependent on them. He promised himself – *again* - that he would run the next operation without them.

His mind was stuck in a loop, reliving the flight from the restaurant. How could he have been so stupid as to ignore the protest? He should have insisted they leave the restaurant as soon as he got there. He knew better, even if his sister didn't.

He sent her a message letting her know he was home. She replied that she was going to bed and they'd talk soon.

He stripped off his sweat-soaked shirt and pants. The reek of riot gas filled the room. He stripped naked and dumped everything in the laundry chute. He feebly waved his hands in the air.

"Shower, please" he requested.

The shower rolled out of the wall and the glass walls fogged as the water started.

He stood, letting the hot water run down his upturned face. It was his second of the day, which meant he was being charged by the minute. The daily expense total he ran constantly in the back of his head crept upward. It was close to his anxiety threshold. But he needed to feel clean. He hit the soap dispenser and started washing.

He sighed as he looked over his thin frame. His veins snaked over the top of muscles like piano wire. "One more job and I'll start eating more," he promised himself.

He pumped the soap dispenser again and washed his hair. The woman from the protest bothered him. Who was she? Why had she scanned him? The pulse didn't feel like the police. It was too subtle. Was Homeland running deep cover? Was he now on the Feds' radar? Why had he followed that sick man? He should have walked away. Why the hell hadn't he walked away?

The adrenal flood clawed at him. He tried to breathe. His heart slammed against his ribs, trying to break free of its narrow cage. His head spun. He sank down and hugged his knees to his chest, waiting for the wave to pass. The warm water flowed around his face, as he fought for control.

He managed to slow his breathing and he realized the shower debit alarm had been chirping for a while. It had been an expensive anxiety attack.

"Shower off."

He fell into the bed as the shower wheeled itself back into the wall. He wanted to curl up and sleep, but he couldn't stop his hands from twitching, and his heart rate kept surging. He had to ride out the last of the anxiety. It would be hours before he could sleep. He needed to rebalance his neurochemistry. But drinking alone was a path to a dark hole he didn't want to fall down again.

He chose his black jeans and his new iridescent blue shirt. The nano material reflected the light in a shimmery fold. From a distance it looked like the spider silk fabric fashionable among the upper classes. Putting it on made him feel better. He pulled on his shorter civilian jacket and put his boots back on.

"I'm going out. Set the alarm..." he said. He paused. "And if I'm not back in three hours, signal Keema to ping me."

He wanted a drink. But if he was longer than three hours it would mean he had fallen into the bottle. Keema would be able to get him out and take him home.

"I will set the security alarm, and I've set the reminder to call Keema if you are not home in three hours," his room replied.

The whine of the cleaning bot scurrying out to pick up his towel and vacuum leaked out into the hall as he closed the door.

He ignored the video of Emily again asking him to come to the coffee shop and walked out into the fog engulfing the city. Liam took a deep breath, savoring the cool, moist air and started down the street. The sidewalks were empty and only single G-Cabs glided past.

Cocooned in the fog, his shoulders began to relax out of their hunch. An occasional tremor still rose up out of his midsection, but they were less frequent now. He walked down the street, past the local chain shops and restaurants. He ignored the screens in the windows offering drinks, food, companionship, acceptance. He turned away from the new apartment towers and walked deeper into the older part of the city.

The sign for Oscar's Pub emerged from the fog. Outside, among the tables and chairs, a few older men stood vaping, mixing their steam with the city's fog. Liam nodded to a few familiar faces as he passed, and quickly ducked inside.

As he passed through the door, the pressure of the constant advertising queries faded. Liam touched the network filter in gratitude. The dim reddish light inside felt inviting and created deep shadows.

Oscar nodded to Liam as he walked in. The big man with a shock of receding red hair rarely spoke. Liam nodded in reply and took a seat at the pitted oak bar next to a tall muscular man with a blond flattop.

"Sergei," he said, patting his shoulder. The hard carbon fiber inserts of his shoulder felt as though he was patting a table. Liam wondered how far the implants extended under his leather jacket.

The man at the bar lifted his drink in a toast with the slight hiss of an artificial muscle. His four carbon fiber fingers wrapped around the ceramic mug.

"Liam. How is life?" he said. Liam had to focus on understanding Sergei's thick accent.

His sharp cheek bones and angular features were so Russian he seemed a caricature out of an old Cold War movie. Liam remembered watching one about a boxer with his dad when he was very young. Sergei resembled the villain. Liam swallowed the sadness that followed the thought.

"Life is... exhausting," Liam said.

Sergei nodded and drained his drink. He motioned at Oscar for another round. "Care to join me?"

"No uppers for me, my friend. It's been a rough night. I'll take a Halcyon," Liam said. He wished he could have another tequila. But between dinner and the shower, he needed something less expensive. With grain shortages, the hops virus, and the wine country moving north faster than they could plant new vines. Genuine fermented drinks were expensive. Halcyon was one of the new breed of smart drugs grown in a vat, providing a mild tranquilizer and euphoria without the side effects.

Oscar slid a tall glass of the cloudy red Halcyon in front of him. He drank half of it in one swallow. The sweet, almost fruity liquid made him wince, but the vice around his head loosened immediately. He sighed and set the glass down.

Sergei's arm hissed as he reached for his drink. "Soy for the protein, stim to keep you sharp!" he said, slapping the bar. "Always keep your edge."

He raised the glass to Liam in a toast and took a large swallow.

"Always sharp," Liam replied, taking a sip.

"What is wrong, my friend?" Sergei asked. His eyes were glassy from the stimulants. He leaned closer and whispered, "Is there someone you need removed? I still have some good implants. They didn't decommission everything."

Liam froze, unable to think of a response. He had always wondered what remained of Sergei's military implants. Then Sergei slapped him on the shoulder and sat back laughing.

"Nothing I need right now. But thanks for the offer," Liam said, with a small laugh. "Maybe soon, though."

He had been drinking with Sergei for almost three years now after Keema had brought them together for a job. As fellow veterans, they had struck up a drinking relationship, although their wartime experiences had been vastly different. While Liam had stared at computer screens in an air-conditioned room, Sergei had been on the front lines. The big

Russian had come to San Francisco after the Sino - Russian war of 2028. When Russia's collapsing population in eastern Siberia created a power vacuum, the Chinese corporations had filled the void. When Russia decided to nationalize Chinese assets, China responded with Russia's own playbook.

With encouragement from Beijing, the ethnic Chinese population in Amur began campaigning for independence. Their paramilitaries attacked police stations and started separatist government councils. The Russian president sent in Spetsnaz operators with full military hardware. The neural implants dialed their empathy down to zero and turned their propensity for violence to eleven. The squads of uncaring super soldiers left a trail of bodies and demolished villages in their wake. The Chinese responded with their own special forces. The struggle was violent, dirty, and quiet. No one wanted to admit two nuclear powers had engaged in direct warfare over territory. The Chinese eventually backed down. Men like Sergei had been partially decommissioned and sent home.

Not that Sergei ever talked about it. All Liam knew was what he had read on the news feeds and a documentary he had watched by a Chinese historian. Liam doubted Sergei slept very well, if at all.

"So, Sergei. How is life? As you say," Liam asked.

"I have new job!" Sergei replied.

"That's great news. What are you doing?"

"I'm a doorman at Piper! Lots of easy women and beautiful money," Sergei said with a smile. "Or was that easy money and beautiful women. I get them confused."

Liam rolled his eyes. Piper was the hottest new nightclub with the finance clique in San Francisco. Only a few months old, tables were reserved weeks in advance. Liam could imagine the kind of money thrown around there. "That's great news. How's the side action?" he said.

"The left hand is good, and the right hand doesn't care. You want to come to the club one night? I get you in. I even get you VIP table and some company. The boss doesn't care. He only cares about making sure we have as many rich capitalists as possible. It's like the old country. The bankers, they are so easy to make feel important. If they can spend money on it, it must be good, eh? We even have staff to make sure everyone has a good time," Sergei said with a wink.

"That sounds fun. It's been a while since I had a night out," Liam said.

"Yes! This is good. It's a great place, lots of fun. Maybe you bring a date?"

"We'll see about the date," Liam said. "I'm a little out of practice." He wondered about the girl from the protest. She didn't seem the type who would go to a club like Piper. But Emily from the ad might.

"Well, maybe I will find you a girl," Sergei said with a laugh.

"No, but thanks."

"Anyway, the bosses are great. They even gave me new legs. Look!" Sergei pulled up his pant leg. The carbon fiber was flat black in the warm light of the bar. The leg was intricate in a way Liam had never seen before. The internal structure looked organic, intertwined spindles of fiber in flowing shapes. There was something almost alien about the design.

Liam whistled in appreciation. "That looks expensive. Latest model?"

"I don't know what model. All I know is it interfaces with my old neural outputs. I can run faster, jump higher, it doesn't crash, and it doesn't fucking hurt when I stand," Sergei said.

"How much did that cost you?" Liam said, sounding harsher than he intended.

"Nothing. I do my job and sometimes run some errands for them," Sergei said.

"Errands? What kind of errands?"

"Nothing much. Just be here at a certain time, pick up this person, take them here. Take a package here. Lots of packages to bad neighborhoods, but I'm Spetsnaz, no one messes with me," Sergei said.

"You aren't running drugs, are you?" Liam asked.

"I don't care. What is it you Americans used to say? Don't ask, don't tell? They gave me new legs when my old ones froze on me at the club. They gave them to me like it wasn't any big deal. But they make crazy money, so maybe they don't care."

Liam looked at Sergei, his brow wrinkled in concern. He hoped the big Russian wasn't getting himself in trouble. When they met, Sergei was near his lowest point, trying to sedate himself into oblivion. The withdrawal from the emotional blockers had been devastating as the memories of what he had done almost overwhelmed him.

"Well, you deserve some good luck," Liam said.

"Here's to good luck," Sergei said, draining the last of his glass. "Now I must go. I have package to pick up and deliver across the bridge. A different kind of fun from the nightclub," Sergei said, winking. He got up and walked out of the bar with a slight whisper of the artificial muscle. The stiffness of the old Russian legs was gone. He looked more powerful. Liam wouldn't have guessed Sergei was missing both legs above the knee.

The warmth of the Halcyon had spread beyond his neck and reached down into his arms and belly. He downed the last of the drink and waved his hand over the bar to pay. As he added his usual generous tip for Oscar, he wondered how much longer Oscar could keep the place open as the new high rises marched closer.

He walked out into the gray night, warmed by the cocktail of drugs. He failed to notice the small tracker drone drifting high above him as he made his way home.

11

HOSPITAL

Cold, bony fingers held his wrist with a supernatural strength. Liam tensed, holding down the urge to fight free. She looked at him, her eyes sunken into her head. Her hair was thin and stuck to her forehead with sweat. Waves of pain, grief, and washed over her expression. He surrendered and melted into her. She held him tightly to her as she took her final breath.

Liam bolted upright, gasping. The late morning sunshine streamed through the window, drilling into his brain. He slowed his breathing. He lowered his clenched fists from his face.

When he reached his apartment the night before, he had made himself a depressant from his home bar. Then another. Then he overrode the liability warning and had another. As usual, he set his bodynet to dose him with the counteragent if he took things too far.

Finally, the weight of the drugs had pushed him under. Usually, the drugs were a recipe for a few hours of utter blankness in an unconsciousness deeper than any sleep, but not restful. But last night the recurring nightmare had filled the emptiness.

"Good morning, Liam. The time is currently 9:45 am. You slept for five and a half hours last night. Your weekly average is down to five point three five hours per night. For optimal health and performance, please try to sleep at least seven hours per night. Would you like me to identify methods to help you sleep more?" the apartment asked, with its usual cheerful tone.

"No," he said, clenching his jaw. It was the third time in a week the apartment had asked. "Start the morning checklist. Hold the news feeds," he said, as he got out of bed. Once his weight was off the mattress, the bed folded itself back into the wall. The apartment projected his morning routine onto the wall. He subscribed to Ferris Industries' morning rituals feed. It provided him with a structured system of exercise, meditation and positive psychology. He opened the drawer and put on a shirt and shorts placed there by the laundry bot yesterday. He began the exercise routine prescribed by the feed.

As he started his program of push-ups, sit-ups, and squats, he replayed his bodynet's recording of the protest before. Who was the woman in the crowd? Why had she scanned his ID? Was she Homeland? He did not want to be on anyone's radar right now. The NewReal job could be a turning point for his reputation score. A few more points and he would have a shot at the higher paying jobs.

The apartment interrupted his reverie. "You are not activating your glutes enough on the squats and your knees are tracking over your feet. This could lead to long-term knee injury. Would you like a refresher on proper squat form and mechanics?" The house overlaid the video of him squatting with a wire frame of the ideal posture.

"No. Thank you," Liam said. He focused on squeezing his butt until his image came within the acceptable margin of error. The apartment cheered as he complied, earning it a glower from Liam.

A few more exercises later, his apartment checked exercise off his morning list. The shower rolled out of its place in the wall and the water started up. He stripped off his shirt and shorts and placed them in the laundry chute. He stepped into the shower, letting the warm water roll down his neck and back.

The apartment chimed with an incoming call. All he wanted to do was finish his damn morning routine. He considered ignoring it. If it was important, they could leave a message. He'd get back to them after the twenty-two minutes he needed to complete the checklist.

He squinted through the steaming shower door, trying to see the caller ID projected on the wall. The hair on the back of his neck stood up as he saw the name. He turned off the shower and stepped out. It returned to its location in the wall. "Go ahead and answer," he said.

His specs were in their cleaning holder next to the bed, so the apartment projected the caller on the wall. Whoever was on the other end would see an animation, rather than his naked body.

"Hello?" he said. The caller was wearing a plain blue shirt, with a small logo stitched over the left breast.

"Mr. Baron? I'm calling from Glaxo Hospital in San Francisco. Are you Liam Baron?" the man asked.

"Yes. I'm Liam Baron," he said, wrapping a towel around his waist.

"Mr. Baron, I'm calling you because you are the emergency contact for Julie Baron. Is this correct?" he said. Liam swallowed the acid rising in the back of his throat. He started to dry himself off as fast as he could.

"Yes. Is there something wrong with Julie? Is she OK?" he said.

"You should come in. She was admitted last night, and she is asking for you," the nurse replied, his face unreadable.

"What happened? Is she ok?" he asked. He threw down his towel and snapped impatiently at the wardrobe, willing it to open faster. It presented him with an outfit, chosen for the day from his wardrobe by his clothes service.

"I can't disclose any more. When you get here, come to the fourth floor on the south wing. Ask for the isolation ward," the nurse said, closing the connection.

"Oh shit," Liam muttered. The isolation ward could only mean one thing.

12

THE WARD

THE MOMENT THE G-CAB STOPPED, Liam ripped open the door and ran across the neat courtyard. He yanked the door open and ran down the hall. The route to the isolation ward appeared in his specs. He ran down the hallway in the direction indicated. He arrived at another elevator. He tried not to pace as it came down to him.

The doors opened. A middle-aged man in a wheelchair, pushed by a young orderly, slowly rolled out. Liam held the elevator door, willing them to move faster. The orderly smiled at Liam as they passed.

"I'm sorry we need to discharge you already, Mr. Harrison," she said to the man in the wheelchair. "It's a shame your insurance couldn't cover another round of treatment."

"It's not your fault," Mr. Harrison replied. "You took great care of me. But you can't work for free and I'm all out of credit. Hopefully, I'll be able to pay some of this off and come back for another round soon."

The elevator doors closed. Liam hoped Julie had some money saved. He assumed Biotron offered decent health coverage. But there were always co-pays, out of network doctors, maximum payments. They had a hundred different ways to milk the unfortunate.

The elevator doors opened onto the ward. Half the lobby was screened off by a plastic tent. Inside, five people were sitting with flu-masks over their face. Nurses wearing face shields, flu-masks and full hazmat suits moved among them. A nurse called out as she caught an elderly man collapsing in front of her. From the other side of the tent, two orderlies in similar protective gear wheeled a stretcher through the airlock and gently laid the man on it. They wheeled him out of the airlock into the corridor behind the tent.

As Liam watched in stunned silence, a nurse handed him a flu-mask. Numb, he put it over his face and tightened it.

"Can I help you?" she said, her voice muffled by the layers of plastic and paper.

"I'm looking for Julie Baron. I was told I could find her here? I'm her brother," he said.

"Let's see," she said, her eyes flicking over the data layer in her specs. "She's in room 21. You can't go in, but you can see her through the plastic. Put a suit on and follow me."

"Do not take off the mask. The visitor hall should be safe, but we are taking no chances. Once you have finished your visit, exit through the decontamination area. If you don't follow the rules, we will quarantine you as well."

Liam nodded his understanding. "There are a lot of people here," he said.

"We're running out of space. Your sister's lucky. We just had a bed open up."

"Is it as bad as it looks?"

"It's awful. We can't do a damn thing to help except make them comfortable and pray. If it keeps up like this for much longer, we're going to get overwhelmed," she said. She blew out a breath. "Anyway, ready to go see your sister?"

"Yeah," Liam replied.

Julie lay on her side, pale and racked with a cough. She spit a hard lump of mucus into a tissue and dropped it onto the pile in the trash can next to her bed. The tattoos from her bodynet stood out in sharp relief against her pale skin.

She noticed Liam and rolled over, waving weakly. "Hey bro, how's it going?" she asked with a small smile.

"I'm fine. How are *you*?" he said.

The nurse patted him on the shoulder. "Ten minutes. She needs to rest. I'll come back for you," she said.

"I've been better," Julie wheezed. Her normally pale skin was paper white. Her eyes were sunken, and her hair stuck to her forehead with sweat.

"I can see that. Have you seen the doctor? What did they say?" he asked, putting his gloved hand on the plastic wall. His cheeks flushed as he realized he was relieved there was a barrier between them.

"The doc says I probably won't die of toxic shock since I'm young and healthy. But they can't do anything for the pneumonia. I'll either fight it off myself, or not..."

"What about your research? Don't you have a cure in the lab?" he said.

"Don't say that too loud," she whispered. "I don't want anyone to overhear." She grimaced with the effort.

"Okay, so? What about your research?"

"It hasn't been released yet. They're planning to gear up production now," she said.

"But won't they release some for you?"

"I called David this morning. He said he'd take it up the ladder. They'd need to do a special run in the lab, which needs some of the same people working on production," she said. The effort of talking seemed to exhaust her. She lay back and closed her eyes. Liam watched her, his fists clenched in helplessness. After a few breaths, she opened her eyes again.

"You helped discover it. Doesn't that count for something?" he said, knowing in his heart that it didn't.

She laughed gently, trying not to cough. "You know it doesn't. If I had access to my lab and the data, I could do it myself. We've figured out how to transfer the genes for the antibiotic into a yeast. We let the bugs grow then extract the compound. But they locked me out of the network as soon as they found out I was sick. They said I was a security risk until I recovered. They don't want me to copy the data to make my own drugs."

"So why the fuck wouldn't they make some for you?" he said.

"Because they don't have to. It's all risk and no upside for them. I know it's safe and I'm willing to try. But they're only concerned about the bottom line," she said.

"Fuck them," Liam said. "Can you grow this stuff anywhere?"

"No, Liam. If you get caught, they will disappear you down a black site prison. You can't..." She coughed violently and weakly dabbed at her mouth with a tissue. He could see the light crimson of blood.

"What's the other choice, Jules? What's the other option?"

"Convince them it's in their best interest. Megan, our CEO, is having a party tonight. David is invited. Get her to agree to do it for the good press it would generate. If anyone can talk them into it, you can."

She coughed again and this time it didn't stop. Her face screwed in pain as she grabbed her chest. The nurse ran down the hallway and pushed him out of the way. Two more followed, dragging an oxygen cart.

"I'll go. I'm going to get you well, no matter what," he whispered as an orderly took his arm and led him out. He followed, trying to blink back the tears. He had to focus. There was a party to attend.

13

PARTY

LIAM RUBBED the back of his head, trying to get rid of the tension headache building there. He leaned back against the palm tree growing out of the sidewalk. The brightly painted Victorian house nestled into the hillside behind it. The street and sidewalks were clean and well maintained.

He had watched the house all afternoon from a dragonfly drone perched in a tree across the street. The caterers had pulled up two hours earlier. The jazz quartet arrived an hour before the first guests. He hadn't seen Megan, but he assumed her Tesla had taken her to her garage in the back. Megan had the means and the desire to have her own car, even though it drove itself.

Liam hung back as another luxury Tesla pulled itself up to the curb. A thin, well-groomed couple, dressed in cocktail party finery, emerged and walked up to the house. The dragonfly recorded the guest's invitation code as their bodynets broadcast them to the house. If the house recognized the code, it would unlock and open the door. The drone sent the code to Keema. She unpacked it and sent him his own personal invitation.

"I still don't think this is a good idea," Keema said in his head. "There's no need to confront her here."

"I don't know how long Julie has. If the drug is ready to go, we don't have time to wait. What if Megan agrees tonight and we save Julie right now?"

He took a deep breath, held it a moment and then blew it out. He was dreading the next hour. Entering a house full of wealthy people, he didn't know and asking a high-powered executive for a favor wasn't his idea of a good time, especially feeling almost naked. His coat and tactical boots were too aggressive and definitely not formal enough for tonight. The shirt he was wearing felt like it wouldn't stop a damp breeze and he knew he couldn't run well in the shoes he was wearing. But there shouldn't be any violence this evening. At worst, a large man would ask him to leave and show him the door. Nonetheless, he couldn't stop tensing his shoulders without the reassuring bulk of his coat.

"I'm ready."

"Alright. If you won't listen to reason, then let's get this show on the road. I've got facial recognition up and running," Keema said. "I've ID'd the guests who have already arrived and sent you profiles. I'll pick up anyone we've missed once you're inside. Try to be discreet."

He smoothed his shirt and walked across the street. The scent of eucalyptus and honeysuckle filled the spring air. On another night, he would enjoy being outside. Tonight, he wanted to be anywhere but here. He had nothing in common with the people inside. They might as well be an alien species.

He forced himself to smile as he transmitted the invitation to the house. The door lock popped open, and the door swung inward with a slight hiss. Liam stepped inside. The house would send his ID to everyone inside, a modern version of a gilded-age butler announcing guests. A few heads turned to look at him, but quickly looked away. They didn't know him; thus, he was not important. He moved into the front room. The dark wood polished to a high gloss. The built-in bookshelves held a collection of antique books, sculptures and mementos from around the world. A colorful abstract painting took up a large area on the far wall. Liam choked as Keema overlaid the most recent sale price.

"Not helping, Keema," he whispered.

"Sorry. Couldn't help it," she said with a small laugh. "Oh look, it's Allan Peterson."

Liam turned his head to follow her pointer. Allan was tall and thin, and he wore the new Silicon Valley uniform of a shimmery-blue spider silk shirt capable of stopping a knife attack, loose breeches, and a pair of knee-high boots. Allan's expensive gray graphene bodynet gave the appearance of a subtle tribal tattoo. He looked miserable, surrounded by a pack of bankers, wealth managers, and their spouses.

As the founder of HipShare, he had a net worth greater than the GDP of several small countries. HipShare allowed anyone to create a graffiti overlay in their specs and share it with their friends. The frequently obscene tags caused random outbursts of laughter in public spaces. Another step in the long-term trend of technology making people appear mentally ill. Liam had tried to avoid it but was beginning to feel like a Luddite in most conversations. Talking to someone using HipShare called into question the idea of a shared reality.

Liam scanned the rest of the room. His specs labeled each person with their name and salient details for starting a conversation. Finally, he saw Megan, standing near the kitchen. She was in a heated conversation with a dark-haired man. "*David Suarez: head of ecological research at Biotron*" floated over his dark curly hair. He rubbed his short salt and pepper beard with his hand in frustration as he spoke. Megan flicked a glance over at Allan. She kept track of the man of the hour while trying not to appear too eager.

"Wait until their conversation finishes and you can get Megan alone. It will be easier if she doesn't have to look strong in front of an employee," Keema said.

"I agree. What about David?" Liam responded.

"He'd be an easier target."

"But does he have the pull? I thought he was a research scientist. They don't have a lot of political power."

"I've run a few simulations, based on what we know of her personality from her public persona. There's a better chance of success if David agrees to try to convince her. She'll ask for concessions from him, but he is more likely to have something she wants," Keema said.

"I'll try for David first," he said.

"You need to do something besides stand in the corner and stare at them while you wait, though."

"Dammit. That was my whole strategy for the evening," he replied. "Fine. Find me someone to talk to."

Liam made eye contact with a waiter and grabbed a champagne glass. He took a sip as he glanced around the room. The flavor of apple and citrus, followed by toast and honey stole his attention.

"Holy shit! That's actual champagne. She spent a lot on this party."

"They're gearing up to go public later this year. She's out to impress."

He made his way over to the buffet table, reminding himself this was an upscale party and slowly picked up one of the China plates. Looking over the lavish buffet in front of him, he moved to the platter loaded with Spanish ham and cheeses. As he contemplated how much he could put on his plate without embarrassing himself, he noticed Allan standing next to him with a plate in his hand, picking over the vegetable platter. Allan was a notoriously strict vegan and Liam self-consciously stood holding a plate of animal parts.

"Liam Baron. You're an interesting choice of party guest," Allan said. "How do you know Megan?"

He was about to respond when Keema whispered to him. "Tell him the truth. Trust me."

"I forged an invitation so I could get in," Liam replied.

Allan cocked his head in amusement.

"I need to talk to Megan."

"And why do you need to talk to our esteemed hostess?" Allan asked with a slight smirk.

"Go for it," Keema said. "It can't hurt."

"My sister has lung fever. I'm here to beg for an early release of the drug they are working on for her," Liam said.

"I'm sorry to hear about your sister," Allan said, eyes flicking left and right as he read from his specs.

He muttered something Liam couldn't hear. Liam's hands tingled as the network surged as Allan pulled down an enormous amount of data. He looked past Liam, hands twitching as he manipulated the reality only he could see.

"I wish you luck." Allan picked up several pieces of fruit and turned away.

"Thanks?" Liam said to his back as he walked away.

"That went well," Keema said.

"That went well?" Liam replied, shoving a piece of ham into his mouth. It had been a while since he had had meat like this and the salty, fatty flavor distracted him.

"It did. Check your nine o'clock," she said.

He glanced over his left shoulder. Megan was stalking towards him.

"I thought we were going to go through David?" he sighed.

"Time to improvise," Keema said.

Two large pins with small white flower accents held up Megan's shoulder length brown hair. Her spider silk dress wrapped around a body forged by an exacting fitness and diet regimen. A creeping terror started in his groin and worked its way up to his chest.

Easy tiger," Keema said. "Breathe."

"Hit me. Now, please," Liam whispered as Megan closed the distance.

"Here come the blockers," Keema said as his medi-patch clunked. "It'll take a second."

He took a deep breath and forced a smile on his face as Megan approached. It was showtime.

14

MEGAN

"Hi," Megan said with a tight smile. "I don't believe we've met."

"Hi. I'm Liam Baron. You have a lovely home," Liam said, with a broad smile. He stuck out his hand. Megan hesitated before shaking it once.

Overtly rubbing her hand on her skirt after she let go, she stared at him. "I don't recall inviting you, Mr. Baron. Are you with Allan Peterson? I noticed you were speaking with him just now."

"He's concerned about the same issue I'm here to speak to you about," Liam responded trying hard to keep his face neutral and maintain eye contact.

"And what is that issue?" she said eyebrows rising skeptically.

"Go direct," Keema said. "She won't react well to an indirect approach."

"I wanted to speak to you about my sister, Julie, who works for your company," he said.

"You want to ask for something for your sister? She can't

come ask herself?" Megan asked, interrupting him.

"She's in the hospital with lung fever and she needs your help."

"That's too bad. How can I help?" she said, squinting at him, examining him like a bug on a pin.

"She needs access to the antibiotic she is helping you develop to treat it."

"She told you about that?"

"She's part of the team that discovered it. Of course, she told me about it. I was hoping you might help her get access to an early run."

"Restromycin is very expensive to produce right now, Mr. Baron. My accountants tell me it's several hundred thousand dollars per dose."

"But she's your own research scientist!" he said, trying not to sound as though he was pleading.

"Well, it's unfortunate, but it's not my problem. I have a responsibility to my shareholders. A legal responsibility, Mr. Baron. I can't simply give away the results of our significant investment in this promising new drug."

"But what about the positive press? You save one of your own with a new drug developed in your labs. It would give people hope and you'd be able to capitalize on the goodwill. She and I are more than willing to make sure that story happens," he said.

"No. The positive press would not outweigh the costs and potential liabilities. What if it went wrong? What if Julie was one of the people our models show it won't help? We try the drug on her, and it fails, then what? Our IPO doesn't happen because no one trusts the drug. It's much better to release it worldwide, all at once. The few percentage points it doesn't work on are unfortunate background noise. No, there isn't much upside for us. If she was willing to pay for it, then the optics would be completely different. She'd be taking the risk, not us. But you've said she can't afford it right now, so there's nothing I can do."

"So, you expect her to come up with hundreds of thousands to access a drug she discovered?"

"*Helped* discover, Mister Baron. She was part of a team. A very expensive team. We aren't a charity. We could work out an internal loan for her and deduct it from her salary. We've done that for a few of our employees who find themselves in unfortunate circumstances. She should check with HR to see if they could arrange something," she said, turning to leave.

"So, she can be an indentured servant for the next ten years? What if the press were to get wind of the fact you are refusing to treat one of your own?" he said, feeling desperate.

Megan turned back around and stepped in close. Liam could feel the firm muscle in her shoulder as she gripped his forearm and pressed against him.

"What press? Who would report it with that kind of spin? I would refrain from making idle threats, Mister Baron. Julie violated the terms of her non-disclosure agreement by telling you about it. Assuming she recovers, and wishes to keep working for Biotron, I would recommend you leave now." Letting go of his arm, she gave him a quick smile, as if they had shared a little secret. Then, she spun on her heel and walked over to a group of well-dressed bankers on the other side of the room.

Liam moved to follow her. A large man in a dark suit detached himself from the corner and started to walk towards him. Liam grimaced and shifted into a fighting stance.

"Don't," Keema said. "We won't get through to her. From her point of view, she's right. There's too much risk to the IPO for her to think about it. If you make more of a scene it will blow back on Julie. They could fire Julie right now for telling you about the development of Restro. We need another plan. Let me work on it and we'll talk about it in the morning."

Liam knew she was right. He wasn't going to be able to convince Megan. He grabbed a piece of Parma ham and shoved it in his mouth as the man closed in. He turned and headed for the door before the bodyguard could say anything.

He glanced back as he opened the door and caught Allan Peterson staring at him on his way out. Allan could buy Biotron tomorrow, but all he was doing was staring at him. He shoved the thought out of his head as he stalked into the night air. It was time to do it the hard way. He took a deep breath and walked down the street. He had work to do.

15

THE SCORE

Liam slouched in the G-Cab, fighting the rising tightness in his shoulders and neck. Megan was a dead end. He could find some leverage to get her to change her mind. He could go fishing for some scandal, some whispered rumor but it was unlikely to provide what he needed. She was greedy and callous, traits her social circle admired, but they were not helpful to him. The cab pulled up in front of his building and he got out, still lost in thought. Walking through the lobby, he again ignored Emily's repeated plea to buy coffee. As the elevator descended toward him, the only solution that he could think of was to steal Restro. As he got into the elevator, he pondered how to take on Biotron, one of the biotech darlings of the city. Stealing augmented reality code or other infrastructure tech was risky, but it didn't generate headlines. The tech was too boring.

This would be different. If they caught him, it would be headline news. An intellectual property terrorist, stealing Biotron's new marquee drug. They'd accuse him of trying to sell it to China, India or Brazil. Or all three. Somehow no one would ever hear about him trying to save his sister.

It would be the end of his career. If he was lucky, he would go to jail. If he were unlucky, there were rumors about Homeland and the CIA warehousing people in old container ships slowly cruising in circles in international waters.

He choked down the surge of adrenaline at the thought of spending the rest of his life in a container in the North Pacific. He stretched his arms and slowed his breathing. He needed to focus on creating a plan to get the recipe, and not end up floating offshore. He stripped off his new party clothes, smelling of stress, sweat and food that made him grimace and threw them in the laundry chute.

He signaled for the shower. He stripped and leaned against the wall as the water ran down his face. He took a few deep breaths, letting the heat relax him. Producing Restro while avoiding prison would be difficult, but not impossible. Two years ago, he had covered his tracks on an AI heist by forging a research history. A few weeks creating logs of code, notes, and team communications about a fake simultaneous discovery. His buyer had paid double for a plausible evidence trail. Julie said Restro came from a common soil bacterium. It was possible someone else would discover it. If he sold it with a forged history, he could use that to get the first doses. He might get some off the first lab runs before the major production lines were up.

The shower chimed. He was deep into his extra fee time. He turned it off and toweled off, still focused on planning the mission. He gestured at his bed, and it folded down from the wall. The sheets were a crumpled mess, crushed into the foot of the bed when, in his rush to the hospital, he hadn't pulled them tight before it folded itself into the wall.

He stared at them. Was it only this morning he learned Julie was ill? A surge of panic ran up his spine, amplified by his exhaustion. He needed sleep. His thoughts were slow and jumbled. To have any chance of success, he needed to be at his best. Still naked, he shuffled over to the drink dispenser.

"Give me a drink. I need a sleep aid," he ordered.

The machine whirred, then stopped and announced, "You've exceeded your limit for sleep aids this week according to your health plan. If you wish to pay for an extra dose, please say yes."

"God dammit!" Liam yelled. "I'll pay for the fucking sleep aid."

"I'm sorry, you need to respond yes or no," the machine replied calmly.

Liam took a deep breath, fighting the urge to rip the machine out of the counter and slam it on the floor. "Yes," he said through his clenched jaw.

The machine returned to burbling and a small, hot, soy-milk-based beverage slid out its door. "Your account has been debited," it said.

Liam grabbed the drink and closed his eyes. He took a few deep breaths and downed it. The warm liquid coursed down his throat. The familiar numbness followed. Stumbling into the bed, he pulled the crumpled sheet over him.

The drug began to pull him softly down into the bed. In the quiet, the slide show of him, Julie and his dying mother began, unbidden, to play again. The brown and orange couch in the living room. His mother, her eyes sinking into her skull, her tendons taut as he held her hands. His throat burning as he swallowed his rage at her for leaving him so slowly. His father working late again on a 'client accounting emergency', hiding from his own pain of loss. Julie, sitting close, one arm around his shoulders. He could still feel his jaw clench and his shoulder hunch against her arm. He didn't want her to protect him. He didn't want her comfort. But without her, he was alone on the roiling sea of his grief. He gasped for breath, his eyes opening, the welling tears trickling down his cheeks. The drug held him down as though he were drowning. He gripped the edge of the bed like it was a life raft. He gradually got his breathing back under control. His eyes grew heavy again. More thoughts came, and he was helpless to stop them.

Julie was going to die.

He couldn't save her. He would end up locked in a small cell on a dead, heaving sea. Clamping his eyes shut, he willed the drug to pull him under into the black, dreamless void.

The rest of the night passed with alternating surges of anxiety and emptiness. The bright light of the sun shining into his eyes brought him awake. His mouth was dry and sticky, his eyes glued shut. He groaned as he rolled out of the bed. Pulling on his robe, he padded across the room.

The bar burbled a hot soy and stim into a mug and slid it onto the counter. Liam picked it up and sat back down. The mid-morning sun threw a bright rectangle on the floor, and he stared at it absently. He felt wrung out, too tired to worry, or even think. His apartment chimed and announced an incoming call from Keema.

He felt a mild flash of annoyance as she disturbed his empty reverie. He shook his head, disappointed in himself. Keema would be trying to help. He waved to accept the call and the house projected her avatar on the wall in front of him. She was tall and strong, with bronzed armor. She held a long spear that she brandished when making a point, or when Liam was being particularly dense. Liam liked the representation and the fact that it was very consistent. She looked like she would run a spear through the gut of anyone who got in her way, or his.

He had never seen her in person, only her voice and her animated representation. He had no idea what she looked like or where she was. He assumed she was a she. When his first agency assigned them to work together, they had agreed it was best if they never met. If he was ever caught, he wouldn't be able to tell them anything about her, and vice versa. Their communications were always anonymous and encrypted with encryption schemes changed every two weeks when a courier delivered new keys. However, she had seen his face in reflections as she watched through his specs during missions.

It was possible she had a complete record of each of his operations: audio, visual, biometrics, network traffic, and bank records. Only very late at night, when the fear came, did he wonder if he was foolish to trust her. But, given his operational record with her, he kept those worries tamped down.

"Morning, sunshine," said the warrior.

"Morning, Keema," he said. "One sec. Let me get my face on."

He retrieved his specs from their case. His eyes burned as he put them in, but they did that every morning. He blinked away the tears and transferred the call to them. The flat projection became a full 3-dimensional representation of her warrior. The system even rendered the gleam of the sunlight off the bronze armor when she walked by the window.

"That's better. I like being 3D," she said and thrust the spear at him. He flinched and swatted at the image of the blade. His hand passed through it.

"Funny," he said. "I've been through the wash cycle all night. Do you have something important?"

"Of course," she said, sounding annoyed. "After the party last night, I started working the problem. Megan is a no-go. We need another plan."

"We?" He took another swig of his drink. The stimulants were beginning to burn through his fog.

"Yes, *we*," she said as if she were speaking to a particularly slow child. "I'm going to help you, so you don't get killed, or worse, get me arrested."

"But there's no percentage. I can't pay you."

"After everything we've been through together, did you think I'd hang you out to dry on this? No way. Besides, Restro has value. We can figure out something on the back end. I'll help you for an even split if there's an upside." Her avatar waved its hands at the unknown possibilities of the future.

He hadn't expected this. Liam took a sip of his drink to give himself a moment to recover. "So, what do you have in mind?"

"Well, Julie said she could make it herself with access to the data, right? So, we get a copy and get her a lab. Or we find someone who knows how to use a lab. We make enough for her, and a few friends, then figure out what to do with it," she said with a shrug. "We keep it quiet. It will look as though she recovered on her own. Then we see if there's a way to scale it up while avoiding detection by Biotron."

"We'll need to create a research history, too. That will make it more valuable for any potential buyer. If they can pretend, they discovered it at the same time, it will be harder for Biotron to shut them down," Liam said, swirling the last of the drink. He let himself feel a small bit of hope.

"See? We make a great team," Keema said. " I put my

gremlins on the problem last night. Biotron is buttoned up tight. But we managed to get a basic map of the organization, their offices, and a few other goodies."

"You have gremlins?"

"I called in a few favors, got an AI to look for hidden connections, you know...spy stuff."

"It doesn't sound like the usual spy stuff, Keema. It sounds like you went through a load of effort." Liam locked eyes with the avatar and added, "Thank you."

"Like I said, Restro has value. There might be a few interested parties. We will figure something out." She pointed her spear at him and narrowed her eyes.

"Point taken."

He could tell she was lying, but he couldn't decide why. She might not want to reveal her true feelings for him. Or she was planning to screw him on the score of a lifetime? Either way, he didn't have much choice. Her avatar presented him with a wooden box. Liam grimaced. She had a taste for anachronistic visual analogies.

"Here's the operational folder. Review it and get back to me. I have a few ideas for the approach, but I want to get your reaction first. I've taken the liberty of organizing it for you. Call me back later this afternoon." With a blink, she disappeared.

The box remained on the floor in front of him as viewed through his glasses. He couldn't help but smile as he pushed the key encryption into the keyhole.

The box popped open. He unrolled the scroll sitting on the top. The parchment looked worn and stained. It held a list of interlinked pointers to more information. He glanced at the list of text, video, biographies and the networks of connections and communications. His system analyzed the data set, pulling together correlations and relationships. He waited for it to organize itself. He felt breathless. He was going to steal Julie's work, and make sure she had what she needed. He would have the cure for himself as well. When he sold it, he'd have enough money to pay off the rest of his debts. He would then take some time off and find a different line of work. He moved over to his more comfortable chair and explored the data space.

Megan was the spider at the center of the web of relationships at Biotron. Keema highlighted David Suarez, the lead researcher he had seen at the party, and Julie's boss.

David knew Julie was sick, but he hadn't done anything for her, despite her obvious feelings for him. He had access to the genetic code, the recipe for creating the drug at volume. Liam weighed his options. He could try to break into his security and take what he needed. He would do it quietly to spare Julie's feelings.

But he might need to make David the patsy in this game, make it look as though David had sold Restro to someone. A few anonymous wire transfers, some poorly erased messages, and he would be the obvious suspect. No one would bother to come looking for Liam. It would sting for Julie, but she would live. A surge of electricity rose out of his gut. He loved this moment when he saw the plan. If time allowed, he could spend days working on the little details. But now he needed to move fast. He started sketching. As he worked, the thought of destroying David to save Julie stilled his rising excitement. He had used people before, but never anyone this close. The thought of Julie's disappointment if she could see him planning David's destruction weighed on him. He'd make sure she never knew.

16

OUTSIDE BIOTRON

LIAM PULLED himself deeper into his coat, trying to ward off the chill as the fog flowed down the bay. It scattered the ballpark lights, creating a warm, diffuse light that belied the cold. The wind hissed through the manicured landscaping. "Glorious summer in San Francisco," he said to himself.

He took one last glance around. No one was nearby. He and Keema had spent the last two days planning this moment. All the planning in the world couldn't prevent a random encounter. But for now, he was alone.

His target was an anonymous glass and faux brick two story building. During the day the area was full of very smart people manipulating molecules for the betterment of humanity, or at least the parts of humanity who could afford lifestyle cures and longevity drugs.

Liam switched his specs over to night vision and reached out with his hands. His fingers pulsed and tingled as he felt the security systems talking to each other. He could feel the security guards' radios as they wandered the building on their rounds. He walked down the sidewalk, mapping the building from different angles.

He switched his visual channels, peering into the building with infrared. The heat signature outline of a guard by the front door shimmered in yellow and orange. The radio of the other security guard on his rounds upstairs moved closer.

Satisfied, he moved back to a small garden about a hundred meters from the front of the lab. "The area is clear," he said.

"Go for the next step," Keema replied.

The bench in the garden wasn't perfect, but it was the only public space close enough to the building. Sitting in a G-Cab would be warmer, but that was a fast way to prison. The car would even drive him there itself. He hoped anyone who saw him would mistake him for one of the growing multitudes of the homeless.

He pulled a large glasses case out of his coat pocket and popped it open. The dragonfly drone inside unfolded its wings and rotated them into flight position. Its carbon black body had a cluster of small cameras at the head. It was a slightly larger model than the one he had used at the party. He ran through his pre-flight checklist. Everything was green. He closed his eyes and connected to the drone's camera array. The image filled his vision. He had the disconcerting feeling of sitting in his own hand. He connected to the small network packet sensor tucked inside its underbelly. It was charged and ready to record.

Preflight completed, he opened an overlay of the office building. He was waiting for a security guard to open the door and start their patrol of the grounds. He didn't know when that would happen, but then, neither did the security team. The building AI randomly generated their patrols, avoiding predictable holes in the coverage. They would head outside when their specs told them.

He hoped it would be soon, as he was starting to shiver. Using the heater in his coat would drain the batteries, so he pulled the coat tighter and tried to ignore it. "I should have worn another sweater," he whispered.

"Yes, you should have. I told you it was going to be cold tonight," Keema replied.

"I know. I just hate feeling constricted. Hopefully it won't take long to get the listener into Suarez's office. You've got the flyby ready for tomorrow?"

"Yes. I'll do a pass by his window around noon. The listener will relay the traffic as I pass by. We should have all of the data analyzed just after lunch and we can figure out what to do next."

His fingers tingled as they caught a new radio signal, and he nearly dropped the drone. He switched out of his drone's-eye view and ordered it to perch on his shoulder.

The new signal pinched and itched in a way he knew by heart. Someone was remote operating a drone somewhere very nearby. He knew the pulse of a course correction and the tingle of the new heading, and the monitoring heartbeat throbbing underneath. He swung his hands in an arc, trying to locate the source. It was coming from somewhere off to his right, in the green lawn in front of the labs across the street. He couldn't decrypt the feed. It could be a security patrol, or someone else moving in on one of the labs.

"Are you getting this?" he whispered to Keema.

"Yeah. I'll keep an eye on it. You better get going," she said.

"Dammit! We don't know when the security team will open the door for their sweep. What if that signal is a security drone? I'm sitting out here in the park with my ass in the breeze," he said. "This doesn't feel right."

"Do you want to abort? We can try again tomorrow night."

He sighed. "No, Julie doesn't have time for us to wait. I'll get the package in place."

"I'll watch your back while you're in."

He closed his eyes and switched back to the drone-eye view. He twitched his shoulders and the drone clicked into the air. It flitted toward the front door of the lab, correcting for the breeze off the water.

As he neared the door, Liam flipped so its head was facing down, tail in the air. He grabbed the top doorjamb, feeling the magnetic feet lock into place. He set the drone to watch the door for movement. He left the audio feed from the drone piped to his audio system and opened his eyes.

The orange and yellow heat signature of the second guard descended the stairs. He risked a glance over to his right, to the low hedges that ran along the other side of the sidewalk across the road. He thought he could see a slight variation in the temperature. Was someone lying on the other side of those hedges? The ground could be warm because of a sewer, or it could be a dry spot the sprinklers missed. Or there could be someone with good thermal shielding lying there.

"No change in the drone signal. It's not coming towards you. Focus on the mission," Keema hissed in his ear.

"Yes, ma'am," he said. "I hope you have bail money ready when it turns out it's a security patrol. Cause I will let them take me alive."

He glanced back at the offices. The guard was heading toward the door. He brought his vision back to the drone's camera.

The guard walked right below him. His dark hair was parted to one side, thinning in the back. "Hey, Crosby. I'm going to do the perimeter check. Next round is on you. It's cold out here tonight," said the guard, holding the door open as he looked back inside over his shoulder.

"It's summer. It's cold and damp every night, Paulino," said Crosby.

Liam released the drone's landing magnets and flipped the tail over. He flitted inside the building as the guard let the door close behind him. He flew as close as he dared to the drop ceiling, the white tiles a centimeter over his head. Beyond the entryway, the building opened into a glass atrium framing a wide staircase. He banked and flew to the top of the atrium. The drone signaled that it had found its programmed flight path and Liam relinquished control. The drone flew better than he could in most situations. At the top of the atrium, it rolled over and turned toward the main second floor hallway. Gaining speed, it pulled up hard and folded in its wings. It sailed through the grate of the air conditioning duct.

17

DOGFIGHT

He let out a sigh of relief as the drone cleared the grate. Small drone intrusions were frequent enough that some companies put screens over their ducts, but physical retrofits were expensive, and usually done after an incident. Liam smiled at the thought. This might be the last time he could pull this off before they closed this particular barn door.

Inside the duct, the video stream began to degrade. He blinked out of the drone, trusting it to follow the mission plan. He took another glance back across the street. He zoomed in. There was a small thermal variation behind the hedges. He wished he had another micro-drone with him to check it out. Next time, he'd make sure he had two. But he couldn't risk moving and losing contact with the drone inside.

He forced himself to take a deep breath and rolled his shoulders. He had a strong urge to get up and leave. If there was someone on the other side of the hedge, he wanted to move to a better position to deal with them. But he forced himself to sit still and concentrate on the mission. He made sure the sensors on his coat were at full sensitivity.

Finally, the drone emerged from the duct and reestablished contact. It was sitting on the edge of the grate in the ceiling of Suarez's office. He switched back to the drone's eye view.

Clinging upside down to the ceiling, he looked down into Suarez's office. It was small, with only enough room for a large bookcase, a workstation table, and a love seat. The wear pattern in the carpet told a story of days of pacing, working complex puzzles in his mind.

The bookcase was a curious affectation. Everything Suarez could need would be available in his specs. But there were large textbooks, reference books and shelves of notebooks. The clutter would provide a useful hiding spot. He highlighted a place on the top of the bookcase.

The dragonfly flitted over to the square Liam had highlighted. The dust suggested the cleaning crew knew it was out of sight. That should keep the listener from discovery for at least a day. The drone landed on the shelf and released the listener. Flicking the wings, he took off easily without the heavy load. He turned once, to make sure the listener was out of sight.

He opened a channel to Keema. "Listener placed," he said.

"Good. Hold station for a second. Let's make sure we have good signal," she replied. He rolled his eyes. Of course, she was going to check the signal.

"We may need you to reposition it on the shelf if I can't get a good read."

He tapped his foot, while she tested the signal from the listener. This was taking too long.

"Okay. We're good," she said. "Head for the duct but

hold at the entrance. I want to take one more look to make sure everything is alright."

"Starting drone egress."

He circled the room once, pushing the wings hard. Then as it lined up on the grate, he folded its wings back in and shot through the gap. Once through, he flared the wings and spun back to the entrance of the grate.

"Great. I'll hold here," he said. He checked over the drone's energy levels and reviewed the exit path. Something moving in the room caught his eye. He connected to the drone's view again, turning the insectile head to try to catch it again. A small shadow flickered on the wall and then disappeared. He walked the drone to the edge of the vent. Something passed right in front of him. He tracked it. Another dragonfly alighted behind the crown of the bookcase and deposited a large listener.

"Oh shit, Keema. We have company," he said.

"I see it. Watch them from your location. I'm getting good signal on our listener. If they plant and go, we'll leave them. Can you feel a signal?" she said.

"Hold on." Liam shifted his attention from the drone and reached out. Listeners passively soaked up information from the target until its memory was full. It would only broadcast a signal in response to a specific command from someone nearby.

Any other agent worth their contract advance would make sure they had good signal as well. So, he waited, feeling for the activation check signal and response. A moment later his hands tingled with the other signal check. The other operator was nearby.

"Is there an open contract for Biotron?" he asked Keema.

"Not that I've seen. I may have missed it last week while we were working," she said.

"Should we leave it?" he asked.

"There's no reason to interfere. If there is an open contract it gives us some cover," she said.

"That's what I was thinking."

The other dragonfly, nearly twice the size of his and dark blue, turned and perched above their listener. Its large antennae swiveled, scanning the room.

“Don’t do it,” Liam whispered.

The other drone picked up their listener and took off.

"Dammit!" he hissed. “Keema, are you getting this?”

“Yes. I’m trying to track the signal. Go get him,” she said, her voice flat and steady.

He pushed his drone off and out of the grate, diving towards the other bot. He aimed for the left wings, hoping to knock it out of the air. With any luck, it would let go of the listener and he could retrieve it.

He dove hard. The instant before he made contact, the other drone dipped its wings, and he shot past. He spread his wings and pulled back hard to break out of the dive.

"Above you!" Keema shouted.

He looked up, the drone's head tracking his movement. The blue dragonfly barreled down at him. He cursed and ducked to avoid the on-rushing insectile robot. The motion put him back into a dive. He flicked the wings as fast as they would go, needing to gain altitude. A red warning flashed in the periphery of his vision. He was running out of power. A drip of sweat rolled down the back of his neck, momentarily bringing him back to his physical body. He fought to stay with the drone, his stomach churning with the split sensation.

Straining his shoulders, he maxed the wing speed. The drone's flight leveled out millimeters above the beige carpet. The drone wobbled as the automatic systems overshot their control parameters. The wobble increased, threatening to roll him. In the park, he threw his shoulders back, flaring the wings. He gained a little altitude and his flight leveled.

Out of his peripheral vision, he saw the blue drone turn back around towards him. He pulled up, trading speed for altitude. He shot upward, racing along the wall, but it wasn't enough. Liam staggered as the blue dragonfly slammed into him. It bounced off the wall and plummeted towards the floor. The room spun around him. He slid off the bench. He felt cool wet grass on his face as he plummeted towards the floor.

Finally, everything went black.

Liam opened his eyes, trying to re-orient himself. He pushed up onto one knee and put his hands on the ground to create a physical anchor. His vision spun as his inner ear tried to figure out what the hell had just happened.

"Breathe, Liam. It's okay," Keema said. His medi-patch clicked. A warm rush of anti-motion sickness medication flooded behind his eyes. He grabbed onto the bench, took a few breaths and levered himself up.

"Thanks. God, I hate crashing those things. It must take a year off my life each time," he said.

"As soon as you can walk, you need to get out of there. Whoever planted that other bug has to be close."

18

BARKLEY

When he stood up, his motion alarm flashed a warning. In less than a second his coat stiffened to protect him. Across the street, a figure stood up and walked around the hedge toward him. The figure waved as he crossed the street, "Liam! Am I surprised to see you!" he called out.

Liam froze. The man walking toward him was just over six feet tall, with thick, muscular arms and legs. He looked like a troll emerging from the fog in a Norse saga. Liam swallowed as he recognized the man's ambling swagger.

"Barkley? What the hell are you doing here?" he said, his voice much higher than he wanted.

"Probably the same thing you are. Was that you inside?" Barkley said, stopping about five feet away, knees flexed, the weight on the balls of his feet like a kickboxer. Hands by his side, palms turned toward Liam, he gave a little shrug. They had crossed paths a few times before, and it had generally not ended well for Liam. Liam felt a cold tight anxiety grip the back of his neck.

"Yeah, that was me," Liam responded, crossing his arms

over his chest. He realized he was already curling into a defensive posture. He grimaced and made himself lower his hands.

"I cleaned up the mess you left on the carpet. I also removed your ridiculous little sensor." Barkley smiled and winked. "You know there are better models, right?"

"Yeah, I know. So, looking for anything in particular in there?" Liam asked, jerking a thumb toward the lab building. He tried to keep his voice even and confident, but he heard himself quavering. He clenched his teeth. It was one thing for Barkley to screw up a payday for him, but now he had put Julie's life in danger. He balled his fists, fighting the urge to scream.

"Probably the same thing you are. You know you're not going to win this, right? Remember Denver?" Barkley watched him like a cat watches a mouse.

Liam felt his heart quicken, ears filling with the sound of rushing blood. He had barely escaped Denver. They had competed to steal a new algorithm for improving shale oil fields. Barkley had stolen it the day before and then set a trap for him. He had called in a tip about an eco-terrorist who remarkably, like Liam, was planning to bomb the building. Getting out of Denver with his face in every police heads-up display had cost him a lot of money. The damage to his reputation had cost him even more.

"Easy, Liam," Keema whispered in his ear. "Be smart. He's baiting you. We can still get something out of this."

"I remember Denver. I learned a few lessons," Liam said, stretching his neck, trying to find a way to bring his heart rate down.

"I bet it will," Barkley said. He exhaled and extended his hands.

His medi-patch clicked, and he felt a surge of energy run

through his arms and legs. Everything became sharper. He felt light and fast.

"A little boost. Kick his ass," Keema said.

Liam's fingers tingled with a new signal. An intrusion alarm floated up in his vision. Barkley had sent his first probing attack.

Barkley stared at him, just out of arm's reach. Liam focused and took a deep breath. Two could play this game. In electronic combat, he might have a chance.

He twitched his right hand, sending his own probe at Barkley. If he could find a piece of equipment with a security flaw, he could easily break in. Once inside, he could figure out who hired him and why. His bodynet analyzed the responses from the attack, looking for an opening. But Barkley's systems were a solid wall.

"What the hell?" Liam whispered.

"He's got some serious new kit. But new kit means new security holes. Keep him busy while I look," Keema said.

Liam gestured to launch his network attack routines. In his specs, arrows of malicious code flew toward Barkley. Most disappeared, blocked by Barkley's defenses. A few lingered as they found a small weakness. They disappeared moments later as they were neutralized by the next layer of defenses.

As he pushed his attack, the intensity of the tingling in his hands increased. The edges of his vision turned red with warnings. Barkley opened new attack vectors, probing Liam's older, patched-up systems for a hole. The thought of Barkley gaining full access made his mouth dry. Barkley could send his mission logs to the police, cut him off from the network and leave him here to be arrested. He prayed they hadn't missed a hole in his systems.

"Shit, he's fast," Keema said. "So far, the defenses are holding. I still can't find an opening, though."

Liam reached out, dedicating more bandwidth and power to the attack. He expanded his attack on Barkley's drone systems, hoping to get lucky. Nothing was working.

Barkley stared at him, his eyes tracking information in his specs.

"You know you can't win this, right?" he said as he extended his arms as if he were passing a basketball. Liam's specs flickered, overwhelmed by the sudden surge of energy. Liam blinked, trying to refocus.

"He's brute forcing the specs. I may need to shut them down," he said.

"Not yet," Keema said. She sent him a flaw in the watchdog in Barkley's pocket. Liam accessed the bot's control systems, and he muttered a series of commands.

As he sent the last command, the world disappeared behind a wall of static. He instinctively threw his hand over his eyes and staggered backwards. A huge boulder of code barreled down on him, pounding his collapsing defenses. He closed his eyes, but the static was in the specs, behind his eyelids. He fought down rising panic.

"Dammit, I'm locked out," Keema said. "I've lost control."

Blinking, Liam tried to clear the static. As fast as it had gone, his vision returned.

He found his bearings and looked at Barkley. The larger man was swearing and batting his smoking pocket. Liam's attack had caused the watchdog to overheat, and its batteries had exploded. Liam wiped the tears away from his watering eyes and refocused his attack.

"I have an idea," Keema said. "Hold him off for 30 seconds."

Liam sent another probe, searching for an opening. His hands burned as his embedded antennae overheated from the strain. He couldn't keep this up much longer.

He felt Keema use his bodynet. She sent Barkley's test signal to the listener in the office. The listener responded, sending out the password request. Keema relayed the request to Barkley's system.

Barkley snatched the dead watchdog from his pocket. With a grunt, he threw his open palm toward Liam. Immediately the static returned. Liam stumbled back.

"Hurry up, Keema," he said. "He's close to the main network!"

"Almost done," she replied.

Liam rapidly changed settings on his specs. He gained a moment of clear vision until Barkley again swamped it with noise. He was running out of options.

Barkley's network finally replied with the listener's password. She then relayed the authentication to the listener, pretending to be Barkley. The listener was open to them. Keema changed the password, locking Barkley out.

"I've done what I can," she said. "Get out now."

"I can't see," Liam said, staggering through the haze of static.

He grabbed the specs out of his eyes. His vision returned. But he had lost his primary interface to his bodynet, and the fight.

He blinked away tears as he stumbled toward the edge of the park. The cool night air burned his eyes. Barkley had a look of quiet concentration as he directed attacks on Liam's still functioning bodynet. His tattoos burned as massive amounts of data passed back and forth. "Fuck it. Keema, get me out of here."

"I have a G-Cab waiting for you a block to your south. Turn right and it should be there."

"Got it." Liam felt his left arm stiffen as Barkley overwhelmed the armor interfaces on his coat.

"Running away again, Liam?" Barkley called out. "I don't think so. We aren't done talking."

Liam turned and tried to run. His coat tightened around him, restricting his motion. The normally comforting weight of the coat began to suffocate him. He had to act fast. With full control, Barkley could lock him in his coat and leave him helpless.

"Time for a Hail Mary," Liam muttered. He turned back towards Barkley and took a deep breath. He held it for a second, then let it out sharply as he drew his right arm up from his navel and stretched it towards Barkley. The power flowed down his arm through his outstretched fingers. Barkley staggered as his systems faltered under the onslaught of the small directed electromagnetic pulse. Liam felt his coat relax as it depleted its power supply.

The two security guards started running toward them from the office building. Barkley had his back to the building and hadn't seen the guards.

"I called in a report of suspicious activity to Biotron security. Run," she said.

Liam used the last of his power to throw a large amount of electronic noise at Barkley. It would take Barkley's system precious milliseconds to filter it out. As the last of his power drained away, he lost contact with Keema and the rest of his systems shut down. Liam turned and sprinted away from the park, his coat flapping limply behind him as he ran.

Behind him, there was a shout and the crackle of a taser. He risked a glance over his shoulder as he reached the street. One of the guards was down, clutching his groin. The other was thrusting a taser baton at Barkley. He made contact and Barkley stiffened. The guard closed and gave another thrust of the baton.

Liam grinned as he ran toward the waiting car. Barkley was going to have a long night.

19

KEEMA

Liam woke with a gasp. He lurched off the bed, looking for the source of the intrusion.

"Liam!" Keema voice rattled his skull. "Wake the fuck up! We have work to do."

"Dammit!" Liam jumped.

While he slept, his mattress had recharged the internal batteries tucked into his lower abdomen. Once they had enough power, his communications systems automatically restarted and reestablished the tactical communication link to Keema from the night before.

"I fucking hate it when you do that."

"If you didn't sleep until the middle of the morning, I wouldn't need to. We have things to discuss," she said.

"No talk before caffeine and glucose," he said. "And pants. I need two minutes. The world will not end in the next two minutes, right?" The apartment, registering that he was awake, opened the shades revealing a bright burning morning sunshine. The kitchen chimed as it finished readying his breakfast.

He put on last night's crumpled pants and shoved his specs on his eyes and shuffled over to the kitchen system. A fresh cup of soy and stim flowed out of the brewer into the waiting mug. He picked it up and slurped the top off it. The torpor fled in front of the stimulants.

"I can focus now. What's up?"

"I grabbed the data from Barkley's listener this morning."

"Good thinking," he said. Last night's activities would have the lab on high alert. They would sweep for bugs. "Did you get anything? Do we have a lead?"

"I got a surprising amount of data. Something's not right. We should go through this together," she said.

Liam took another swig of his drink. The mix of anticipation and dread churned his stomach. "Hit me."

The data structure appeared in the middle of the room along with Keema's avatar, the files arranged in a timeline, running from left to right. Fainter lines connected people and topics. Liam gestured and swung the axis of the view so the files rearranged themselves by social connection. Megan's name appeared in many of the files, but none with 'Suarez' or even just 'David'.

Liam scowled and bit his lip. Most of the files should link to David. They were hacking into his workstation after all.

"This is strange," Keema said. "I could only copy data in the buffer. When the buffer filled, the system started overwriting the oldest files, first in, first out."

"So, we should have, what, a couple of hours of data from his workstation? Whatever he was working on plus some messages? Right?"

"We should. But we don't. These are archive videos pulled from the company database. It looks like he downloaded these recordings a few minutes before I got there. It didn't seem like he was in the office when I flew by either. I think he downloaded this and then left," said Keema. She squinted and tilted her head.

"I don't understand. He downloaded a bunch of video archives and then took off? What is he up to?"

"Let's take a look at one from the beginning of the timeline."

She opened a video. Megan, tense like a violin string, was in a video conference with a man of South Asian descent. The man's black hair was carefully slicked back and framed by the upturned collar of his shirt.

"Vinge, what do you need?" said Megan.

"Hey, Megan. I'm looking at the first two quarters of the post-Restro launch and I can't make the numbers work. The board said we need ten million in revenue by the end of Q2, right?" said Vinge, incredulously.

"That's right," she replied.

"Well, I can't get there with any sort of reasonable growth rate," Vinge said, shaking his head. He smoothed his hair back and stared at Megan.

"What are you using for the projection?"

"I'm using ten percent of the infected population with access in the first eight weeks, growing to about a third by the end of the second quarter," he said.

"Can we accelerate production?" she asked.

"That's our max production capacity," he said.

"What are you using for a price?" she said, her mouth drawn tight.

"A thousand a dose, like we agreed."

"We can charge whatever we want. No one else is even close to a cure. We'll have the patent on the molecule soon," she said, frowning at him.

"But won't increasing the price bring down demand? And what about the press?"

"Willingness to pay has nothing to do with this," Megan said. "What if we rolled it out more slowly?"

"What do you mean? I can't make the numbers work as it is." His brow wrinkled in confusion. "If we roll it out more slowly, we'll make less money," Vinge said.

"What if we have a great launch, great press about how the cure is here. But then we run into technical production problems. Maybe scaling the production line isn't going as well as we hoped."

"So, people know it's available, but they can't get it. We release it at a thousand. Run into scaling problems so we must increase the price. If we get through the first and second quarters at five thousand a dose... then we take it from there. I'll run that through the model and see where we get."

"Good. We need to make those numbers. The board is getting anxious about the IPO," she said. "Get me the new model by Monday. I'll loop Don in on the production side." She cut the connection.

Liam stared at the frozen image; mouth open. Keema stood, arms by her side, spear tip lowered.

"Well..." Keema said.

20

CHAT

"THAT CAN'T BE THEIR STRATEGY," Liam said. "There's no way they would do that deliberately."

"You really think they wouldn't?"

The kitchen dinged at him and his bowl of fortified oatmeal slid onto the counter. Liam pushed it aside. He wasn't hungry anymore.

Keema pulled up a video voice mail. A man with a soft, round face and curly hair spoke: "Hey Vinge. Looked at the scaling issues. How long do you want them to take?"

The next video up was Vinge's reply. "Hey Don. Four or five weeks should get us where we need. Thanks! How about Tuesday for the sushi I owe you?"

"Well, shit." Liam said. "I'm wrong."

"Here's one from later in the week. It's labeled *Megan, Don, Vinge, George.* George Stillman is the board chair."

George and Megan were sitting together at a small conference table. The glass walls of the conference room were on the full privacy setting. Megan was in full professional mode, hair pulled back, suit crisp. They stared at the camera until Don and Vinge appeared in two separate windows. Each was calling in from their offsite offices.

"So I've reviewed the market development proposal outlined by Meg. I like the approach," George said. George was late middle aged, balding in a monks pattern, but lean and tanned. His subtly striped shirt suggested wealth without screaming it.

Then, a private message, from Don to Vinge: *"Yesss. Quarterly bonus, here we come."*

Vinge replied with a high five animation. : "*Srsly. Dinner at the Chop House on me. Maybe you can finally find a date.*"

Don: "*V. Funny. I have a date for tomorrow night.*"

Vinge: "I meant one you didn't pay for."

Back on the call, George was saying, "So we don't think the price increase will blow back on us?"

Don and Vinge snapped back to looking directly at their cameras, trying to fight smiles.

Megan cleared her throat and set her jaw. "We don't think so. We release the PR about the drug production difficulties after week four. We claim the initial price was too low to support the ongoing development. We'll promise to drop the price once we have the production difficulties ironed out."

Vinge nodded. He continued, "My model shows enough demand at the higher price to maximize revenue over the following two quarters. So, we should hit our targets."

George leaned in to the camera. "And Don, we can develop a plausible rationale for the delay?"

"We'll be lucky if we have to create one, to be honest." Don said, his round face flushing slightly "We've isolated a molecule from a soil bacterium that doesn't like growing in the lab. This bug likes its dirt, not a petri dish. We have copied the genes for the antibiotic into yeast and the initial cultures are starting to grow. The problem will be scaling up for large quantities. But it's tricky. A contamination event would set us back months. So, we can just be careless for a moment and let nature take its course."

George then leaned back in his chair, staring at the ceiling. Megan gave the two men on the video screen a small nod. She knew which way this was going to go.

"Then it's decided," George said. "We go out at $1,000 a dose, then run into production problems.

"Of course, George," Megan said. "And this goes no further, yes?" She waited for them all to agree. It didn't take long. Smiling now, she said, "Thank you, gentlemen. I'm sure you both have work to do."

The call ended.

Keema looked away from the video and straight at Liam, her lip curling in disgust.

"Now we know what David was after. He must have copied the evidence," she said.

"The question is: Is he going public, or does he want a piece of the action?"

"We can work with this. If he's looking for a piece of the action, we threaten to expose him. He gives us access, we keep quiet."

"And if he's going public?"

"He makes a bigger impact than just bad press by giving us the data."

"Wait... you see a conspiracy that will kill tens of thousands. All to ensure they make their quarterly targets. And you aren't angry?" Keema said, gripping her spear.

"Of course I'm angry. These guys deserve what's coming to them. But we still have a job to do and I need to get the data out for Julie. Once we have the data, we can do what we want - get Julie a lab and make it for ourselves, sell it to the highest bidder, both. But first, we have to get it."

"What if we released it globally? Put it out there for anyone with a synthetic biology lab to make it? There are thousands of people with home labs who can grow yeast. Distribute it, make it in every neighborhood," she said, swinging her spear like a conductor.

"If we release it publicly, we get sent to a shipping container floating in the middle of the Pacific. Probably before we can get Julie the medicine she needs. Besides, how will we get paid if we open it up to everyone?"

"You'd rather get paid than save lives?"

"No. But we are going to need money to get ourselves out of this one way or another," Liam said. "And we'll still have a copy we can release."

"Yes. We'll have a copy. Didn't you listen to Megan? There is no price curve for medicine. It doesn't work that way. Either you need it and you get it, or you die," Keema said. Her shoulder sagged and she hung her head.

"We'll figure it out when we get it. David is the place to start," Liam said.

"My data suggests he's home. That's where we go next. Figure out what his plans are and see if we can gain some leverage there."

"I'll start the prep to get into his place and get access to his home system. Hopefully Barkley doesn't have the same idea."

"What do we know about his contract, anyway?" Liam asked.

"Not much. He's been getting steady work as we've been rebuilding after Denver. I don't know who is backing him," she said.

"If he's still active, he'll get in our way. I really need to upgrade some of my defensive systems," Liam said, his voice tight.

"I've shipped you a new bodynet router. He used a weakness in your current system to gain access to your visual systems. He was very close to gaining complete control of your systems," she said.

"You don't need to send me a new router, Keema. I'll figure it out," he said, a little hurt by the implication.

"There isn't time to figure it out, Liam," she snapped, throwing her hands up, exasperated. "I've got a supplier who gets them for me cheap. You can pay me back after our big payday." Her lip curled as she spat the words.

"See. This is why we need to get paid, Keema. I'll pay you back. Just let me know how much it is," Liam said, trying not to clench his teeth. Why did she have to make him feel like he couldn't take care of himself? He couldn't afford new hardware, but he could have leased it on credit.

"I need you to be effective in the field. That's all it is."

“Let's try for David's place tonight. Can you get access to his spending habits so we can see if there's a pattern for when he's not home?"

"I've got it. I'm also sending you some extra security patches. I'll be available later and we'll start the mission prep," she said. She cut the connection and disappeared from his living room. The videos from the data dump hung in the air in front of him.

21

HOME INVASION

LIAM STROLLED DOWN the street outside the fading Victorian house for the third time in an hour. He checked the feed from the watchdog sitting on the fence outside. Nothing had changed. Liam sighed and stopped to pretend to tie his shoelaces.

"You there?" he asked.

Keema replied immediately. "Of course. Here and waiting. Switch to infrared. Let's see if we can find him inside.".

Liam blinked his specs into infrared. The walls of the building were blue, the same temperature as the outside air. The front window glowed orange. There was a spot of brighter yellow in the lower right corner where the caulk needed repair. Inside, a small electric space heater gave off a white-orange glow. Glancing up at the second-floor apartment, he detected what appeared to be a small child playing in the front room.

"The upstairs neighbors are home. Checking David's downstairs apartment. I can't see him on IR."

"He's probably there. If he keeps to his pattern, he

should leave for dinner within the next half hour. That will be our window of opportunity," Keema said. Liam wondered what it would be like to walk into a warm restaurant where everyone knew him. But patterns create weaknesses.

He reached out with his network traffic sensors for David's signature. The signal surge cramped his hands, and he quickly damped it down. His own bodynet felt strange to him. Keema's new router felt sharper and faster, like upgrading from a Toyota to a Ferrari.

The initial rush subsided, and he felt a steady thrum from the house. "His net signature is there. He's still home," Liam said.

Liam kept his focus tuned to the signature. "I can feel him moving." The prickle in his fingertips increased. David entered the front room, his orange and yellow outline visible, as he searched the room. Liam couldn't help but laugh as he watched David absent-mindedly pat his pockets and then find his keys on the desk. Liam stood up and walked down the street, away from the front door.

"Watch him after he leaves. He'll turn right and walk down the street. At the end of the block, if he turns right, he's going to the Italian bistro. If he goes left, he's going for Korean barbecue. Italian usually takes him an hour. Korean is usually forty-five minutes, unless he gets takeout. If he does, he'll be back in twenty. That's your operating window," Keema said.

"More time would be better. I don't know what I'm looking for," Liam said.

"We only get one shot at this. So, make it count."

Through the watchdog he saw David leave the building. He turned right towards the row of restaurants on the next block. Liam turned back and watched him walk down the block and turn left towards the Korean restaurant.

"Well, that's inconvenient," Liam said. "Can you still see him?"

"No. I don't have access to the street cameras in this neighborhood. They upgraded the systems in the last few weeks, and I haven't figured out how to get in yet," she said.

"Figures. I'll set the timer for 20 minutes. Here we go."

Liam hurried back up the street and up to the front of David's house. The door had a standard electronic lock with a wireless key. He placed his finger on the pad and waited. His finger tingled as his bodynet ran through his database of known master codes.

The streets were completely empty, no one out walking, no G-Cabs visible. He was the only thing moving on the street. In a crowded city, other people were usually the best concealment.

"C'mon, c'mon," he hissed at his system.

Finally, the lock popped, and the door indicator turned green.

He took another watchdog out of his pocket and placed it next to the door.

He then entered a short hallway with a door to the right and a stairway heading upstairs. The entryway smelled of damp wood and old cooking oil. Dishes clinked and voices filtered down the stairway.

He placed another small bot in the dark corner by the front door. It rolled itself into the deepest shadow it could find.

Next, he turned his attention to the old wooden door to David's apartment.

"Huh. Haven't seen one of these in a while," he muttered.

It was a brass doorknob with a physical lock.

Extracting the automatic lock-picker, he slid it into the

door and pressed the trigger. The small unit vibrated and then slid into the key bolt. He rotated the tool and the lock clicked open.

He took his last watchdog out of his pocket and opened the door just enough to roll it in. He switched his perspective; the other bots would alert him if anything changed. He rolled through the entry hall, scanning with the infrared laser for motion sensors or cameras and saw none.

The skin on the back of his neck prickled as he wondered if he was missing something. He scanned with the watchdog again, but there was nothing.

"Get moving," Keema said. "You have 10 minutes."

Liam pushed the door open, stepped inside, and closed it softly behind him. The entryway was a small hallway with three closed doors along the sides ending in a kitchen in the back of the house. An old light brown runner carpet covered the middle of the hall, fraying at the edges over the dark wood. The floor was clean and smelled of polish. David had expensive taste in housekeeping robots.

"I'm going to assume he works in the front room," Liam said, fighting the growing tension in his jaw. He was missing something – he knew it - but he had to find the data.

"Calm down, Liam. Your heart rate and respiration keep spiking," Keema said.

"Sorry. I hate rush jobs," Liam said then took two deep breaths. He brought his focus back to the hallway. "How's that?"

"Looking better. Now focus and get the hell out of there," she said.

"I'm moving into the front room," Liam said. He opened the door to the study and gestured for the watchdog. The bot rolled into room. Liam repeated his sweep for a security system but found nothing.

Liam began to relax. Either he had missed something and was already screwed, or David didn't have a security system. He switched back and walked into the study. The room was warm with an overstuffed chair and paper books on the shelves. A workstation lay on a table facing the street by the front window. It looked a lot like the one he had stolen from NewReal. Liam realized he had completed that job just three days ago. It felt like weeks.

Liam crossed the room and picked it up. It was an older model, slightly scuffed around the edges. "I've got it," he said.

"Great. Five minutes."

"Time's fun when you're having flies," Liam muttered. He pulled out a small plastic square from the inside pocket of his coat and attached it to the bottom of the unit. "Bug's attached."

He hid a small listener in the corner next to one of the books. He pinged the listener and got a good response.

"I've got a good signal from the listener," Keema said. "Get out of there."

"I'm going to have a look around," he said. "I feel like we're missing something."

"Liam, you don't have time to screw around."

He walked out of the front room and back into the hall. "I'm not screwing around. I just have a feeling."

"Alright, I can't force you. Four minutes."

He slowly opened the next door down the hall. He checked the bathroom and the hall, then came to the bedroom. The closet was open, revealing a few plain suit coats, trousers, and older, unfashionable work shoes. A pair of running shoes were placed neatly next to the closet. The carpet was older, but clean.

Liam found an electronic photo frame on the dresser.

There was a picture of David with a few other adults in a tropical location. His breath caught as he noticed Julie standing next to David. She looked relaxed, tanned, and happy. They were all smiling at the camera, lifting drinks. David Suarez was a handsome man, with dark eyes and wavy dark hair. Liam could see why Julie liked him.

He found the advance button on the frame and started scrolling through the pictures. Most were from conferences and work functions. A few pictures seemed to be of family. David and his parents, siblings, nieces and nephews at family gatherings.

Liam sighed and put down the frame, a growing ache creeping up from his chest. He couldn't believe David was part of the conspiracy to risk so many lives for quarterly earnings.

He scanned the bedroom, looking for evidence to the contrary. A small, obsolete tablet sitting on the bedside table caught his attention. Curious why David would keep a relic like this, he picked it up and flicked it open. The system flashed a lock screen, with a passcode prompt. "Keema, any known security flaws in this model?" Liam said.

"Database is searching… Yes. There's a known backdoor through the manufacturer's update system. Here you go. Three minutes. Don't fuck around," Keema said.

"Understood," Liam said, flipping open the tablet. He scanned through the library of technical papers and notes for experiments. Then he noticed the video diary app. He then tapped the icon. David's face appeared, dark circles under his eyes. He looked right at the camera and sighed.

"I've been keeping this journal for years. Now I question the wisdom of it. If anyone finds this it will be the end of my career. I won't erase my own memory to protect myself from these idiots. A few days ago, Vinge called asking about the environmental conditions for the yeasts making the antibiotic. It wasn't an out of the ordinary request, but it was the way he asked it. How long could the system be out of range before the whole population crashed? What would happen to production yields if the temperature was off? All these questions about how to stop the growth. But there's no way the tank would be out of temp range for more than a minute. It would either correct itself or scream for help."

Liam started recording with his specs. "Keema, can you get a copy of this too?"

"Yeah, I'm recording," she said.

David paused, glancing around him. "I left a little bug in Megan's office. I know. It was illegal but I have now stolen six weeks' worth of meeting recordings between high level people at Biotron. They are planning to restrict access to the antibiotic by faking manufacturing problems." David's brow furrowed and his lips tightened.

"This is the worst plague humankind has seen since the Middle Ages. And they want to maximize their quarterly revenue? Jesus Christ, we are so close to an uncontrolled pandemic. The death rates in India and Nigeria are about to skyrocket. Unchecked, the disease will kill hundreds of millions. The resulting social breakdown will kill a billion more. And that's if we're lucky. What the fuck do I do? How do I get this out?"

David sighed. The anger and tension drained from his face, replaced by a flat expression. "I need to find a way to get this out to more people. Enough that Biotron can't stop it. I know it will be the end of my career. I'll have to go into hiding. But that's a small price to pay. How the hell did it come to this?" David's face froze in a grimace of disgust, and he disappeared from Liam's view.

Liam placed the tablet back where he found it.

"Well... I think we know where David stands," Keema said. "I've cloned the tablet as well. Now get the hell out of there. You have less than a minute to clear the front of the house."

Liam left the bedroom, closing the door behind him. He retrieved the watchdog from the study. He scanned the room while his system checked to make sure nothing was out of place. The deck on the table glowed. It was a centimeter off. He nudged it back, so it aligned with the original image. Then he backtracked out of the apartment and closed the door.

As the lock clicked, an alert from the watchdog in the front yard flashed across his specs. It had detected motion, noise and heat. Someone was out in front of the house.

"Shit," he whispered. "Ideas?"

"Get back into the apartment and out the back door, now," she said.

He pulled the lockpick out of his jacket pocket and tried to get it back in the lock. He missed his first attempt.

"Slow is steady, steady is smooth, smooth is fast," he repeated, forcing himself to calm down. The lock slid into the door. As he waited for the tool to buzz its way into the lock, he checked the feed from the watchdog's camera. A figure stood at the bottom of the front steps, with outstretched arms, fingers twitching like the antenna of an insect. Liam recognized the posture. Whoever was out there was looking for network traffic. Then they stopped, lifted their hand and waved at the watchdog.

22

RETREAT

LIAM'S STOMACH CHURNED. He recognized the silhouette looming over the watchdog as well as the posture.

Barkley smiled, raised a large boot, then the world went black. Liam's head jerked as he snapped back into the hallway.

A message flashed in his vision. Barkley was requesting a private communication channel. He accepted the connection while he worked the pick.

" Long time, no see, eh? Biotron thought it might be a good idea if I kept an eye on the place." Liam could hear him through the front door. He only had a moment before the larger man broke it down.

"Biotron?" Liam asked as the pick finally slid through the tumblers. He twisted it open, trying not to make noise.

"Yeah. Thanks for setting up the meeting. After the guards took me to their leader, we had a little chat. After some mutual negotiation, they've hired me as a security consultant," Barkley said.

Liam pocketed his tools and slipped through. He quietly shut the door behind him and re-locked it.

"I'm glad it worked out for you," Liam muttered. He scurried down the hall into the kitchen. He switched channels.

"Keema, now what? Same exfil?" he asked.

"I don't have visibility into the alley, but the exfil plan is the best bet. There are four G-cabs in the area. I'll guide you to the nearest."

The front door slammed open. The watchdog in the entryway sent an alert, then disappeared from his specs. He unlocked the back door and stepped out onto the damp and mossy patio. A row of overgrown planters screened a six-foot privacy fence. Behind the fence was an alley, just wide enough for a car.

He ran across the patio, leapt onto a planter and grabbed the top of the fence.

The rotten wood crumbling in his hands, the top section gave way. Liam was quick to grab the crossbar of the fence. He hauled himself over the top, then bailed off, tumbling as the whole fence gave way beneath him.

Liam had taken two wobbling steps when his coat sounded its projectile alarm. It ballooned away from his body faster than he could react. The movement changed the fabric's angle just enough to deflect the twin taser darts.

Liam spun around. His coat sealed up around him, shifting its armor pattern to face the threat. Barkley ran toward him down the alley, reloading without breaking stride. Liam shuffled back, looking to buy time. He sent a network attack at Barkley's bodynet. Liam's new system felt sharp and light; his attacks were fast, but Barkley kept coming.

Liam scrambled backwards faster, pulling a dragonfly

out of his coat. The drone surged towards Barkley as he brought the taser up to fire again. The radar in his coat detected the needles the instant they left the launcher.

Liam raised his arm to block them. The fabric tried to shape itself to deflect the needles again, but they found purchase. The coat shuddered as a jolt of electricity surged through it. It shorted out and hung on him like a heavy blanket on a summer night.

Barkley swatted at the dragonfly. The drone swooped and dove with random evasive maneuvers. It banked hard and landed on Barkley's back. It hammered directly onto his bodynet. Barkley grunted and staggered as malicious code overwhelmed his systems.

"Run, now," said Keema.

He turned and sprinted down the alley.

Liam risked a glance back over his shoulder. Barkley was charging after him, a long combat knife in his hand.

"Keema! Right now!" Liam panted. He cleared the end of the alley and sprinted up the block.

"Working on it. The nearest G-cab is three minutes away," Keema said. "Let's buy you some time."

His medi-patch clicked, and energy surged through him. His lungs opened and the air felt sharp and cool. The world slowed down. He'd pay for this later, but now he flew over the pavement, down the empty street, away from Barkley. Most of the houses had their blinds pulled, their occupants' home for the night.

Without his coat's radar, the dart took him by surprise. There was a sharp, piercing pain behind his left ear. A warm flush radiated out from the point of impact. He staggered. The sensation spread down his neck and into his shoulders. The street bowed in front of him. He tried to run on, but he couldn't seem to control his feet.

He stumbled, catching himself on a light post. He turned as Barkley barreled toward him. The knife gleamed in the soft light.

"Trying to find a counter agent. Keep fighting," Keema said, her voice strained.

Barkley slowed, a half-grin on his face. He crouched into a fighting stance, weight on the balls of his feet. He stabbed out with the knife. Liam threw himself back, the blade skimming over his coat. He swung at Barkley's face, reaching for his eyes. Barkley easily blocked his drug-addled swing.

Barkley recoiled and stabbed out again. The knife flicked in and out like the needle on a sewing machine. Liam twisted and stumbled backward, trying to block again and again. The knife slashed his forearm. Burning pain shot up his arm, taking his breath. Liam kicked out, contacting the inside of Barkley's left leg.

The larger man took the blow, letting his leg twist to absorb some of the energy and slashed back across his body. Liam ducked under the swing and staggered back.

"Found it," Keema said. "Dumping the counter agent now. Keep moving, breathe."

He gasped as the icy counter to the tranquilizer hit his brain stem and the world returned to its standard orientation. The two men stared at each other, inches out of arm's reach. The blood ran down Liam's hand, pooling on the ground. His breath came hard.

Barkley smiled. Moving like a boxer, he closed the distance. Barkley threw a hook, knife out like a spike. Liam stepped inside the swing, blocking upwards, punching hard midsection. Barkley threw an uppercut, smashing Liam's cheek.

Liam staggered. His vision filled with a white light. He swung blindly, trying to buy time. Barkley advanced again.

He feinted with the knife and threw a hard left underneath Liam's rib. Liam doubled over, searing pain flooding him. He screamed. Barkley hit him across the back of the head, and Liam hit the pavement hard.

Warnings blinked red as his bodynet registered the damage. His internal diagnostic indicated internal bleeding, a broken rib, and a high probability of concussion.

Barkley stood over him. "Don't worry, Liam, I'm not going to kill you. At least not right now. You may want to get that liver looked at, though. I think I broke something important."

"Hang on, Liam," Keema said. "Giving you something for the pain and the shock. Help is on the way."

The cramping agony in his abdomen subsided as his system flooded with painkillers. He coughed, feeling something shift in his chest.

"What do you want, Barkley?" Liam said, spitting out blood.

"I want to know what you learned in Suarez's apartment. Then I want you to go home and give up the gig. Go back to your shitty little jobs," Barkley said, smiling.

He knelt next to Liam, frowning at him. "You really shouldn't have gotten in my way the other night. But now it's your turn." Barkley picked Liam up by his collar. "Now, what did you find?"

"Nothing. All I did was hack the network. We were waiting for him to get back," Liam said.

"Really? That's all you did in the twenty minutes you were inside?"

"Yes. We hacked the network and planted a listener. We didn't know when he'd be back. I didn't have enough time," Liam groaned. He swallowed against the rising urge to vomit. Even with the drugs, the pain was threatening to overwhelm him. He couldn't catch his breath.

"See... You failed to mention the bug last time. I still think you're lying," Barkley said. "But I don't have a lot of time. The police will be here soon. I'm sure someone saw your pathetic attempt at self-defense."

He pulled out his knife and showed it to Liam. "I need to make this quick. I'm going to have to cut out your data store. This is going to hurt... a lot." Barkley put a knee on Liam's chest and reached for his arm. His bodynet data store was embedded under his skin.

"Wait... I'll give you access. Use your reader. You don't need to cut it out," Liam said.

"I know I don't need to. But I want to," Barkley said. Liam felt the broken rib shift and gasped. He couldn't get enough air to scream.

There was a clap of thunder and the pain and pressure eased. Liam smelled ozone, as if a massive lightning strike had occurred near his head. He looked up groggily. Barkley was stumbling as fast as he could away from Liam. He heard footsteps. He couldn't move his head. He rolled his eyes up, straining to see behind him. "Sergei? What are you doing here?"

23

RECOVERY

In time, the ceiling came into focus. The orange-peel texture was stained yellow by years of cigarette smoke. The wallpaper was thick and looked plastic and the smell of antiseptic stung his nose.

Underneath the blanket of narcotics, his jaw throbbed. Liam watched his vital signs twitch on a display on the bedside table. He tracked the tube from his arm to an IV stand dripping a clear liquid into his veins. This place looked like a bedroom, not a medical facility.

He had a hazy recollection of Sergei appearing over him in the thunderclap of an electric arc weapon, the metallic smell of ozone coating his tongue. Sergei's hidden Russian military implant was more powerful than anything he had seen before. Keema shouting at him and dumping the last of his medi-patch into his system as Sergei dragged him down the sidewalk. Sergei placing him in the backseat of a waiting G-Cab. Then strong hands lifting him and placing him on a stretcher. Someone had removed his coat and cut off his clothes, despite his feeble protests. Finally, a needle slid into his medi-patch, and he faded out.

He tried to sit up. The stabbing pain in his abdomen made him gasp, and the edges of his vision turned dark. He sank back down. Pulling back the bed sheets revealed a large bandage covering his lower rib cage. He pressed on the gauze and felt the stitches. The room spun and his mouth watered with nausea. He decided not to press there again.

"Keema?" he said, hoping the connection was still open. His chest tightened in the silence. Her voice was gone from his head. The bodynet must be either too damaged or out of power. His specs were gone. He fought to keep his breathing under control.

"Hello?" he called out. He rolled on his side, struggling to sit up. "Please calm down, Mr. Baron. You'll tear your stitches," the IV machine said.

Liam struggled to sit up. The pain brought tears to his eyes. The IV sighed and he heard the click of a valve. Warm relaxation flowed into his arm. He gasped as it rose up into his neck and overtook his brain. He faded out.

The next thing he knew, someone opened the door to his room.

"Mom?" The moment he said it he knew he was wrong. The woman was too short. He stared at her dumbly. She approached the bed. He slowly realized she was holding a needle.

He couldn't think straight and needed the drugs out of his system right now. With his bodynet offline, he couldn't access his medi-patch. He wanted to get up, but his body was not responding. He fumbled with the IV feed, trying to pull the needle out.

She gently pulled his hands away. "It's ok," she said. She stuck the hypodermic she was carrying into the port on the

IV and pressed the plunger. An icy cold shock ran up his arm. He laid back as the sensation crept toward his heart.

Then the feeling of fatigue lifted. He could think again. He stared at the woman.

"Ah, good. You're awake," she said. "How are you feeling?"

With a jolt he recognized her from the protest.

"Who are you?"

"My name is Lilah. I'm a friend of Keema's."

"Bullshit," Liam said, still trying to peel off the tape holding the IV needle in place. "You're a cop, or a spook. I felt your ID ping."

"I'm neither. I pinged you to make sure you weren't a cop, or a spook. You were very curious about what we were doing at the protest. I needed to be sure."

"Only the government has that kind of access. What do you want?"

"The government created the back doors. But they forgot to hide the keys. Now stop picking at your tape or Hospital will sedate you again for your own good."

Liam sighed and laid back. Even if he could get the needle out of his arm, he wasn't going anywhere. The effort involved in sitting up made him dizzy. He wanted to go back to sleep. They couldn't question him if he was asleep.

"We've patched you up," she said. "Your liver was split, and you were bleeding internally. You also have a mild concussion and lacerations on your hands, forearm, and face. Do you remember what happened?"

"I'm not talking to you," he said and turned over, facing the wall.

"Don't be stupid, Liam. I'm not a cop. My name is Lilah Araya."

Liam rolled back over and studied her face. "I do know

you. You developed the core bodynet systems, the protocols, the implantable routers and the circuit tattoos. But that doesn't mean they haven't recruited you."

"True. But I'm not a spook. I'm OP."

"Open Party?"

"Yep, joined up about five years ago. I helped build this hospital that just saved your life."

"What do you want?"

"I want to run a diagnostic on your bodynet, upgrade your systems and get you back in the fight."

"Why? What's in it for you?" He knew how this went. They would pretend to be on his side. Then when he talked about the plan, they would arrest him. Or they would infect his systems and grab Keema too. He was not going to make this easy for them.

"Think about it, Liam. The fever is accelerating. We are weeks away from the point of no return. If there is a cure, we need to get it out as fast as possible."

"What does that have to do with me?"

"The OP is reinventing the future. There are thousands of biohackers working to set up distributed production plants. There are a hundred microbreweries cleaning tanks right now to grow the cure. All we need is the DNA sequence. A few thousand letters and we can save millions of lives."

"So, you want me to trust my sister's life to a bunch of basement hackers?"

Lilah frowned. "These are some of the world's top scientists and engineers. Yes. It will be in their basement because their universities shut them down. Your sister would be first in line. We'd owe you that much."

"Is that why I'm here? You want to recruit me? I'm not much of a follower."

She laughed. "You're here because Keema vouched for you and your life was in danger. Yes, you're one of our best chances to get Restro. But we would have done this for anyone Keema asked us to."

Liam's head was swimming. It didn't make sense. How was Keema involved in all of this? How had he gotten here? And how the hell had Sergei known where to find him?

"Just patch me up so I can get out of here. Julie needs me. And I need to talk to Keema."

"Your systems are pretty fried. It's a risk trying to talk to either of them right now. Talking to Julie right now makes her an accessory. I'll see if I can get an encrypted channel to Keema."

She closed her eyes. Her hands twitched as she muttered under her breath. After a moment, she opened her eyes. "I've got a line to Keema. You have two minutes."

24

CHECKING IN

KEEMA'S AVATAR appeared on the screen hanging from the IV stand. "Hey, Liam. How are you feeling?" she asked.

"Is that really you? How can I be sure? My net is fried, so I can't check the cryptographic signature."

"We met on a contract two years ago. I introduced you to a guy named Sergei. You managed to escape Denver by spending 10k on a fake ID that got you as far as Cheyenne where you took a bus to Omaha and caught the train back from there."

"You could find that out through research. How do I know you aren't a spook pretending to be you?"

"I guess you don't. The best I can do is tell you what you like for breakfast, the contents of your medi-patch, your family's names, birthdays, addresses. There's nothing I could say that couldn't be learned some other way. So, you'll just have to fucking trust me. You're being pig-headed right now, Liam. Let them help you."

"I don't know who to trust."

"Look, if we're all spooks, then you're already fucked.

We're inside your net, inside your head and we have you in a hotel room in the middle of Oakland. We can do whatever the fuck we want and there's nothing you can do about it."

Liam grimaced. She, even if it wasn't Keema, was right. There was no way he was going to get out of here on his own. In the back of his mind, he knew this was Keema. But the voice in his head kept asking the same questions. How could he tell? What if this was just a machine simulation? At some point, he needed to make a choice

"Okay. I give up. How's Julie?"

"She's through the early critical phase. They are going to send her to home quarantine soon. We have a few days until the pneumonia gets bad."

"Oh, that's good news. What now?"

"Do what Lilah says. You need to rest and heal. Just take care of yourself for the next day or so."

"I don't have a lot of choice about that."

" I have to go. I don't trust we can keep this line secure."

"Thanks for everything, Keema. You saved my life."

Then she was gone. Lilah looked at him and arched her eyebrows. "You ready? I need to run the diagnostics to prep for the repairs."

He was too tired to care. "Go ahead," he sighed, "You've got me over a barrel for the hospital bills anyway."

"No, we don't. This hospital is free to anyone who needs it."

"What?"

"Most of the care is delivered by machines. Your vitals are constantly monitored by Hospital, our digital medical system. We grow most of the drugs we need in bioreactors downstairs. We import the rest. The nurses, doctors and surgeons are part of the movement. Most are refugees who can't find a medical job. We put their skills and training to use."

"And the FDA doesn't shut you down?"

"We're small enough that they haven't noticed yet. But a raid is always a risk. Being in Oakland helps too. No one cares much what happens here." She took his arm and pressed her fingers on his net tattoos. Her hands were covered in a fine spiderweb of light gray graphene tattoos. The graphene was a lot more expensive than his metallic system, but it was a lot faster, and more aesthetically pleasing. His arm tingled as she sent a surge of current into his network.

"What are you doing?" The warmth of her touch centered his attention. He glanced at her face. Her eyes were closed in concentration. Her long dark hair fell around her face as she tilted her head. His net surged and twitched. He looked away before she could catch him staring.

"Sorry. Needed to focus there for a second. I've identified a few places where your network overloaded during the fight. That shock took out more than your coat. There are a few improvements I can make as well. Your system is good, but not great," she said, nodding to herself.

"You can fix it?"

"I invented it, so yeah, I think I can fix it."

"You're going to give Restro away once I steal it, eh?"

"Yes. We are. To be honest with you, that was going to happen anyway." She took his hands and peered at the sensors in his fingers.

"What do you mean?"

"Keema was going to make sure we got a copy of the data," Lilah said as she put his hands down. She stood and walked over to the window.

"Why would she do that? Once we got the cure for Julie,

we could sell it on to one of the big Indian or Brazilian pharmas."

"Look, Liam. I know you. I know how tempting the money from this would be. But there are other priorities. Eventually you'll see that."

"But I could have paid off everything and gotten out," he said, laying back into the pillow. "God I just want to get out."

"No, Liam. There is no ticket out. There's no way to win. You have to quit playing. Anyway, get some rest. Julie still needs you. And so do a lot of other people."

Julie. He closed his eyes. Maybe getting her the medicine she needed was enough. With his eyes closed, the exhaustion overtook him, and he drifted off.

The dream came again, but this time the drugs held him down. Her cold, bony hand gripped his arm. He couldn't look at her. The thin, yellow skin clinging to her skull filled him with revulsion. He didn't want to feel this way. He wanted to feel love, or compassion, or anything other than this. Instead, it was only the gut churning rage at her and himself. He looked around for Julie, but she wasn't there. He was alone. He forced himself to look at her face. Julie stared back at him; eyes filled with sadness. She opened her mouth to speak and drew a labored breath. She tried to mouth the words, but nothing came. The hand gripped him tighter and then went slack.

25

THE DISAPPEARED

He opened his eyes, gasping for breath. The sheets were twisted around him and cold from his sweat. The heart rate monitor on the IV bleeped and flashed a warning.

A warm yellow light filtered in from around the blinds. He had slept through the night. He called out, "Hello?"

"Good morning, Liam," Hospital replied from the IV, startling him. "Would you like to sit up?"

"Sure," Liam said. The head of the bed lifted with a hydraulic hiss.

"I've let your team know you are awake," Hospital said. "Is there anything you need?"

"I'm hungry and I need a shower."

"I'll let them know."

The door opened, and a man walked in with close cut dark hair and an olive complexion. He was followed by a tall, rectangular robot on wheels. A door on the side of the bot opened, and it extended a tray with a covered plate. The man took the tray and clipped it to the side of bed over Liam's lap. "Good morning," he said.

"Morning," Liam replied. The smell of roast potatoes made Liam's mouth water.

"I'm Sayed. I'm your nurse."

"You work for the OP?" Liam asked. He picked up a fork and speared a few of the potatoes. They were crispy and light. A warmth spread through his shoulders as he savored his food.

"I'm a member," Sayed said. "We don't really do the whole 'work for' thing. I contribute where I can. I was trained as a nurse in Lebanon before the drought."

"Not sure I follow." Liam shoveled another fork full of potatoes into his mouth.

"I'm sure you don't. But I'll leave it to Lilah to explain. I have a lot of people who need my help. I'll come back in a little while and help you get cleaned up." He turned and left, the bot following him like a puppy.

Liam ate, a little insulted by Sayed's dismissal. He could understand if someone would explain it to him.

After Liam had finished his breakfast, he rested with his eyes closed but Sayed returned, this time followed by a larger bot with two triangular treads and large arms.

"Ready to bathe?" Sayed asked.

"Sure," Liam said.

Sayed removed the IV line. "Hospital says you don't need this anymore as long as everything continues to improve. And I need it down the hall."

Facing the bot, Sayed extended his right arm. The robot mimicked his motion. "I'm going to use Ralph to help you get up and assist you. Go ahead and lean on him and use him for as much support as you need." The bot wheeled over, and Liam grabbed hold of the extended arm. Mimicking Sayed's motions, it gently pulled him out of bed while the other arm swung around behind him to support his back.

Sayed extended his arms, and the machine moved him gently into the shower. "I'm going to let Ralph take over from here. He's programed to help in the shower and will retrace his steps to get you back to bed. There will be clothes waiting for you when you are done."

Liam grunted and the door closed. He untied his hospital gown and let it fall to the floor. As he stepped into the shower, he looked himself over. There were two small suture marks where they had gone in to repair his liver. The bruise over the area was an angry purple and red. The pain when he twisted to wash his back made him want to curl up on the floor of the shower. He braced himself against the bot and let the water run over him.

He turned off the water. Ralph extended another small arm with a towel. Liam gingerly dried himself off and put the towel back in the waiting bot's still extended arm.

Naked, but clean, he shuffled back to the bedroom. A set of sweatpants and a T-shirt with the logo of a band that had broken up three years ago were on the bed. The clothes were worn, but they fit well enough. Finished, he sat down on the bed, tired from his efforts.

Ralph folded in his arms and backed out of the door, closing it behind him. Liam gently lay back on the bed and closed his eyes. He still wasn't completely sure he was safe. It seemed an overly elaborate ruse if they were trying to entrap him. He doubted Homeland would be so subtle. Their methods of ensuring cooperation were usually more obvious.

He wished he could connect and talk to Keema and Julie. The quiet of the room made him jumpy. He opened his eyes and cautiously rolled up into a sitting position. A dim light filtered around the chase of the small window across the room. He forced himself to stand up and shuffled over.

The manual shade seemed out of place in a talking hospital full of robots, but he pulled on it and let it roll itself up. His room was higher than he expected. He estimated he was ten stories up. He stared out the window. The hills to the east were still blackened from the fires last year but he could just make out some green shoots of new growth. He leaned against the glass, looking west. The jumble of buildings was interrupted by the fault lines of the freeways. In the distance, the super towers that dominated the San Francisco skyline gleamed in the morning sun. If he squinted, he could make out his own apartment building just off the eastern shore.

The door opened. Lilah entered the room. "Good, you're up. Let's go. We need to get you patched up. And there are some people you should meet."

"I meant to ask you. What happened to the guy from the protest? Obviously, you brought him here," he said.

"We got him here and into isolation. He died the next morning. Nothing we've tried so far has worked. This thing is scary..." she said, staring past him out the window.

"So, we've got to get moving. Have we gotten anything off the bugs? Is anyone tracking David?"

"Here's the thing, Liam," she said. "He's disappeared. We haven't been able to pick up a trace of him since the night you broke in. But no one has reported him missing, either."

"They have him," Liam said. "They're hiding him somewhere, whether he wants to be there or not."

"We don't know that," she said.

"It's what I would do. Use the break-in as a pretext to move him to a secure facility. Then I can't reach him, and we're out of luck," Liam said. He felt dizzy. He shuffled back to the bed and sat down.

"You okay?"

"Just a little lightheaded." He swallowed the lump rising in his throat. He was going to fail again.

"Hospital says you should finish healing in another day or so. But it would be good to get you up and about. And we need you to get back in the fight."

"I'm ready," he said, wishing he could believe it.

"Good. I'm taking you to our shop. We'll get your network fixed. You'll also get temporary access to our network resources. We're here to help."

"Keema and I can handle this," he said. "We don't need your help."

"Yes, you do Liam," she said with a sigh. "As kick-ass as Keema is, even she needs help."

"How do you know Keema?" he asked.

"We go back a way. Now let's get you patched up," she said firmly as she took his arm and led him out of the room.

26

TATOOS

A FEW BOTS moved up and down the hall with trays of food and medicines.

"I know you don't want a recruitment pitch, Liam. But look at what we are doing here. The hospital has the potential for a hundred rooms once we finish renovations. The bots and the hospital system give us the ability to deliver services to a lot more people. Everyone gets the treatment they need. Some choose to pay it back with money, labor or in-kind donations. Others can't and that's fine too."

"How do you afford the medicines? The doctors?" he said as they stepped into the elevator.

"We grow the vast majority of the medicine we need - from pain killers to insulin - in big bioreactors full of modified yeast in the basement. I'd show you, but they're big, boring metal tanks. The staff have free food, shelter, clothing - all provided by the OP. They also get paid in our internal currency. For most, being able to do the work in an environment of freedom is enough. The AI takes care of monitoring, simple diagnosis and basic treatment," she said. "We help the people we can."

They got out of the elevator and headed out into the bright sunshine. Liam closed his eyes, enjoying the warm sun on his skin. The pain and fear of the last few days seemed more manageable in the bright light of day. A G-Cab rolled up and they got in.

"We're heading to our network node here in the city. The mechanic shop is there along with a few others," she said as the car accelerated away from the curb. They drove for a while in silence, Liam watching the yellow grass and dry, dusty yards slide past.

The car pulled into a faded strip mall. A scaffold covered in solar collectors shaded the cracked parking lot. The car rolled under the scaffold and stopped. Liam followed Lilah as she walked to one of the storefronts and pulled the door open. A small gust of cool air pushed out of the door, as they entered. Empty display racks still hung on the walls of the old store. They walked through the empty shop and exited through the back door.

They entered a larger space that had once been back storerooms for several businesses. The air smelled of solder and hot plastic generated by the individuals and small teams working among rows of high workbenches filling nearly all the space in the large area.

"Welcome to the workshop. Everyone here is working to solve community problems. That team is working on improving larger scale energy storage. The team over here is working to improve our nutrient recycling in the greenhouses," she said.

"How do you pay all these people?" he said.

"They are here because they want to work on interesting problems to make life better for a lot of people," she said.

"They've given up on the old economy. We're building something new here."

"They're working for food and shelter?"

"Anyone can leave any time they want," she said as she walked towards a bay at one end of the row of workbenches. "If they've donated money, they can choose to get it back. So far, there haven't been a lot of takers. We live better than most people on the outside."

They arrived at the bay. A large industrial robotic arm loomed over a worn tattoo artist's chair.

"I don't have money for upgrades," he said, rubbing his sutures.

"The community has decided to provide the equipment you need," she said. "So, we are going to trust you to do the right thing because Keema vouched for you. Do you understand? She's put her reputation on the line, and all we have is our reputation." Lilah motioned for him to sit in the cracked and taped chair next to the table. "Your choice..."

"What do you mean she's vouched for me? Isn't she a friend?" Liam asked.

"Let's just say she's got a bit of credit that she's decided to use," she said.

Scowling and with hands on her hips, she pinned Liam with her eyes. "Choose. Sit or walk out that door over there."

Startled by her intensity, Liam glanced around, then sat.

"Alright, let's get to work. Take off your shirt first. We'll start there," she said while rooting around on her worktop. Liam hesitated. He hated taking his shirt off in public, especially in front of someone he found attractive. But she needed access to his bodynet tattoos.

With a sigh, he pulled his shirt over his head, conscious of his thin frame and pale skin.

She turned around with a digital meter in her hand. "Ouch!" she said as she stared at the purple, yellow bruise on his ribs. "Who did this to you?"

"A guy named Barkley. I've known him for a few years. It's the first time I've had to go toe to toe with him. I think I hit him once before Sergei saved my life," he said. "I don't remember a whole lot. I was too busy bleeding."

"Well, your tats are definitely messed up. You overloaded some and broke some others. I'm going to find the exact points," she said. She moved her stool next to his chair. Taking the probes from the meter, she touched them to his tattoos, starting on his forearm. The cold metal probes were a sharp contrast to her warm hands. She stopped every few moments and circled a spot on his body.

Liam sat in silence, uncomfortable with not speaking but unable to think of anything to say. She moved in closer, tracing the lines on his torso. Her hair smelled like mint and chamomile. A few moments later she leaned back and put down the probes.

"I've got your upper body marked out," she said, leaning back.

He looked down over his torso and laughed.

"Yeah. Your network is fried. I can put you back together. We'll need to replace your antenna. I have a new design that will be a big improvement."

"I thought those designs hadn't changed in years."

"Our AI cluster evolved it. I have no idea how it works. I can't even draw it well enough. No one has the required dexterity. We'll need to get you into the printer. But I can do the easy stuff here." She picked up a tattoo gun from the tray attached to the back of the chair along with a bottle of gray ink.

"Graphene ink? How can you afford that?" he asked.

"I told you. We make and grow just about everything we need," she said. "We decided as a community to invest in this capability. The machines aren't hard to make, and we can make all the raw materials here. No external supply chains to make us vulnerable."

"But doesn't that take a huge amount of energy?" he asked.

"We can make this out of carbon dioxide, sugar, and solar energy," she said. "Now lay back and try not to move. This isn't going to be pleasant."

He made himself lie still and not wriggle as she applied the tattoo gun. The buzz made conversation difficult. But he didn't want to stop.

"So how did someone like you end up joining the Open Party?" Liam asked.

"Like me!" She broke into a smile. "I was a hardware hacker. Too much cyberpunk and not enough sense. I invented a few of the items you have embedded in you right now. I got a couple of patents, started a company, found investors and sold parts to other hackers. Then it started to take off. I sold for an obscene amount of money. I had more money than I knew what to do with and I was miserable. Someone else owned my life's work."

"But that's the way it works. You got the money, and they got the intellectual property," Liam replied, trying not to pull away from the burn of the tattoo gun.

"I know. The investors wouldn't have let me turn down the buyout anyway. What I realized later was I didn't have the right to sell it in the first place. Intellectual property is a fiction invented to keep printers happy in the 18th century, but we've perverted it beyond reason. What we learn about the universe, about how to make things better for humanity can't belong to a few people."

"But how do you pay for it? R&D takes time, money, equipment," he gasped as the tattoo needle slid over his spine.

"Yep. And how many scientists and researchers are motivated by money? We just want to do the work, solve the next puzzle. The industrialists learned how to harness that impulse. They give the technicians enough to live better than most. But they own what we create. I thought I owned a company. I was a master of my own destiny. But I belonged to the investors and then our buyer." The pressure on the gun increased. "I did it to myself because I didn't know any other way."

"And the OP?" He flinched away from the gun, and she eased the pressure.

"Sorry about that," she said, rubbing the area to ease the pain. "The OP gave me a new outlet. I don't have to worry about keeping a roof over my head. I have time to invent new things, or work to build things other people here find useful."

"What if you don't? How do you prevent people from just goofing off all day?"

"A few people do that when they first arrive. But most people want to contribute to something larger than themselves. When the benefits are shared by everyone and we celebrate each contribution, people tend to want to help. I'm glad I'm not in the greenhouses harvesting tomatoes. But without the person who does, I don't eat. Does that make them less worthy? Not to me." She patted his shoulder, and he turned over. He was acutely aware of being half naked in front of a woman he wanted to impress. She was Lilah freaking Araya, and she was building his new bodynet.

She took his arm and pinned it to the chair. The gun hummed as she retraced much of his network there. He tried to think of something to say, but the burning in his arm from the new tattoo was too distracting.

"There is so much potential in our human ingenuity. No one has to be hungry, homeless or ignorant. Those are bugs in a system with fundamental design flaws. We are building a new system and giving it away because we can. If you don't have to worry about starving, you can afford to be generous and think about the future."

"But there's only so much to go around," Liam said. "How do you make sure no one takes more than they should?"

"We use energy as the basis of exchange. I need a certain amount of energy to live, to grow my food, clean my water, provide heat and light. We produce more than enough. You need to live it to understand. We want to build a new economy, not some utopia. This is a real industrial civilization built on physics and democracy, instead of finance and oligarchy," she said. "Anyway, I'm done with the repairs here. Do you want a new antenna?"

"I don't understand, but I need an antenna if we are going to find David and get Restro out to people who need it," he said.

"Great. Once you get the antenna, I'll hook you into our network. Then you can see what we are trying to do," she said, helping him up off the chair. She led him over to a large medical bed covered in plastic in the next bay. She motioned for him to lie down on his stomach.

"I'm going apply the ink first," she said. "Then the laser will burn it in."

She applied a thin layer of gel across the base of his neck and stepped back. The robot arm swung down from the ceiling. "Lie very still," she said. "This is going to hurt."

27

THE NETWORK

THE ROBOT ARM DESCENDED, positioning itself millimeters from the base of his neck. The gel was warm, and the sensation of her touch lingered. Then the burning started. He held his breath, forcing himself not to move. The pain was like a sharp, hot, needle scraping across his back. He gripped the table and tried not to whimper.

"Almost there," she said.

Then the heat was gone. He opened his eyes, trying to blink away the spots in the edge of his vision. A surge of energy flowed across his network, and he felt whole for the first time in days.

"Okay. You're done."

"That sucked," he said, as he sat up.

"We're working on the process," she said. Her attention shifted to something in her specs. "Your diagnostics are all good now."

She pulled a lens case out of her coat pocket and handed it to him. "Put these in. I've tied them into the network. You have provisional access to our internal systems as well as regular public access. Just be careful connecting outside of this network."

He pulled down his lower eyelid and put the specs on. The familiar burn as his eyes adjusted was comforting. He blinked a few times and they integrated with his network. It felt different. The signal from the new antenna was stronger, faster. His sensors seemed more expressive.

"Wow, this is great," he said. "Can I connect?"

"Sure," said Lilah. "I'll give you a few minutes." She turned and left for her workstation.

It took him a few moments to adjust to the new interface. When he finally found the communications system, he tried connecting to Keema, but she didn't answer. Disappointed, he applied a few layers of misdirection and opened an encrypted connection to his feeds.

An image popped up taking up his whole field of view. He stumbled backwards in surprise. "What the fuck?" he said.

"I forgot to warn you. Everyone else got that while you were offline," he heard Lilah say.

The image was a graph, entitled "A gift from the Worm". For a moment, he didn't understand what the sharply rising curve with a large red curve underneath it meant. Then an icy nausea rose in his throat. It was a Centers for Disease Control simulation of spread and death rates of Lung Fever. He checked again. Millions were going to die in the next few months.

"These are real?" he said, finally able to close the image.

She came back around the corner, wiping her hands on her overalls. "They're real. After the image popped up, someone leaked the whole report."

"Why isn't anyone talking about this?"

"The press doesn't seem interested and the CDC and WHO aren't reacting the way we expect, either. We know they're on a shoestring budget, but they've been watching for something like this for years. There's something else going on."

"What do you mean, something else?"

"Who knows? They might not want to panic people, or they are taking the rosy scenario, or ..." she shrugged.

"What? You aren't telling me something. What are you hiding?"

"The Worm also released some additional stolen messages. They haven't been verified. But it seems some very powerful people are willing to let this happen," she said.

"What are you talking about?" he said. He had an empty feeling in the pit of his stomach. She was a conspiracy nut. He hoped she hadn't damaged his network. He started looking for the exits. "What do you mean, let this happen?"

"They know they just need to delay for a few months. Then this accelerates and it shaves a few percentage points off the human population."

"Why would they do that? That's stupid! The social breakdown will be worse than the disease."

"A few of the wealthiest have already moved to their retreats."

"How do you know this? That sounds nuts." He stood up and started looking for his shirt and coat. He needed to get away from her. She waved her hand at him. A large package of data was loaded into his system.

"The Worm isn't the only one gathering data. We've quietly picked apart some of their networks. We've been using the data from our nightclubs, like Piper, to run network analysis and first-level intrusions. That gets us in. Then we bootstrap our way up the ladder through a combination of social engineering and hard hacking. So we're reading a lot of people's mail."

"But why? Why would they want to kill so many people? That makes no sense."

"Really? You can't figure that out? They have their lifeboat, so the rest of us can go ahead and drown. Sooner rather than later would be better for them."

Liam started to argue but stopped. The signs had been there for years. Billionaires building retreats and bunkers. Buying up huge amounts of land in remote places. Investments in private security, and weaponized drones. The crowds of not-quite-rich trying to get close enough to ride their coat tails through the coming turbulence. He felt empty, suddenly exhausted.

"What do we do? It's not like we're going to start a revolution," he said.

"Just get the recipe for Restro. We'll take care of the rest."

"And where does that leave me? I'm left dangling in the breeze. When they come for me, will you be there?"

"You won't be alone, Liam," she said, putting a hand on his shoulder. He was acutely aware he hadn't put his shirt back on yet.

"They will come for you. They will come for all of us. You know they will," he said. He stood up, and she let her hand fall away. "I'm going to take care of Julie. What you do with Restro is up to you. Keema was going to give it to you anyway and there's nothing I can do about that. But once Julie has what she needs..." His thoughts trailed off. He didn't know what he would do then. But he didn't have the energy to figure it out.

"Would it help to talk to Julie?"

"I can talk to her now?"

"Your new antenna is secure, and we'll obscure your location. If her room isn't bugged, you'll be safe."

“Then let’s do it,” he said.

Lilah closed her eyes and raised her hand. A connection request popped up in his specs. "I've routed you through a few different points and spread the connection out. It should obscure your location for a few minutes. Don't take too long."

"I won't. I just need to check in with her. There's so much going on."

"I'll leave you alone. Come find me at my workbench when you are done." She left the little alcove and drew the curtain across the opening. He was alone with the robot arm and the plastic covered bench. He thought he could sneak out now if he wanted. But he had a call to make first.

28

AN ORDER

Liam closed his eyes and tapped the connection request floating in front of him. A moment later, he was looking out of the camera on the communications tablet on Julie's IV stand.

"Hey, sis."

A half-smile lit up Julie's face. She was pale and her hair clung greasily to her head. She waved. "Hey, bro."

"How are you feeling?"

"I've been better. But the fever is bearable now."

"I'm glad. They tell me you're through the initial danger."

"That's what they say. How are you doing? Where have you been?"

"I've made some new work colleagues. They are very interested in your work."

"Really? How much are they offering you?" she said, raising her eyebrows.

"Nothing. They are offering me nothing. But it's your work, so it has to be your decision."

"I'm glad you came to that realization," she said, her voice hoarse. She started to cough, shallowly at first, then deeper, as if her body were trying to expel her lungs. Finally, she managed to spit out a chunk of solid yellow-green mucus into a tissue. It joined the pile on the table.

"What do you want me to do?" he said. He reached out, wishing he could touch her.

"These people are offering you nothing, what will they do with it?"

"They say they'll release it publicly, give it to a bunch of biohackers and breweries. I think they're sincere, but I don't know. It's never been done before."

"What's the other option? Selling it to a rival?"

"That's pretty much what I was planning to do. We also have some potential leverage over Biotron. They aren't good people."

"No shit," she said with a rueful grin.

"What do you think I should do?" he asked.

"What do you think you should do?" she replied. "You need to believe it's the right thing or you won't be able to see it through."

"I want you to get well," he said. "That's all I care about. I can use the leverage to get them to make enough for you."

"And if I get better, but the disease spreads past the point of no return? If it hits the elbow on the curve? I couldn't live with that," she said. "You said they're a network of biohackers?"

"It's more like they have a network. I'm not totally clear. But they think once everyone gets going, they will produce more than any single facility could," he said. "At least, that's what they tell me."

"Even if your network of home brewers can't produce enough, there are giant facilities in India and Brazil that could. It wouldn't help here, but it would help globally," she said, lying back. Her eyes closed, and her breathing slowed.

"Jules?"

"Sorry, just thinking it through," she replied, not opening her eyes.

The way she lay with her eyes shut and her hands folded over her chest pulled Liam back to the agony of waiting for their mother to pass. He felt the weight of the shame of waking each day hoping she had faded in the night. He would lie in bed, listening. But then he would hear their father's voice, the forced cheerfulness as he brought her tea and some plain toast. He would hear her croaking thanks and the door closed. The disappointment would come with a surge of nausea, fear and anger pointed inward.

"Jules?" he said again.

"I'm still here. This needs to get into as many hands as possible."

"But what if I can't pull this off? We might all get arrested before we can get it out. Or it could take weeks before we can make enough. And I didn't want to tell you this, but David is missing."

"What do you mean, missing?"

"No one has seen him for a few days. I was keeping an eye on him, and he's dropped off the radar."

"You have to find him. He's the only other one who really understands how this works."

"I know. We're trying. But it keeps getting harder."

"I can live or die, and it doesn't matter. Making sure people have access matters. Making sure this disease doesn't push us over the edge is what matters. We are so close to the edge. So close. It feels like we have built everything out of sand. All it will take is one more grain to collapse the whole thing," she whispered. "This doesn't have to be that grain, not because of someone like Megan. Not if I can do something."

"It matters to me. How can you ask me to risk losing you?" he said. His throat closed as he fought the tears.

She opened her eyes and dragged herself up to a half-seated position. She started to cough again but managed to force it down after a few rasps. "It's my legacy, Liam. If I don't make it, you need to make sure it survives me."

"But if I can get them to make some for you. We need you to get better. Then you can keep working, keep creating new medicines."

"Listen: I won't take anything from Megan, or you if you just get enough for me. So, no. If you make a deal, I won't take the drugs. Like you said, it's my decision."

Dammit, Julie! You are such a stupid idealist. It's not how the world works. People like Megan run the world. There's not a damn thing anyone can do about it. So if we can make them throw us a bone, we take the bone."

"No. I won't," she said. "Not anymore. Being sick has made me realize... I don't care about their rules. If I play their game, I lose... we all lose. I'm taking my piece off the board. I can't sweep the whole game off, but I can refuse to play."

"But...," he said. The set of her jaw and the look in her eyes told him it was useless. He had a vision of her dead on her couch at home. Stick thin, skeletal, unmoving. The sour but oddly sweet smell of the final hours of life still hanging in the air. He choked down the acid that rose in the back of his throat.

"No," he said. "I can't do it again." The lump in his throat swelled, threatening to cut off his breath. He inhaled deeply, trying to get air around it.

"You can't do what again, Liam?"

"I can't fail again," Liam said. The tightness in his throat had expanded into his chest. He was struggling to breathe normally. Tears sprang to his eyes.

"You didn't fail. There was nothing you could have done," she said. She reached out, trying to touch him through the screen.

"I shouldn't have wished for her to go at the end," he said through clenched teeth.

"She was suffering so much. She wished she could go too. There was no hope in those last months. She saw how much pain she was causing you," she said.

"But she was the one who was sick!" he said, in nearly a shout. "I should have hidden it. I should have swallowed it like you and Dad. Then you left, Jules. And Dad.... You have no idea what it was like in that house after you left. He was a ghost," Liam hissed through clenched teeth. He swallowed hard, trying to choke down the lump in his throat. But the pressure underneath was too great; he wasn't strong enough to close it back down. He shuddered and his hands went cold.

"I know, Liam. I regret that every day. I'm sorry. I couldn't handle it anymore. Dad checked out. When you were home, you were so angry and withdrawn. Then you enlisted and I didn't understand. It took me years to realize you were angry with yourself and not with me," Julie said. "You couldn't have saved her, and you couldn't save Dad. You know that, right?"

"Not really. I still hate that it all happened," he said, he slumped back in his chair. A lethargy spread through his limbs.

"Look at me! I've watched you gnaw at yourself for a decade. Are you ready to be done? Because I am. I forgive you, Liam. I forgive you for hoping she died, for feeling disappointed when she hadn't. Because I felt the exact same damn thing. Every night. And she understood. She loved us for it. She loved us for wanting her pain to be over. If she could have, she would have ended it herself. She told me, towards the end. She was sorry she put us through it. But she couldn't find a way to leave," she said, her own tears falling now, dripping onto the white blanket.

"I had no idea, Jules," Liam said. He wanted to take her hand and lean against each other like they had done often before. "I thought I was the only one."

"I know. I never wanted to admit it. It was foolish and hurtful. It took me a long time to forgive myself. I was afraid of saying it out loud. Because then it would be true. But I've said it now, and I just feel sad that I didn't say it earlier," she said.

"I wish she could see what you've done, Jules. She'd be proud. Now it's my turn to make her proud," he said. His arms felt heavy, and he sobbed.

"It's time to make yourself proud, Liam. She's gone and Dad's not coming back. It's just you and me," she said. Her back shook as she fought to keep from coughing.

"What if I fail? What if we can't get Restro from them? If you go, then it's just me," he said, the old, familiar icy grip on the back of his neck.

"Then you better not fucking fail. I know you can do this. I know you can, and you have allies now. Use them... and kick Biotron in the nuts. Now get to work," she said and severed the connection.

29

LUNCH

LIAM WALKED out of the tattoo room and found Lilah's workstation. She was hunched over a circuit board, the tip of her tongue sticking out of the corner of her mouth. Solder smoke curled up as she touched the iron to it. She looked so focused Liam decided to wait.

She blew a strand of hair out of her face as she applied the iron again. Then sat back and inspected her work. When she was satisfied, she looked up.

"How's Julie?"

"She's weak, but she's through the immediate crisis. I need to move *now*."

"Let's get some lunch," she said. "You need to eat. I can show you some of what we're building here. Maybe that will help you understand."

He followed her through the workshop. There were people at most of the workstations busy fabricating electronic parts.

"Why are you doing this here? You could all be out making a killing."

"Because making a killing is killing us. Things are going to get very bad over the next few decades. We need to help as many people as possible to have a chance of avoiding another dark age."

She opened the door to the corner shop that had been a Chinese restaurant. The smell of the food in the steamer trays made his stomach rumble. A few of the tables were full of people chatting and eating. The majority were in their twenties or early thirties. A few gray hairs were scattered around the room.

"Do you really think there will be another dark age?" he said as they joined the serving line.

"Our current civilization is doomed. Whether we make the transition to something new or something worse is still up in the air. I just hope some of what we do here helps prevent it. Anyone can copy what we are doing, make a little seed community and adapt it locally."

Lilah led him over to the serving area and handed him a plate. "The veggies come from the green houses and everything else is made in the bioreactors."

He looked over the available selections. There were a lot of curried greens, fresh salad, chili, berries, and a potato and cheese dish. Unable to decide what he wanted, he loaded his plate with a bit of everything. Lilah eyed his plate and raised her eyebrows.

"How can you mix like that?" she said.

"What? You don't like your food to touch? It all looks so good I can't decide," he said, noticing the sauces had started to run together.

They found two seats at a table next to a woman with an unruly pile of curly salt and pepper hair. She stopped her conversation with the man next to her as they sat down.

"Liam, meet Mike and Sylvia," Lilah said. "Liam is a new associate on the network."

"Nice to meet everyone," Liam said. He shoved a large forkful of food into his mouth.

Mike extended a hand to Liam. "Always nice to meet a new member," he said. His hand was rough and scared like a farmer, but his protruding belly and the slight softness to his face suggested a more sedentary lifestyle. He had dark nut-brown skin and close-cut dark curly hair.

"You were recruited by Keema?" Mike asked.

"I've worked with her for years," he said. "I don't know that I've been recruited yet, though."

"What will you do with Restro once you have it?" Sylvia said.

"Julie wants you to have it. I just hope you can do what Lilah says," Liam said. His answer made him flush, and he looked down at the table. He felt as though he was a child, and everyone else at the table was patiently waiting for him to find the right answer.

"I promise you, Liam. We will spread this as far and wide as we can," Sylvia said. "Just get the code and we'll have a thousand production facilities up and running within a month."

"And what about Julie?"

"Julie will get our first batch made here. We'll owe her that much. And we need to get her somewhere safe. She'll be vulnerable at home."

Liam sat back. His appetite was gone. Sylvia was right. As soon as he was a threat, they would use Julie against him.

"What will you do?" he asked.

"Lilah will get her from the hospital. We'll take her someplace safe and make sure she has the proper care."

"Where?"

"I don't think it's a good idea if we tell you that, Liam," Sylvia said, peering at him over her glasses. "If you are caught you can't reveal what you don't know."

"So, you're asking me to trust you with my sister and you aren't going to tell me where she is?" Liam asked, jabbing a finger at her.

"Do you think it's a good idea for you to have that information?" Sylvia asked.

"Go easy on him, Sylvia. He's new," Mike said.

"How will I find her afterward? What's to keep you from using her against me like you say Biotron would?" he asked.

Lilah pursed her lips and shook her head. "You have to trust someone, Liam. It's up to you. What do you want to do?"

He closed his eyes and took a deep breath. Lilah's hand on his knee grounded him. He opened his eyes and stared at Sylvia. "They'll be after her no matter what. So get her someplace safe. But if you try to use her as leverage, know I will burn you."

"I wouldn't expect anything else," Sylvia said. "Do you have something Lilah can give her so she will trust her?"

Liam opened his library in his specs. He pawed the air as he paged through his collection of photos and videos. He found one of the four of them in happier times. He sent it to Lilah.

"Good. So, you'll go get Restro for us?"

"I'll do it. I don't know that I have another choice."

"There's always a choice, Liam," Mike said. "Whether you realize it or not. You get this done and we'll help you get out from under your debt."

"You can do that? How?"

"It will probably be a good idea if you disappeared afterward."

"You want me to give up my life?"

"Do you really live now?" Mike said. He pushed back from the table and stood up. "I'm going to get back to work. "

He turned and walked out the door. Sylvia looked at Liam and shook her head. Her pursed lips reminded him of his grandmother when she was disappointed in him for failing to do his chores. "I don't know why, but Keema trusts you. Know that the people here are putting a lifetime of work, their freedom, and potentially their lives on the line. What are you willing to risk?"

Liam stared at her, unable to find an answer. She sighed and followed Mike out the door.

He jumped as Keema's voice sounded in his head. He had forgotten he was hooked back up to her communications network. "Hey, Liam. Will you and Lilah find a place we can talk in private? I think we have a plan to find David, but it's going to take some work," she said.

30

CLUBBING

THE NEXT NIGHT, the full moon lit the city as Liam waited across the street from the Piper nightclub. He leaned against the wall of a new apartment block with the requisite artisan bakery, organic clothing store and yoga studio on the ground floor. The area was very different than it had been when he first moved to the city. An influx of money had pushed out the artists and lesbian communities who had colonized it from the drug dealers and homeless in the timeless ecology of economic succession in the city. Someday there would be a financial fire and the cycle would start over again.

He shivered slightly in his thin shirt. The last day had been a whirlwind of preparation. It was too risky for him to go back to his apartment. So, Lilah had requested some clothes for him. The pants were from a thrift store, but the shirt was new spider silk from the vats. It glistened as the fog beaded on it and dripped onto the street.

"Hey Keema. Any update on Julie?"

"We have her safe and sound. Now focus on the mission," she said.

He checked one more time on her monitor. They had set up a fake signal from Julie's house to make it appear she was home. She wasn't allowed to leave while she was under quarantine, so hiding her in a safe house had required some extraordinary measures.

Three women in short party dresses walked up to the door. Sergei let them in after scanning their ID's with a camera hidden in his flashlight. The AI's ingested the information, updated their social databases, measured preferences, and cross-referenced them with commercial data sources. Within a half second, they had generated a complete profile. The club would use the information to create a perfect evening for them. This was what made Piper so popular. No one realized their lives were analyzed as soon as they walked in, but they knew they had a great time, every time.

Liam shook his head. They were so careless with their personal information. He watched the women walk inside and then he scurried across the street. A G-Cab at the end of the block slowed to let him pass with the minimal amount of velocity change. The protests had grown steadily since the night Julie got sick. Traffic was slowing to a crawl around the city. The routing algorithms seemed a little desperate to him now, trying to make up for lost time. The car passed a few feet behind him, closer than a few weeks ago.

Liam nodded to Sergei as he walked in. Tonight, they would get their first access to the Biotron network. Yesterday, he had sent VIP invitations to Don and Vinge. Vinge had gotten on the waitlist weeks ago. Now they had won a drawing for a table on the club floor.

A bit of embedded code had phoned home when Don and Vinge opened their invitations.

Liam walked into the club. The large dance floor was

flanked by two sets of tables with white tablecloths and small electric candles. The walls were painted black, with large dark violet curtains hung every ten feet around the room.

In the back, the DJ stand seemed to float above the floor, working with the machines creating a slow, throbbing beat hinted at desire and promised release.

The patrons all had sleek grey graphene bodynets. The men were wearing shiny silk shirts, in bright reds and blues. Most of the women were either in skintight party dresses, printed in just their size in the last day, or elaborate outfits of smart fabric that moved with their mood. Liam ducked as one woman extended a set of wings from the back of her jet black insectile outfit. Liam was glad for the social camouflage his blue silk and black breeches provided. He skirted the edge of the dance floor and went upstairs to the balcony where another set of tables waited for the evening's festivities. Just reserving the table cost more than Liam made on his last job and that didn't include the bottle service. He walked along the back wall and pushed through a small door. Walking down the hall, he passed the doors on his left until his specs signaled him to open the last door. As he reached for the handle, his bodynet exchanged password keys with the door system. As he touched the handle, the door unlocked.

Inside, Lilah sat in a large, comfortable chair with her eyes closed. An invitation to join a shared display floated over his head. He waved and a stream of data from the club below flowed over the dark wood paneling.

"You ready?" Lilah asked. Liam's heart raced. He knew he was reading more than he should into their time yesterday, but he hoped there was something more than just a repair job between them.

"I'm as ready as I can be. I spent all afternoon rehearsing, so I think we're good," Liam said. He hoped Lilah hadn't noticed the blood rising in his cheeks. "I still can't believe this club is an OP front."

"It was Sylvia's idea. She realized we were going to face organized opposition to what we are trying to do, so she hired the right people to start several clubs like this in a few global power centers."

Keema's avatar appeared next to Lilah's chair. "Take a seat, dummy. Let's review the operation one more time. We're targeting both men to ensure we get in. Then we bootstrap our access to Biotron through their systems. We let them walk us into the facility and then find where they are keeping David."

"It's a good plan, but I'm not big on using a honeypot," Liam said.

"Honeypots work. Phaedra is a highly trained member of the team, skilled in self-defense. She's dedicated to the mission, and she'll have backup the whole time. We aren't sending a lamb to the slaughter here. We're luring the lamb in for dinner," Keema said.

"Yeah, I know it's a useful tactic, and it's not like they wouldn't do the same to us," Lilah said. "Still, I hoped *we* could be different."

Keema looked at them and shook her head. "It's not like we're targeting them for drone strikes."

"If you say so," Liam said. "I assume I'm still on for Don?"

"Yep. You've got about an hour before they show up," Keema said. "They won't want to seem too eager. But they'll be excited enough that they'll arrive as early as they dare."

31

TABLE SERVICE

The club was starting to get busy. The AI controlling the drink dispensers was slowly increasing the amount of alcohol in each drink. Liam watched as the club registered the increased emotion and energy in the crowd. The playlist feed updated as the machines switched to faster beats and increased danceability. Liam watched the multidimensional graph display of the machine's interpretation and manipulation of the club's emotional state.

The system had been evolving for the last year and could now manipulate the crowd in any way the club manager wanted. The night could be mellow and smooth, frenetic and urgently sexual, or seamlessly transition from one to the other.

Liam selected one of the women he had seen enter the club and tracked her data. She had consumed one standard unit of stimulants, targeted for her estimated body size with no added sugar. He idly traced the model back through her personal history, everything the club computers had linked from the moment Sergei scanned her ID.

A surge of nausea constricted his throat as he realized how much he now knew about a woman he had never met. He swiped her profile away and switched over to the background on Don and Vinge. Don was short with sandy-brown curly hair. He had the look of someone who was naturally pudgy and wasn't working all that hard to keep it off. The frequency with which he used euphemisms for drugs in a party context in his social feeds was well above the average for a man of his background. He had profiles on the largest three dating sites, but successfully connected only once every few months.

"This is one of the guys who determines who lives and who dies in the next year?" Liam said, sharing his view of the profile with Keema and Lilah.

"Unfortunately, yes," Keema said. "You wouldn't know it, but he has a master's degree in mechanical engineering from Cal. He's in charge of the production facility's mechanical systems. From what we can tell, he's competent in his job most of the time. He looks hung over on Mondays but seems to keep it under control during the week."

Lilah rolled her eyes. "His kind drives me nuts. Still wants to be a college frat boy, behaving like an idiot during the weekend. But he has ridiculously important responsibilities that he just doesn't seem to care about. The only reason he has his job is because of his connections and educational background."

"We can only play against the team in front of us," Keema said. "If they want to put a soft target in our way, who are we to argue."

"Still doesn't make me feel any better about what comes out of their production facility," Lilah said.

"Hopefully you won't have to for much longer," Keema said with a smile. "Vinge is just as easy, but in a different way." She motioned to the shared display and Vinge's target profile appeared. He was a tall, thin man, with dark caramel skin and short dark hair.

"I see why his dating profile is so popular," Lilah said. Liam tried not to let the twinge of jealousy show.

The feed from the outside door camera blinked for their attention and Liam flipped over his view. Sergei was frowning slightly at Don as he scanned in his ID as he did with all the guests. It made them feel like they had passed a test when he eventually let them in. Vinge stood next to Don, talking excitedly. After a moment, Sergei handed Don back his ID, and admitted them into the club.

A club hostess escorted the group to a table near the dance floor. As they settled in, Lilah activated the pin head microphones embedded in their table.

"There are advantages to being one of the hottest IPOs in the city right now," Vinge said with a wide smile glancing at two beautiful women walking by. His hair was perfectly tousled, his spider silk shirt iridescent in the flashing club light.

Don sat quietly at the other side of the table. His knockoff silk shirt was too big in the shoulders. His slightly tousled hair was already starting to fall into its normal curly mass. Liam felt a twinge of sympathy for him.

A waiter approached the table. "We'll take a bottle of champagne to start. The real stuff," Vinge said, he waved dismissively. "And hurry up.".

Liam watched as Phaedra brushed by Vinge. Her long black hair was pulled up in a high ponytail and she wore a skintight dress with translucent patches that slowly moved around the dress in random patterns. Vinge looked up, his eyes fixed on the dress, watching to see what it revealed. She smiled slightly, then looked away. She made her way to the bar, glancing back once. Vinge watched like a hungry lion. They wouldn't have to wait long.

Don was sitting at the table, his head resting on his hand enviously watching the exchange. "You should find someone to dance with, Don," Vinge said across the table.

"Yeah. I just need to get my courage up. But that hottie by the bar keeps making eyes at you," Don said.

"I'm just letting her marinate," Vinge said, sneaking a glance at Phaedra. "You can't rush these things."

Liam fought the urge to storm downstairs and punch him.

The waiter reappeared with the bottle of champagne. As he peeled the foil and slowly worked the cork out, Vinge glanced back at Phaedra. He gestured at the bottle and his eyebrows raised in the unspoken invitation. Phaedra smiled and slowly walked back to the table. Vinge gave Phaedra Don's glass and asked the waiter for another.

Deep in the inscrutable logic of the AI, a parameter reached a critical threshold. The tempo and pitch of the music crept up, building the anticipation of the drop. Four club employees planted in the crowd, prompted by notifications in their specs, made their way onto the dance floor. The AI had decided it was time to dance.

As the planted dancers started dancing, the music reached a frenzied climax, paused and then the bass drop tipped the balance. The woman with the black wings danced out onto the floor, her wings flexing to the beat. Liam watched the two women who had come in before him grab their male companions and start dancing against them. The dance floor was suddenly crowded with bodies, all moving in sync with the beat. The emotional display for the club moved back within expected parameters. The AI continued its vigilance.

Don watched the surge onto the dance floor and sighed. He pushed back his chair. "I've got to take a leak."

"I'll catch you later. Don't worry, buddy. You'll get some tonight," Vinge said, putting his arm around Phaedra.

"Sure," Don stood and walked toward the bathroom.

"I think that's your cue, Liam," Lilah said.

32

THE PATSY

LIAM LEFT the comfort of their operations center and descended back into the club. As he moved through the edge of the crowd, a warm sensation spread through his limbs. He started nodding his head to the music. Synchronizing his movement to the rhythm of the crowd, he passed through unnoticed. He felt light and tall, a god of the city.

He made his way into the men's room where Don was just finishing at the urinal. Liam adjusted his hair in the mirror. He waited until Don finished and turned toward the sink. Then he took out a bag of white pills and pretended to pop one in his mouth. He turned toward Don with a smile.

"Hey, bro. How's it going?" he said.

"I'm okay," said Don, his eyes tracking the baggie as Liam put it back in his pocket.

"You want one?" Liam said.

"What is it?" Don moved towards him. His eyes never strayed from the bag. Liam could feel his need to get out of his own skin. Don wasn't an addict in the classic sense, but Liam knew he took every chance he could to escape.

"Molly. Fresh off the boat from Amsterdam," he said.

"If you don't mind..." Don replied.

"Naw, bro. I've got plenty."

Liam handed a pill to Don. As they touched, Liam resisted the urge to connect to Don's bodynet. He could flay him open in an instant, but it wouldn't be subtle. They needed him unaware.

"Thanks! We've got a table over by the floor. Come by later and I'll buy you a drink," Don said. He popped the pill in his mouth and dry-swallowed it.

"Sounds great. I'll see you around," Liam said, punching him lightly on the shoulder.

Liam made his way back across the crowd, trying to sync back into the rhythm of the music, but he couldn't seem to find the energy. He awkwardly pushed his way through a group gathered near the bar and headed back up the stairs.

He relaxed as he entered the quiet operations room. Rolling his shoulders, he returned to his station. A quick search located Don at the bar. It would take another few minutes for the drug to take effect.

Vinge was with Phaedra; she sat on his lap.

"Well, Phaedra is making progress," he said.

"Yep, that hook is set," Keema said. "She just made net-to-net contact. We've started looking."

"Here's hoping his digital hygiene isn't as good as his physical," Liam said.

Liam turned his attention back to Don. He was in the middle of the dance floor, moving slowly in his own world. Liam reached out and connected to the chip now making its way into Don's gut. The chip absorbed energy from radio waves generated by the club, and rebroadcast data from Don's bodynet.

"Keema, ready to go on Don."

"Take him," Keema told him.

Using the data from the chip, Liam drew a map of his systems. Don's router was new, but he hadn't run security updates in a few weeks. A few other peripherals were in similar shape. Liam reached into the club's network, targeting a stream of commands into Don's net.

"We've got everything, full root access," he said.

'I can see,' Keema replied.

The club systems siphoned up the data, laying open Don's life like a dissected corpse.

A map of Don's life appeared in front of them. Liam swallowed against the rising unease in his gut. It wasn't often he had, or even needed, this kind of full access. Usually, a bit of social engineering gave him what he needed to know, but this was a level of detail that made him deeply uncomfortable. He took a deep breath. Julie's life, and thousands of others, were at stake. He needed to focus.

Liam analyzed Don's movements and communications. Had anything changed in the last few days? Don primarily moved between his apartment and the Biotron production facility in the south bay. He took a G-Cab back and forth, usually spending only enough time at home to sleep. Two days ago, he had stopped going home. He now spent all his time in the lab.

Liam frowned. Maybe Don was feeling the deadline pressure and putting in extra hours. But the change coincided with Suarez's disappearance. He checked Don's communication logs. The number of requests for help to the research team had dropped off significantly at the same time. Either they had made a breakthrough and he didn't need help, or he had assistance from another source.

"I think David is in the Biotron facility," Liam said.

Lilah connected to his feed. Liam felt his cheeks flush with the strangely intimate data sharing.

"I agree," she said. "They can keep him isolated while they get what they need to go into production. I wonder what kind of pressure they have to get him to cooperate."

"They've probably convinced him we're the outside threat, who wants to steal his work and keep it for ourselves. Or hurt him. We did break into his apartment," Liam said.

"It's possible," Keema said.

"I think Liam's right. Getting caught was a bad break. I'm sure they've used that to make us look like the bad guys," Lilah said.

A thrill of energy shot through Liam with Lilah's agreement. Keema raised her eyebrows and shook her head as she registered the change in his vitals.

"What do we do?" Keema asked.

"I'll go in and get him tomorrow night," Liam said. "I can use Don's credentials. Can we make sure Don has a date tomorrow night to keep him out of the facility?"

"Sure. I'll spoof a date request on one of his dating profiles," Keema said.

"How are you going to get David to walk out with you if he thinks you're a threat?" Lilah asked.

"If he knows Julie needs his help, he'll come voluntarily," he said.

"And if not?"

"Then he'll come along involuntarily," Liam said with a sigh.

33

BREAK-IN

LIAM AND SERGEI crouched behind the stormwater swale outside the Biotron production facility. Overhead, the nearly full moon cast its pale light. The fog stayed north tonight. Liam wished it had spread down the peninsula.

Liam switched his tactical view to the condor drone loitering high above them. Keema had deployed it hours ago. It hovered over the facility, listening for electromagnetic leakage, tracking radios and network traffic. They had tracked five security personnel over the last hours, as they made their rounds. Two pairs were on patrol with the final guard stationary inside the building. Keema and the OP analysts agreed this was probably where David was being held.

"Time to move," Keema said. Sergei tapped Liam's shoulder as he passed, and they hurried up the slope. Across the small drainage field, the production facility seemed to glow in the moonlight. Liam and Sergei ran, keeping low, across the open space up to the door of the facility. Liam waved his hand over the reader, using Don's key code. The reader beeped and the fingerprint scanner glowed red. He placed the plastic fingerprint glued to his glove on the scanner. It chimed and the door on the lock popped open.

They slid inside and found themselves in a small lobby, with an empty reception desk in front of another glass wall. Behind the glass a complex maze of tanks and pipes filled the cavernous warehouse. Liam moved across the lobby to the side door. He scanned Don's identification code again. The door buzzed as it unlocked, and Sergei pushed through. Anyone watching the building security system logs would think Don was entering the building. He wasn't scheduled to be here tonight, so there was a strong chance security would investigate. Speed was now their best weapon.

Sergei sprinted through the factory floor, heading for the stairway up to the office level. Liam pushed himself to keep up. Sergei's powered prosthetics hummed as he hit the stairs and bounded up them four at a time. Liam took every other stair, panting as he hit the top of the staircase. Sergei was waiting for him at the corner to the hallway. As Liam approached, Sergei extended a prosthetic finger with an embedded camera around the corner and nodded. The guard was right where they expected him.

Liam jogged up next to Sergei. "Go," he whispered.

Sergei spun around the corner and raised his taser. The guard didn't have a chance as the darts stabbed into his chest and brought him down with a whiff of ozone. Sergei charged down the hallway.

Liam caught up to Sergei outside the room as the Russian was securing the guard, binding him with zip ties. The building would notice the guard's vital signs had changed and would raise the alarm in a few seconds.

Liam moved to the door of the office. He waved his hands over it. The door bleeped at them but remained locked. Liam tried again with the same result. A bead of sweat trickled down his neck into the collar of his coat. He quietened his mind, made sure the broadcaster was set properly and tried again. Again, the door didn't budge.

Sergei pushed him aside. "I've got it," he said. He took a step back and launched himself into the door. It burst open and the two of them charged inside. Across the blonde wood conference room, a single figure sat in a high-backed chair, facing away from them. Liam ran over and stopped suddenly. A cold chill raised the hairs on his arms.

Don slumped in the chair. His curly hair was matted to his head, his face contorted in surprise. Liam reached forward tentatively and touched Don's hand. It was stone cold. He reached forward and felt for a pulse in his neck. He was dead.

Sergei came around the table. "We need to leave, right now."

"Wait," Liam said. "We've come this far. Watch the door." Clenching his teeth, he gripped Don's cold hand. He reached out and fed power from his own system to activate Don's bodynet. He closed his eyes, as Don's bodynet sprang to life. The cold from Don's hand seeped into his fingers. He pushed deeper into Don's network until he found the memory core of his router dumping Don's core into his own storage. He skimmed the contents as they flew by. Buried deep in the file directory was a large, encrypted file labeled "Research". Liam examined it while the rest of the data flowed into his systems. Don was the last person to access it, but the file author was David Suarez. A thrill passed through his body. They might have the Restro data if they could find the key to open it.

Keema's voice made him jump. "Liam, Sergei, the police

are swarming toward the building right now. You need to get out. It's a setup. MOVE!"

Sergei grabbed his arm and yanked him toward the door. Liam stumbled, trying to bring his attention back to the room.

Liam found his feet and started to run alongside Sergei. He switched his systems into full active mode. Keema brought up a wireframe of the facility and the grounds in the lower left corner of his vision. There were two police cruisers out in front of the building and the two Biotron security teams were running through the door. She highlighted another four inbound cruisers and the SWAT van as they approached the main drive. "Shit! ... shit, shit, shit, shit". Liam muttered as they sprinted back towards the stairway.

Sergei stopped at the top of the stairs. Two Biotron security guards were sprinting toward them across the factory floor.

"Not that way," Sergei said. He spun Liam around and pushed him back down the hallway.

"K, we need another way out."

"Working on it," she said. A line appeared in their vision, leading back into the offices. "Follow the line."

They raced back past the conference room where Don's body was still slumped in the chair. They followed the line past the room and around the corner of the corridor. Sergei got to the corner first and peered around as Liam made up the ground. Sergei took off down the hall as Liam panted behind him. Liam's legs burned from the exertion and stress. Sergei was barely breathing hard, and still outpaced him as they ran down the hall. As they neared the next corner, the path indicator suddenly turned around.

"Security in the hall in front of you. They anticipated my move," Keema said.

They spun around and Sergei surged past Liam again to take the lead. As they passed the hall, they had come down moments before, they heard shouts behind them.

"Stop! Stop or we'll shoot!"

Liam's coat shifted the armor to his back and flung his collar all the way up over his head. Sergei made the next corner ten feet in front of him. He was about to make the turn himself when he was thrown to the ground.

He heard the echo of the shot as he hit the floor. His ribs ached deeply, and he struggled to his hands and knees. He heard footsteps behind him as the guards ran forward to claim their prize. He tried to catch his breath to stand and face them.

His medi-patch clicked, and a surge of amphetamines flowed through him. One of the guards grabbed his arm from behind. Liam bellowed with rage as he lashed out with a backward elbow. The security guard jerked back, narrowly avoiding the blow. But Liam was already turning, catching the guard with a spinning punch. Liam kicked up with his right leg, catching the guard in the groin. The security guard bent over with a grunt and Liam hit him in the face with his knee.

The man crumpled to the ground, blood spewing from his broken nose. Liam turned to face the second guard when he realized Sergei already had him on the ground and restrained.

"Nice work," Sergei said. "I didn't think you had it in you."

Sergei grabbed both men and sent a surge of electricity through their bodynets. They groaned as the circuits tattooed on their bodies overloaded and burned out. "That will keep them off net for a while."

"Let's move, gentlemen," Keema said. A path appeared

in his specs and they both took off sprinting. With the amphetamines still coursing through him, he felt as fast as a gazelle.

"SWAT is pulling up out front. Keep moving," Keema's voice was calm.

The corridor dead-ended in an alarmed fire door. "What now?" Liam asked.

"Crash it. Out the door, down the stairs and toward the bay," Keema said.

Sergei hit the door at full stride and with one forceful bound leapt over the railing of the fire escape. Liam leaped through the door and bounced off the railing on the narrow fire escape landing. He recovered his balance as he threw himself down the stairs, barely managing to keep his feet underneath him. He heard the buzz of a super capacitor discharging and risked a glance at Sergei. He had landed cleanly on the ground below the landing just as the other security team came around the corner. Sergei reached out with both hands and launched a full electric arc, using their bodynets as conductors. Both men let out a scream as they went down under the onslaught.

"Jesus, that Russian tech is nasty," Keema said.

Liam hit the bottom of the stairs and stumbled into a sprint across the wet grass behind the production facility. He could hear the sirens of the police cruisers and vans as they pulled up to the front of the facility.

"Shit," Keema said. "I'm being traced. They've tagged our comms and are triangulating. I've got to drop off. Head for the water." Then she was gone. Liam looked at Sergei as they raced for the water. The Russian's expression was unchanged as his arms and legs pumped furiously.

The ground became muddier as it sloped gently into the bay. Liam tripped over a stump he saw too late. He went down in a heap, the wind knocked out of him. Sergei reached down and picked him up by the back of the coat, barely breaking stride. Liam scrambled back to his feet as Sergei pushed him toward the water.

They reached the water's edge. Liam scanned for the exit Keema had promised. He looked back over his shoulder. Two SWAT team squads were creeping around the side of the building. He hissed at Sergei and they both hit the deck, the mud and water splashing up underneath his coat. He figured since they hadn't been shot, they hadn't been seen.

A direct confrontation with the SWAT team was out of the question. Any attempt to shoot their way out would end with them dead in the mud. In a moment, someone would notice their footprints and the game would be up.

34

ABANDIÑOS

LIAM CAUGHT a motion out of his peripheral vision. He shifted to get a better look. A small inflatable zodiac crept up along the shore, its electric motor silent. It was empty but it pulled itself up behind them, its bulbous black rubber snout bumping the soft muck. He belly-crawled over to it and slid over the side. Sergei slid in on the other side.

Liam held his breath as the boat backed up and then accelerated back the way it came. Sergei reached down and pulled a tarp from the stern of the boat over them. The boat would be nearly invisible in the fog as it made its way back north along the shore.

The boat ran along the shore for a few minutes, then turned out to the bay, away from the police on land. It opened the throttle, pushing Liam into the hard bottom. The motor whined slightly as it pushed its maximum output.

Liam fretted in the enclosed space of the zodiac. He hadn't heard anything from Keema since the comms blackout. Was she safe? Had they found her? He needed to get back to the OP, but lying in the bottom of the launch, muddy, wet, and cold, there was nothing he could do.

He closed his eyes as the boat bucked over the waves as they tried to cross the bay. The image of Don's pale face frozen in panic came back to him. Don's need for acceptance had given Liam the opening and he had pushed through it. Megan and Barkley must have killed Don to cut the trail and give them leverage. They'd have evidence from Don's bodynet to link him to the drugs and time to frame him for everything else.

The motion of the boat combined with his rising anxiety. His head swam and acid bubbled up in the back of his throat. He mentally reached into his medi-patch and hit himself with a motion sickness drug. He wished he could talk to Keema.

A dull ache grew behind his eyes as the nausea faded. He tried to sink into the bottom of the boat, hiding from the disaster this had become.

Liam brought up the map of the bay and their current projected path. They were drifting southeast away from Vallejo. From the boat's current projections, they would pass south of Alameda Island, drifting into the channel between Alameda and Bay Farm. At least the tide was coming in, not rushing them north towards the Golden Gate and out to sea.

They needed to get off the water as soon as possible. Sergei dropped a pin on the map at the end of the channel on the eastern edge of Oakland.

"Here. If we can get here, we have a chance," Sergei said.

"What's there?" Liam asked.

"Abandiños..." Sergei said. "It will be fine."

Liam shivered in the damp of the bottom of the boat. "A squatter camp? Won't I stand out?"

"We can get help there," Sergei replied.

Liam hoped Sergei knew what he was doing.

He tasked the boat with finding the best route to the pin and watched as it simulated ten thousand possible combinations. The potential lines gradually narrowed down. The system identified a route with the least potential for detection and the greatest number of escape routes.

The boat shifted slightly underneath him. The motor spun up, taking them perpendicular to their previous heading.

Liam used the time to investigate the database he had stolen. It was a large, encrypted file. According to its own meta-data, someone had made changes a few hours before he made his copy.

He moved the file into a safe box he created; it might have a weaponized payload or have a phone-home feature. He double checked the security around it. Anything military grade would likely overwhelm his defenses before he could delete it. He hoped he could deal with anything less potent.

The file was locked. It required an encryption key. He trawled through his copy of Don's systems and found his list of keys. He clenched his teeth as he tried the first one. It failed. Two attempts left. Liam read through each key, looking for hints.

He identified a key he thought looked promising and fed it to the system. It failed. He had one shot left. He paused. He didn't know what the file would do if he didn't guess correctly. Would it delete itself? Lock itself down and refuse all of Don's keys? Or would it simply time out and make him try again later? Should he keep trying? Or wait until they got to safety and get some additional help?

He had to know what he had. Julie was running out of time, and now the police were involved. If he had the files, he had leverage. If he had junk or worse, then he might as well jump out and drown in the Bay.

He looked over Don's list of keys again. One of them was labelled "Rpo". Could it be Restro Production? he wondered. He decided this one was as good as any. He held his breath as he copied the key. For a moment, nothing happened. Then the system opened. He let out his breath and dove into the data.

He found production schedules and schematics for fermentation tanks, process diagrams and other production data. Finally, he located the section entitled "biology". He reached into it, but it wouldn't open. Liam groaned in frustration. They had everything they needed except the actual DNA sequence.

He reached into the administration layer, looking for the permissions. He found the user access list. Don had access to everything except biology. Obviously, they didn't trust him with the family jewels. Only David and Megan had access to the sequence. And both of those locks were DNA-encrypted. It would require a DNA sample from one of them to open that side of the file.

Liam had a momentary fantasy about collecting the sample from Megan. It involved sharp instruments and screaming. Then he let it go. If they could find David, he would probably just give them the sample.

"Hey, I've got the data. I can get access to the production but not the DNA sequence. We need either David or Megan for that," he whispered.

"Fuck," Sergei hissed. "Did we get anything on David's location from Don?"

"No, nothing. They kept him compartmentalized."

"Ok. When we get connected, we'll get the teams working on it. He has to be somewhere."

There wasn't anything more to say. Liam worked to unclench his teeth as the boat crept across the bay. Slowly they entered a channel. The steady thrum of human network activity returned.

Neither of them dared to connect to the network. It would be like turning on a flashlight in the middle of the dark water. He had no idea whether their encryption was safe or how much their pursuers knew. If the police or Biotron security found them before he could connect to a network, the whole mission would be a waste. He willed the zodiac to move faster, get him to shore. He wanted to get this data out of him.

The boat rode the currents, kicking on the motor occasionally to adjust course. Finally, after what seemed like days, the boat bumped up on the shore. Sergei and Liam unclipped the tarp and stowed it back in the stern. Liam groaned as he stretched his cold, tight back and helped Sergei push it back out into the water. It turned and made a short sprint back out into the water, putting distance between itself and the two of them. It would gradually make its way north, waiting for the outgoing tide to give it an assist. If it couldn't make it back, it would sink itself and wait for someone to retrieve it.

Liam and Sergei scurried away from the water's edge into the mud flats. Liam shivered as they picked their way across the sticky bay mud. Sergei eyed him. "You are cold? This is not cold. Kamchatka in January. That is cold," Sergei said.

"Yes. I'm a soft California boy," Liam sighed. "Can we get out of here and figure out how to upload the data I'm carrying, please?"

"Come on, soft boy," Sergei said with a smile and started off up the embankment. As they came over the rise, they entered the edge of an Abandiños encampment. They crept between the cardboard houses. Each small house was the size of a small trailer, but higher than they were wide. Most had clear plastic sheeting pulled tight over the openings. The light from the LED bulbs over the doors illuminated part of the street. They moved between the shadows as much as they could.

The major streets ran east to west, and the houses were lined up with their long edges facing south. All of the houses had large, clear plastic columns lined up against the south wall. Liam realized they were filled with water to provide thermal mass for the buildings. As they moved deeper into the camp, Liam noticed an increasing number of the houses had their own solar panels. The older houses toward the center had a different design. They were less elegant than newer houses toward the outskirts of the camp, encrusted with printed solar panels and water catchment barrels.

The encampment was quiet. He had expected it to smell like smoke and human waste, but it was clean, and the only odor was the slight tang of marshland. The street was paved with a mix of bay mud and chunks of old concrete. Sergei seemed to know where he was going, and Liam struggled to keep up. They moved quickly towards the highway.

35

SHARING

LIAM HEARD the buzz of the quadcopter before he saw it. He dove into the shadow beside one of the houses, pressing against the warm plastic water bladder against the house. The copter grew louder until it was directly over them.

Sergei heard it as well and stopped in the middle of the street. He scanned the sky, then smiled and waved. Liam squinted, barely able to make out the black drone against the night sky. Sergei kept his palm pointed at the drone. A red laser pulsed against Sergei's hand. Sergei seemed to listen for a minute, then nodded.

The copter waggled its wings and started back down the road. Sergei motioned for Liam to follow. Liam followed the Russian at a slow run. A few blocks later, they stopped in front of an older house. It was painted green with a white trim. The windows were clear acrylic, and it had a full array of solar panels on the roof.

The door opened, and a short, thin man with shoulder-length gray hair waved them inside. Liam followed Sergei into the house, and the man closed the door behind them. Along the right wall, there was a counter with a cooking plate and a water oven, a small sink and a little refrigerator. Along the left was a small sofa, and a table. The furniture was made from cardboard but seemed impossibly complex and sturdy. All the cushions were patchworks of fabrics.

"Carlos! Thanks for this," Sergei said.

"Don't thank me yet, Sergei. I don't know what *this* is," he said, gesturing for them to sit on the small couch behind them. Liam sat down on the sofa, surprised at how soft it was.

"We need to get back north, but we need to do it quietly," Sergei said, sitting next to Liam on the sofa. Carlos pulled up the chair from the table.

"How quietly?" Carlos asked. "Can you wait until morning?"

"I'd rather get there as quickly as possible," Liam said.

Carlos looked at him, brow furrowed. "And you are?"

"He's with me," Sergei said. "I need to get him back to the OP, quickly and quietly. Quiet is more important than quick, though."

"Serge, you know we can't have any trouble here. They ignore us because we keep to ourselves."

"It's important, Carlos. I wouldn't be here if it wasn't. He's got the cure for the fever. We need to get it back to the OP and get it out to the network. Our mesh network has been compromised, and we don't know if we can transmit it on our own."

"The cure? You're sure?" Carlos asked, his eyes wide. "What are you going to do with it?"

"I need to get the lock for the final piece," Liam said. "But then we'll get it out."

Carlos leaned back in his chair. He ran a hand through

his hair, revealing his widows peak. He squinted up at the corner of the house, lost in thought. "No," he finally said.

"No?" Sergei said, the tone of his voice higher.

"No. At least not without leaving a copy here. That's my price," Carlos said. "It doesn't hurt you to leave a copy. But my kids and my wife are asleep in the back. If you think I'm going to let their access to a cure walk out of here, you are mistaken. I know I can't stop you from just leaving, but you wouldn't be here if you didn't need me."

"Shit, Carlos. After everything the OP has done for the Abandiños? You're going to negotiate?" Sergei said.

"You said those were gifts, Sergei. This is something else. Yes, the OP has done a lot for us. But we don't owe you our lives because of it. Do you have any idea how quickly the fever would burn through this place? There are a lot of old and sick people here. We'd fall apart in days. So, I'm asking you to leave a copy here. If we don't need it, we don't use it. If we need it, then we'll use it. No one will know. We'll just not get the fucking plague. How does that sound?" Carlos said.

Sergei smiled broadly, his crooked teeth showing. "You drive a hard bargain, Carlos. But we accept," he said.

"We do?" Liam said, jerking away from Sergei.

"Yes," Sergei said. A dull ache started in Liam's leg as Sergei increased his grip. "Carlos and his people will help us get back to Keema as quickly and quietly as possible. Carlos, if we don't make it, I want you to find a way to release the file to the world. The core genetic code is still locked, but maybe there are enough clues for someone to reverse engineer it. We'll also leave the names of the people whose DNA will unlock it. You're our insurance policy. But don't risk it if you don't have to. This will bring down a full pile of shit storm on you."

"I'll make that call if it comes down to it," Carlos said. "Let's have that data now."

Liam clenched his jaw: "Fine. How do you want to do this?"

"Connect to the house network," Carlos said. "Dump it into the network and we'll figure it out from there."

Liam unlocked his network connections, breaking his electronic silence. He reached out for the house network. There was a brief negotiation between the systems and Carlos gestured to the house to let him in. Then he was connected again. Data flowed over him like a warm shower. Pursing his lips, he grabbed the data file and pushed it to the house network. He fought the urge to reach deeper into the flow, to reach out and try to connect with Keema. They couldn't be watching every connection at once, could they?

Deep down, he knew they would be watching. He sighed and cut the connection. They needed to get north.

"Excellent. I've sent out a request for help. We'll meet up with the crew at the community center. We can disguise you enough to get you through the recognition cameras on the BART and get you on a commuter train in the morning. That will get you as far as Richmond. You'll need to get across the bridge on your own," Carlos said. "We don't have connections that far north, but we can lend you a bicycle, if that will help. Now let's head over to the community center before you wake my kids."

36

MAKEUP

THEY FOLLOWED Carlos towards a warehouse on the north end of the encampment. The corrugated metal building had been recently repainted, but small pools of rusty water still lay around the foundation. Light shone through the windows, and the chatter of a heated conversation filtered through the glass. Carlos knocked twice and led them inside a large room with long rows of tables with attached benches. Along the far wall was a serving area that fronted a large kitchen. A small group seated at a table away from the door stopped talking as they walked in.

"Liam, Sergei… meet Claudia, and Chris," Carlos said, gesturing at the two Abandiños. Claudia was solidly built, with dark brown shoulder-length hair pulled back in a tight ponytail. Chris was short and slim, with dark skin and a shaved head.

"Nice to meet you," Liam said with a small wave. The two nodded slightly at him and turned their attention back to Carlos.

"What's the plan, Carlos?" asked Chris. "Who's the ciudadano?"

"A friend of a friend. Not important. What is very important is we get him on a train north at rush hour without being recognized," Carlos responded.

"A full workup?" Claudia said.

"Si. We need to get them through with the minimum chance of detection," said Carlos.

Claudia and Chris stood up from the table and looked over Liam and Sergei. "The ciudadano will be pretty easy. He's got an average face. This one is going to be much harder with the implants," she said, gesturing at Sergei.

"I will make my own way," Sergei said. "Just get him out."

"Wait, what?" Liam said.

Chris regarded him. "It would be better if you separated anyway. If there's that much heat on you, two men traveling together will increase scrutiny. And his augments will make him an easy target. They won't expect mixed genders. So, we need someone to escort this one."

"Good point. Okay, citizen, since you're the package, you are traveling with me," Claudia said.

Claudia grabbed Liam's arm and led him through the kitchen into a large space beyond. The room beyond was stuffy with the smell of old paper, smoke and hot plastic. Large laser-cutting and milling machines crowded the walls. Piles of used cardboard, plywood, and plastic were stacked between them.

Claudia led him to a back corner. A display screen was set on top of a bookshelf filled with tubs of silicone and colorants. She arranged him in front of a green wall, then gestured at a dragonfly drone perched on top of a small workstation next to the green screen. It took to the air and hovered in front of Liam's face. "Hold still a sec," she said.

The drone flew a slow arc around him. On the screen a 3D scan of his head gradually took shape.

"We've got what we need," Claudia said. "Let's change you enough to avoid the cameras."

The projection of Liam's face began to change. Skin color, brow ridge, nose, cheeks all gradually shifted as the machines evolved a solution. He looked at a version of himself he barely recognized. One cheek was slightly rounder than the other, his nose looked as though it had been broken more than once and his brow ridge was heavier, overhanging his eyes. Liam winced.

"We have the same facial recognition software used on public platforms. The machine evolved a look by competing against the algorithm. The printers have started on the prosthetics we can use to build this. Chris will apply them once they are ready," she said.

The printers rattled to life behind him. "Chris will have a new set of clothes for you as well. You need to ditch the coat, and we need to do something about your hair," she said, squinting at him.

"I'd really rather keep the coat. I don't feel safe without it," he said.

"The coat is pretty distinctive. We'll test it once you're made up. Maybe we can dress it up a bit, use it to change your gait," she said, pursing her lips.

The printers chimed softly in the other room. "Looks like your makeup kit is ready. Chris is on his way over," she said, gazing into her specs.

She turned and walked back across the workshop, stopping to pick up the facial pieces. Bits of Liam-colored latex hung like flaps of meat. She led him over to a chair next to a work-table. Chris walked in and put a large briefcase on the table. He opened it carefully, revealing a large makeup kit. He looked over the latex pieces Claudia had laid on the table and nodded.

"Let's get started," he said. He picked up a wet wipe and started cleaning Liam's face.

"You do this a lot?" Liam asked. "You've got the development algorithms, latex printers, and that's a hell of a makeup kit."

"Let's say we have more than our share of people who need to hide," Chris said with a snort. He put down the wet wipe and picked up a makeup sponge. "A lot of people here face jail time for failure to pay simple fines or taxes. In the camp, they are usually safe. But people need to get out to see their family or get to the hospital. It's a risk, but we've got this down pretty good."

"There are people here who will go to jail because they haven't paid a fine? That's ridiculous," Liam said. From the look Claudia and Chris gave him he knew he was wrong. "They could really go to prison?"

Chris started applying makeup to Liam's face with the sponge. "My brother is in Oakland lockup right now. He owes tens of thousands for being drunk in public. Just drunk...didn't hurt anyone. But the cameras tagged him, and they fined him. He didn't have the money to pay the fine, then the interest and late fees stacked up. Then they picked him up for the crime of having unpaid fines. Now, there's no way the family can pay to get him out. None of us has that kind of money. I ended up here trying to help him pay it down, but then I lost my job."

"Shit, Chris. I had no idea things were that bad," Liam said, immediately regretting his choice of words. "I mean, I worry about my rent payment and student loans. But you're helping me, I'll see what I can do to help you," Liam said.

"Fuck that, man. We don't need your charity," Chris said, putting down the sponge. For a moment, Liam thought Chris was going to hit him.

"Sorry," Liam said quietly.

Claudia put a hand on Chris's shoulder. "He doesn't mean anything by it, Chris."

She turned to Liam. "He's right. Just getting his brother out doesn't help. Because there are ten other people in this camp whose families are in the same boat. If Sergei says what you are doing is important, then we'll do whatever you need. But don't think we're a charity case."

Liam nodded, unsure what else to say. There was a moment of silence as the three of them let the tension of the moment dissipate. Chris let out a heavy sigh and opened his case.

"While Chris gets the makeup right, let's go over our operations plan," Claudia said, leaning against the table next to him. "Until you get back inside in Vallejo, assume at all times you are being watched and they are actively searching for us. We can't put a foot wrong."

She paused as Chris pasted on the cheek plate. "I got it, stick to the plan," Liam said while trying to hold his face still. "I can stick to a plan."

"We're going to head out in five hours to make the 7 o'clock train north. It's peak traffic time and the cameras will have a harder time picking us out. I'll hire a G-Cab and we'll hold hands in the cab as well as after we get out, to signal to the cameras that we are a couple. At some point, you should put your arm around me as we walk together in the station. I have two older transit cards we will use, so we don't have to use the facial biometrics gate. Once on the train, it will be easier for them to corner us, so we sit by the door. If I don't like it, the abort code is that I forgot to turn off the oven. We abort and try to make it back here. Got it?"

Liam grunted his understanding as Chris worked to affix the nose piece.

"Great. I'm going to take a nap. I'll be back in a few hours. Chris, you'll have him done by then?" she said.

"Yep. He'll be completely unrecognizable by the time I get done with him. I've got the gimp insert for the boots," Chris said. He looked down at Liam with a grin. "Of course, it's not exactly comfortable. But you won't forget to walk differently."

"Wonderful," Liam replied. Claudia nodded at Chris and walked out of the workshop. Liam watched her out of the corner of his eyes, not daring to move his head. The latex clinging to his nose felt as though he had a heavy scarf wrapped around his head. He was starting to sweat slightly. Chris roughly wiped the sweat off him with a cloth. "The makeup won't stick if you're sweating," he said.

"Sorry," Liam replied. He wished he could think of something to say to Chris besides an apology. He knew it wasn't his fault his brother was in prison, but the guilt was there anyway, sitting on his chest.

Chris finished applying the latex to Liam and began to add makeup, blending the skin tones of the latex with Liam's skin, hiding the seams and adding the natural variation to the printed pieces. He closed his eyes to avoid making eye contact with Chris.

He started to drift off, the light strokes of the makeup brush just keeping him awake but relaxing him at the same time. He had just surrendered to sleep, when running footsteps interrupted his calm. He opened his eyes as Sergei pushed through the door. "We've got to go now," he said.

37

ESCAPE

LIAM SAT up and pushed Chris out of the way. "What? How?" he asked.

"There are five drones over the camp, and the police are on the way. We need to go now," Sergei replied. He threw Liam his coat and turned to glance back out towards the kitchen. Liam stood up and put the coat on, careful not to smudge the makeup. The coat settled over his shoulders and connected with his bodynet.

"I'm up and running," Liam said. "How do we get out?"

"Carlos is working on it," Sergei replied. "I've given you access to the camp network."

He accepted the access credentials, and a new network connection surged through his hands. An overview of the camp appeared in the corner of his vision. Five small red dots of the drones moved across the map.

"They must have predicted from our last known route. They are assuming we've gone to ground here. They probably don't know for certain yet," Liam said. "If we can get out without being detected, they'll move on to the next most probable location on their list."

"But how do we get out of here?" Sergei said. He studied the map. They'd be watching the one overpass over the highway. Running across the freeway would stop traffic. They might as well stand outside with big signs over their heads.

"Do they have a boat?" Liam asked.

"Yes," Sergei replied.

"Show me where," Liam replied. A blue dot appeared close to where they had come ashore. He traced a route on the map with his finger. If they could get across the river, they could disappear in the squatter camps of the Coliseum's huge empty parking lot. "That's our way out."

"Agreed," Sergei said. "The police vans will be here in 10 minutes. We need to be gone by then."

Chris cleared his throat behind them. Liam glanced over his shoulder and froze. Chris pointed the inch-wide barrel of a shotgun at Liam's chest. He trembled slightly as his eyes began to tear.

"They didn't have to guess," Chris said. "I called them."

Liam turned slowly, with his arms raised. The shotgun pellets wouldn't penetrate the coat, but the scatter might catch his head. He signaled his coat to brace but kept the collar down.

He focused on Chris's hand. He set the coat to button up if his finger moved the trigger. His collar could react quickly enough, but it would only protect the lower half of his face. A slight motion of Sergei coiling up in the corner of his peripheral vision drew his attention.

"What did they promise you, Chris?" Liam asked. "Did they promise to release your brother?"

"A bounty for you appeared a few hours ago on a

commission site. It's enough to get him out. They really want someone called The Worm", Chris said.

"It's not the police offering the reward, is it?" Liam asked, his mouth dry. The police wouldn't use a dark commission site. "It's a private party."

"Yeah, probably," Chris said. "What does it matter?"

"Those aren't police drones. You think the drones will just track us? You think they'll just stop with us?" Liam said. He was surprised that he felt sorry for Chris, not angry. Chris was stuck in a web he didn't make - duped into betraying everyone he wanted to help. In a different context, Liam might have pulled the same trick. Biotron might even turn a profit on the operation from the bounties from the other people here.

The color drained from Chris's face, and he swallowed heavily. "Oh shit. What have I done?" Chris said. "Those motherfuckers. No matter what I do they fuck us over." His eyes narrowed and he gripped the gun tighter. He moved the barrel off Liam and looked past them out the window. "You better go."

"Chris... wait," Liam said as Chris pushed past them and ran out the door. Liam started to follow him, but Sergei grabbed his sleeve.

"He's made his choice. We can use the distraction," Sergei said and pushed Liam out of the workshop and out the side door.

Chris screamed and fired wildly at the drones. The deep boom of the shotgun echoed through the night. Liam watched a flaming drone drop onto a house in front of him.

Sergei pushed him to get him moving. They ran for the water's edge. A young woman holding an infant opened the door to her house, scanning the sky, her face tight with fear.

He and Sergei dodged through the growing crowd in the street as they raced toward the boat.

The thumping boom of the shotgun echoed again through the night, followed by two quick, smaller snaps, then silence. Liam fought through the tightening in his legs as his adrenaline surged. As he feared, the drones were armed. Chris was probably dead.

"Shit, shit, shit," Liam chanted like a mantra as he drove himself forward, trying to keep up with Sergei. He could smell the water now. The lights of the encampment ended in a black void as it yielded to the bay. Behind them, shouts and amplified voices echoed from around the workshop and dining hall as the police started to push into the camp.

The two remaining drones moved out in front of the police line. The large six rotor-copters searched for them but avoided direct contact with the police. A second wave of drones, this time marked in blue, began to spread out over the compound. Then the map disappeared in a haze of static.

"They've started jamming the local net," Sergei said, as they ran on toward the boat. He smiled slightly. "And Carlos has started jamming back. It should buy us a few minutes."

Finally, they reached the shoreline to find a small inflatable zodiac pulled up on the beach. Its black rubber sides merged with the dark mud and black water. Liam climbed aboard and into the back, looking for the motor start. He didn't recognize the engine make. His recognition systems were offline with the jamming war in the camp. He felt around blindly for a start button on the motor. Sergei grabbed the large concrete block tied to the boat as an anchor and walked back to the boat. "I can't figure out how to start this!" Liam said.

"I have the key," a voice said from the shore, outlined by the lights of the encampment.

Liam squinted through the glare at the backlight silhouette. A short, burly figure crested the bank. "Carlos?" he said, trying to shield his eyes.

"If you're leaving, you need to take them with you," Carlos said, gesturing at the young man and a young, visibly pregnant woman following him.

"Too many people will draw attention," said Sergei as he placed the block in the boat.

"You'll have to figure it out. But they need to get out of here. They cannot be caught," Carlos insisted, holding up a small metal key. "Or you need to take your chances with the currents and hope you don't end up out in the Pacific. I think the tide has started going out."

Liam flinched as another man, wearing nothing but sweatpants, ran over the top of the embankment towards them.

"What are we waiting for?" Claudia growled. She snatched the key from Carlos' hand and helped one of the women into the launch. She tossed the key to Liam. The other two from the group climbed in and lay on the bottom of the boat, as Claudia clambered aboard.

"Go!" she yelled at him.

Liam found the slot for the key and the engine whined. He threw the throttle into reverse as Sergei pushed the launch into the water. A large drone, white and sleek, raced over the embankment. Sergei saw it at the same time and pushed the boat deeper into the channel. He winked at Liam and turned back toward the drone. Liam turned the throttle forward and the boat moved away from the shore.

The light from Sergei's laser-guided electrical blast left a spot in his vision. The man-made lightning struck the drone, scorching the casing. It simply stopped and fell to the ground. A shot echoed as the second drone flew in to take its companion's place. Carlos fell, grabbing his abdomen. Sergei sent out another blast at the second drone but missed. As the boat moved away, Sergei sprinted towards Carlos, firing at the drone.

"Will your friend be, okay?" Claudia asked, moving to the back to sit next to Liam.

"If anyone is going to be okay, it'll be Sergei," Liam said. He mostly believed it. "I wish we had him with us."

"Thank you for helping us get these folks out," Claudia said. Two men and a woman were huddled in the bow of the boat, keeping low against the inflated sides. Liam realized the woman was holding an infant against her chest, soothing the infant to keep it from crying.

"Not that you gave me a lot of choice." Liam laughed softly. "But thank you. I'm glad you made me. I'd hate myself even more if we had just left them. Even if Sergei would say it increases our mission risk."

"It's best if I don't tell you too much about them, but they are some of the folks Chris was telling you about," she said. Her face went slack at the mention of his name. "Fucking Chris..."

"He was doing what he thought was best for his brother. He didn't know us, we're strangers bringing a threat to the community. I'm sure they told him they would just track us, feed our location to the police. They wouldn't mention armed drones. But there are no rules for these people, believe me," Liam said, surprised by the bitterness he felt. "I used to be one of them."

They ducked as a rumbling boom and flash of red light rolled out of the encampment. Liam looked back as flames from the camp lit the night sky. Screams echoed as he steered the boat into the middle of the channel.

"Dammit," he said, feeling the tears start in his eyes.

"I hope whatever you are carrying is worth it," Claudia said.

"So do I," Liam replied, his shoulders sagging as he fought back the tears. He didn't understand why he was so upset by the destruction of the Abandiños camp. He didn't know anyone there. Chris had threatened to kill him. Now he was responsible for four people in a boat in the middle of a stinking river. But here he was, trying not to sob for the loss of a few dozen cardboard shacks.

As they approached the overpass, he dialed back the throttle to reduce the visibility of the wake. The small boat crept forward against the current. He settled down on the floor of the boat. They all sat in silence, alternating between watching the river and the burning encampment.

38

ENCAMPMENT

THE OVERPASS LOOMED BEHIND THEM, backlit by the flames from the burning encampment, as Liam grounded the zodiac on the bank. Claudia took the tiller from him.

"This is where you get off," she said. "I'll get them to a safe house further up the canal, then see if I can get anyone else out."

Liam looked at the large expanse of asphalt in front of the bulk of the Coliseum. The tarps, cars, and tents of the squatters' camp spread out over the parking lot. Small fires burned throughout the camp. They filled the air with acrid smoke, which barely hid the smell of human waste. His eyes began to water.

"Head for the far side of the stadium and use the old BART overpass," Claudia told him/ "Cross over the tracks, then make your way to the station. The trains should start running soon. You'll have to risk an early morning train."

She pulled out a slightly crumpled ticket with an embedded RFID chip. "Here's the train ticket. Your makeup is still on, and the dirt will make it even more believable.

Just keep moving and try to avoid contact. Now get the fuck out of my boat."

Liam stepped over to the side. He turned and gave the boat a gentle push back into the water as Claudia restarted the engine. She gave him a quick salute and turned the boat back into the dirty channel.

Liam watched them until they disappeared into the night. Then he was alone, crouching in the soft mud of the reeking shoreline. The smoke from the squatters' camp made him cough. He realized just how clean the Abandiños camp had been - no smoke, no reek of human waste. Now it was a faint red glow on the other side of the highway. G-Cabs and self-driving trucks rolled by on the freeway, their robotic minds uninterested in the human misery a few meters away.

He pulled himself out of the mud and sat down on the low concrete reinforcing wall to take stock. The status check revealed his coat was carrying a near full charge, but his remaining dragonfly was throwing an error. He reached out to listen for a local network. The Abandiños network was gone. He could feel the always-present thin, cold cellular network, but any connection he made would advertise his presence. He shut down the antenna.

The camp was an electromagnetic dead zone. Turning on his radar would be like firing off a flair. He was reduced to his own senses.

He stood and started across the open asphalt. The camp was quiet. A few people were sleepily standing next to their tents, disturbed by the noise and light of the conflict across the narrow creek. The glow cast by the fire over the camp sent a shiver down his neck. He hurried to increase the distance between himself and the tragedy behind him.

As he walked deeper into the camp, the smell of the unwashed, urine and smoke choked him. The tents were arranged in neat rows, with a few feet of space between every other row of tents forming the roads of the encampment. The ubiquitous blue woven plastic rain tarps crinkled in the light breeze off the water. Liam hunched into his coat as he moved down one of the makeshift streets.

The familiar wet, racking cough of the fever erupted from one of the tents as he passed. He quickened his pace. This place would be a graveyard in a few weeks unless he figured out how to unlock the file.

He was nearing the stadium when three bright points of light emerged from the gloom. He ducked down and scurried off to the side. Three pairs of booted feet moved down the boulevard. He slowly crept backwards until he could slide between the tents, careful to avoid tripping over the nylon tent ropes.

Inside the tent to his left, he heard someone stir and call out, "Who's there?"

Cursing under his breath he moved back further away from the boulevard, into the space where the tents backed onto each other. He lay down behind the two rows, watching the lights move across the opening between the rows and turn down the boulevard he had just come from.

He inched forward, carefully placing his hands around the tent pegs holding the tension lines. The men holding the lights, walked down the boulevard, stopping in front of the tent. He had managed to put a tent's length between them. He froze in the shadows.

"Everything alright, Mrs. Nichols?" one of the men called out.

"Someone bumped into the side of my tent. No one is supposed to go between the tents," the quavering voice from inside replied.

"We'll check it out, ma'am. Just sit tight." The lights

stabbed into the dark space between the tents behind him. "Greg, go around the side. We'll push through here," he said.

Two of the men started through the gap between the tents behind him. Greg was jogging back, cutting off his exit. Liam clenched his jaw. He did not want to have to fight his way out.

The two behind him stepped into the space between the tents. Liam kept still, willing them to miss his form pressed against the pallet. The shout of alarm from one of the men reminded him again of his lack of telepathic ability.

He exploded onto his feet, jumping between the tents. He sprinted away from the two behind him who were now cursing and pushing their way back out to the street. Greg ran around the corner. The man's eyes were wide as he ran at Liam, the baton held in front of him like a spear.

Liam twisted at the last moment, hitting the side of the baton with his hand. Greg tumbled into the row of tents when Liam shoved him. Liam sprinted toward the looming stadium.

There were shouts behind him. The other two had stopped to help Greg, belying their lack of training. But now they were running after him, ordering him to stop. He turned down another cross-street, and risked a glance behind him as he ran. They were a full block behind him now. Ahead, the ground rose up a grassy hill, the concrete ramp to the overpass running off to his left. Liam raced up the ramp.

The stadium was dark. Liam raced past the gates, the security fencing sagging and torn. Small fires burned inside the entry gates. Liam caught flashes of eyes reflecting in the dark, still, thin forms hiding in the shadows. The otherness of them sent a new surge of energy through his legs.

Finally, he reached the top of the ramp, slowing to try to

catch his breath. He coughed out the dark phlegm accumulating in the back of his throat, stained by the smoke from the fires. He moved towards the concrete overpass that led from the stadium over the train tracks. It would take him directly to the BART station on the other side.

He turned the corner and began to jog. The pedestrian overpass was wide enough for eight people. The crumbling safety walls had spilled chunks of concrete on the pathway. In a few sections the rusting chain-link fence had been cut away, the material used elsewhere in the encampment behind him. Leaves and trash were scattered over the walkway, undisturbed for weeks.

The security team seemed to be losing interest in the chase. They were far enough behind him that he knew he could make it to the other side before they cleared the top of the ramp.

As he crested the top of the bridge, his heart sank. A rusty metal gate blocked his way down to the street. Blue and red lights alternated, reflecting on the concrete sides of the overpass. He hunched down and crept forward. Two police cruisers sat on San Leandro Boulevard while four insectile policemen scanned the few people who made their way into the station at this early hour.

Liam cursed. The police were bottling up the island, waiting for reinforcements for the inevitable sweep into the Coliseum. Climbing over the gate would draw their attention. A drone flew over the end of the ramp. Liam backed away from the cruisers, poking his head up to see the security team from the camp nearing the top of the ramp.

Now he was trapped on a wide concrete walkway, twenty feet above an abandoned warehouse. Liam was confident he could bull his way past the camp security team. They were amateurs. But then he'd be stuck in the Coliseum. Eventually the police would raid the island looking for him, and he would be responsible for more bloodshed. Going forward meant having to avoid the police. He wished Keema could give him a plan and a way out.

"Think, Liam. How would she get you out of this," he whispered. "She would think laterally. She would find the thing no one else saw." He glanced over the side and realized what he had to do.

He retreated a few yards back up the ramp to an opening in the wire fence. He climbed on to the safety rail. Gripping the fence, he inched his way along the outside. He turned around slowly, facing away from the walkway, desperately gripping the fence behind him. His bodynet calculated his projected flight path. Jumping would land him on the concrete twenty feet below, missing the edge of the roof by a good two feet. He needed some more horizontal distance before gravity pulled him into the unforgiving ground.

He re-ran the simulation again and again, trying every option. Finally, his system converged on a solution that sent a shudder down his spine.

He climbed to the top of the fence, crouching precariously on the top rail. He paused to collect himself and pushed himself off the railing as hard as he could, out into the night air.

39

LEAP

THE WIND ROARED in his ears as he fell through the night. He forced himself to keep his eyes fixed on the metal roofing rushing at him. He slammed onto the building with a bang and started to slide, madly scrambling for a handhold. He finally felt his feet hook into the gutter. He slid to the edge of the roof and lowered himself over the side. He hung off the edge of the building, then let go. He couldn't see his landing point, and the ground was a little closer than he expected. He hit it with a grunt. An electric pain shot through his ankle as he rolled to the side.

Cursing, he rolled to his feet. He needed to get away from here as the noise would draw the drone's attention. If he could move fast enough, he could use the distraction. Each step amplified the pain in his ankle. His boot stiffened as his bodynet registered the pain, diagnosis: ankle sprain.

He hobbled through an open door in the warehouse and moved painfully toward the door on the other side of the building. The police drone buzzed overhead, searching around his landing spot. It wouldn't be long before it looked inside. He pushed through a stack of old crates and out through a hole in the side of the building. He made himself walk as quickly as he could across the empty parking lot, trying to ignore the pain in his ankle.

A lone G-Cab slowly rolled by on San Leandro. Otherwise, the streets seemed empty. A faint odor of smoke pushed down his growing exhaustion. He needed to get out of here.

Liam limped across the street after the drone had passed and turned toward the BART station. He pulled his collar up and hunched into his coat. The two police officers were still watching the street, the drone now on a search pattern over the warehouse and the walkway. The sky behind the station was brightening into a new day. He didn't know how much of his mask was still attached, but he could still feel the nose piece. He hoped he hadn't damaged the makeup too badly. He was going to get on the next train, no matter what.

He slowed his pace down the sidewalk, accentuating the limp. He started to mutter to himself, "Damn them all," he grumbled as he neared the two cops. "I know, I know, it's a plot to make us all slaves.

His reverie was broken as he realized that two of the police patrol were staring at him.

"Gotta catch a train," he said to them. "Gotta get my meds." He coughed wetly and wiped his hands on his coat.

The nearest cop shuffled away from him but didn't break eye contact. Liam rooted in his pockets until he found the ticket Claudia had given him. He limped to the cash card turnstile and held his breath as he slid the card in. The transit authority wanted to phase out these older cards for the new facial recognition system. Commuters with the new ID's walked through without stopping. The machines recognized their faces, checked them against their bodynet signatures and then automatically debited their accounts. It made the commute faster, if you didn't mind leaving a data trail with every movement.

The machine spat it back out, buzzing loudly. "Card read error," it said. Its voice echoed in the empty lobby.

"Heh. Fuckin' thing," Liam said, making himself wobble slightly. A cold rush gripped his hands as the cop watching him approached. Liam straightened the card and tried to push it back into the machine, catching the edge on the reader. With a growl he pulled it back, straightened it again and fed it into the machine. The cop was a few feet away now, squinting at him. Liam knew the cop's specs were trying to match him against a known facial profile. Liam smiled obsequiously at the man as the reader mulled over his card.

"Do you need help?" the cop asked, his hand going to the gun on his hip.

"Heh. Noooo," Liam said. "Just gotta catch a train. Gotta get my meds."

"You said," the cop replied. "Do you have ID?"

"I'm not sure. Bob stole it last week," Liam said. The light on the reader turned green and his card popped up from the reader. He heard the turnstile unlock. Liam coughed again, grabbed the card and pushed through to the other side of the turnstile.

He glanced over his shoulder at the cop still squinting at him. The prosthetics seemed to be doing their job or the police AIs would have recognized him by now. Liam suspected the AI guiding the cop's actions was having trouble deciding if he was worth following or not. He checked his timer. Three minutes to the first train of the morning. Too long if the cop decided to follow him. He hobbled up the stairs to the platform.

He heard the gate chime behind him as the cop decided to follow him. If the cop got close enough to get a good look at his face, he would easily see the prosthetics. They were designed to fool facial recognition cameras, not close human inspection. As he reached the top of the stairs, he turned onto the platform and tried to put as much distance as possible between him and the cop.

He reached out to the cell phone network, the thin connection like guitar strings across his fingers. He pulled up a stored burner SIM card from his bodynet database and added a few levels of misdirection to the connection. Checking behind him to make sure the cop hadn't yet gotten into hearing distance, he connected to the police tip line. "The men you are looking for, the terrorists who broke into Biotron yesterday, I just saw them heading north on San Leandro toward 85th," he whispered and then cut the connection. The tip line would digest the message, extracting his tip. He hoped it would be enough detail to get over the reliability threshold and trigger the systems into action.

He heard the cop's footsteps approach behind him. "I need to see your ID," he said.

Liam took a deep breath and let out a hacking cough. He staggered forward, bent over, coughing. The fake coughing fit made his throat burn. He drew it out as long as he could, staggering over to the column in the middle of the platform and sagging against it. The cop took a few steps toward him. "Sir, your ID," he said, his voice level. "You don't have an electronic ID, so by law you are required to carry a photo ID."

Liam coughed again at the cop. The man took a step

back. "Maybe I got it here, somewhere." He kept his head bent, looking at his coat as he fumbled in the pockets as if looking for an ID card. He double checked the emissions control on his bodynet, ensuring it ignored repeated inquiries from the police network. They could use the root demand, but that usually required a warrant. But it was a risk. If the cop saw his tattoos, he'd be arrested and charged with interfering with a police investigation. Then they'd figure out who he was, and the game would be up.

He coughed into his hand again and reached into the pocket of his coat. "Bob took it from me. He's always stealing my shit," he said. How long was the damn police system going to take to process his tip? He had used all the right key words.

"If you don't have ID, I'm going to have to take you to the station and we'll need to process you. There's a terrorist alert, so we need to check everyone's ID," he said, moving forward with his hand on his weapon. Liam sighed. He might be able to surprise one cop, but the drone and the other one downstairs were too much.

The whine of the train pulling into the station drew his attention. He was so close. Pulling his coat close around him, he brought up his combat interface. He took half a step forward, closing the distance.

"Aw man, I just need to go get my meds," he said. "I'll get sick without 'em. You don't want me to get sick in your station, do you?"

"Sir, you'll need to come with me," the cop said, reaching for his taser. The train stopped and opened its doors with a friendly chime.

40

COMING CLEAN

THE COP'S hand closed on the grip of the taser. Liam tensed, ready to spring to keep him from drawing. But the cop stopped and pressed a finger to his ear. His hand came off his weapon.

"Sir, from now on you'll need to make sure you carry ID. If I see you again without it, I'll arrest you." He spun on his heel and ran down the stairs. The drone outside took off up the street followed by both cops.

Liam dove through the closing doors of the train. The few early morning commuters glanced at him and then quickly looked away. The train smelled of urine and old sweat. The seats were torn, and graffiti covered the few ads left above the seats. Liam took a seat against the far wall, where he could see anyone board. The doors closed with a pleasant chime and the train pulled away from the station. The adrenaline of the confrontation ebbed away, and the exhaustion grabbed the base of his skull. His eyes closed and his head fell back, startling him awake. His ankle throbbed dully.

He looked around the train. The seats were mostly empty, a few commuters either napping or listening to music. He curled up in the corner, trying to make himself as small as possible. The train dove into the tunnels under Oakland.

He stared off into the dark as he flexed his foot. His ankle was stiffening, and he could feel it swelling in his boot. He opened the medi-patch interface and tapped the stimulants and pain medication. The kit flashed a low inventory warning but dispensed the drugs. The familiar tapping sensation was followed by the rush of the stimulant. The fog lifted, and the throbbing in his ankle faded to the background. He decided he could live with it.

The door at the end of the car opened. He risked a glance over the back of the seat. Two men with muscular builds, wearing black coats and dark sunglasses walked slowly through the car. They stared at each person for several seconds, obviously letting their facial recognition systems get a good long look. The other commuters instinctively cowered. Liam buried his face in his coat, pretending to sleep. They couldn't scan his face if they couldn't see it.

The two walked up to his row. One of them had stopped. Liam could feel him staring at him. He kept his breathing steady and slow. The communications traffic radiating from the man was heavily encrypted. It felt military to Liam.

Were these guys feds? Or mercs? Not that there was a lot of difference anymore. The feds hired mercenaries as often as the corporations did. Enforcement was frequently only available to the highest bidder.

Liam shifted slightly and muttered to himself. He twisted, ready to react. He waited, willing the man to move on. Finally, he heard them turn and walk up the aisle. Liam didn't move until he heard the door open and close. Then he counted to ten and opened one eye. They had gone. Everyone in the carriage seemed to let out a collective breath.

Liam could stay in place, or he could move to the back of the train, to give himself as much time as possible. He decided to stay where he was and get out at the next station. If he moved now, and they came back, they would grow suspicious. They were out of the tunnel. The whine of the breaks told him they were approaching the West Oakland stop.

Cursing his stupidity at putting himself in such a confined situation, he willed the train faster. They made the last turn. The whine of the electronic brakes filled the cabin. He got up and walked to the door. The bright morning sun shone in through the windows. It was going to be a clear day.

As the train slowed to a stop, the interior car door opened and then closed. Liam didn't dare look. He grabbed the overhead bar and rested his head against his arm. It screened his face as much as possible.

The two men walked slowly down the train, until they were behind him. "Hey, buddy," one of them said, tapping his shoulder. They crowded him, reducing his ability to react.

Liam grunted.

"Hey Baron, nice try with the makeup," he said with a sneer.

Liam groaned and coughed. "Leave me alone," he said. "I don't know any Baron."

"Yes, you do," said the other one. The man stepped in front of him, blocking the door. His open jacket revealed a holster and a pistol. The train rocked to a halt and the door opened. The outside air was cool and smelled sweet.

The identity ping was overwhelming. His system responded involuntarily, the magnetic signature of his bodynet reflecting back to them. But his network was different now, partially redrawn. His new fingerprint wasn't registered with the authorities. The agent in front of him frowned. It was the distraction he needed.

He let go of the bar and sighed.

As the door chimed its closing tone, he leaped forward and drove his shoulder into the man in front of him. He pumped his legs as hard as he could, pushing him onto the platform. The man grabbed his coat as he stumbled backwards. The door closed behind him before the second man could react.

The agent spun him around and hooked his ankle. Liam tumbled. He grabbed the man's knee, rolling into him. The agent let his knee bend and they fell together. The man landed hard on top of him.

Liam lashed out. His fingers grazed the man's eyes. The soft, wet tissue dragged under his fingernail. The agent flinched, shouting in pain. Liam bucked his hips, lifting the man off the ground. He threw his weight to the side and rolled him over. Up on one knee, he drove the palm of his hand into the man's nose.

He felt cartilage give way. A spray of blood misted Liam's sleeve. He used the man's head and groin as a platform to push himself onto his feet. The agent coughed out blood and rolled onto his knees. Liam kicked out, connecting with the agent's skull. The man collapsed back to the ground.

The people on the platform stared at him. Liam sprinted for the stairs. He leaped down the stairway, taking them four at a time, then sprinted through the hall and vaulted the turnstiles. Out on the sidewalk, he sprinted across the street, hoping to lose himself in the derelict neighborhood. His ankle throbbed but he pushed himself on. The shells of former luxury condominiums sagged in front of him. In the distance, sirens grew closer.

A car turned onto the street behind him. Liam risked a glance over his shoulder. It wasn't a G-Cab or a police car. The black carbon and plastic panels seemed to suck up the light. It accelerated up the street toward him.

He willed himself to run faster. His lungs burned. His legs felt like lead. He broke right off the sidewalk, aiming for a gap between the buildings. The car pulled level with him, and he noticed it didn't have windows. The door opened, inside was bathed in a warm red light.

"Liam! Get in the fucking car," said a voice from inside.

He stopped cold. "Keema?" he asked, panting.

41

MEETING

"YES, it's me. Now get in the car. We don't have much time," she said.

"What's the passphrase?" he asked. He couldn't see much detail. The figure was female, but there was something odd about her appearance. A slight mechanical noise followed her movements.

"We don't have a passphrase," she said. "Deliberately so. But Lilah reconfigured your network a few days ago, if that will help you trust me. Now get in the goddamn car. We don't have much time."

The sirens grew louder. He estimated they were less than a minute away. He ducked inside and the door closed behind him. He stumbled into the seat as it accelerated.

His eyes adjusted to the red light. Two bench seats faced each other. There were no driving controls or other interfaces visible. Keema was sitting facing the back of the car. She was covered with a black carbon fiber exoskeleton. Each limb strapped into the support structure. An intricate gold bodynet tattoo swirled around her forehead and disappeared under her close-cut hair.

"So, we finally meet in person," she said, watching him closely. It was the voice he had heard in his head a thousand times.

"I can't believe it's you!" he replied. He reached out to touch her hand. His hand brushed the hard carbon fiber. She gently pulled her hand back slightly.

"When we got hacked, I had to drop comms and change encryption keys. They knew where I was, so I bugged out. Fortunately, I was able to, er, borrow this car. But we need to get off the streets as soon as possible," she said.

"How did you find me?" he said. "I haven't been on the net since last night."

"I followed the police reports. Once they raided the camp, I guessed this is how you'd try to get out. The fake sighting was a nice idea. But there were only two trains you could have taken within that window. I was driving the gap between them when the call went out to the police. It had to be you," she said.

"They must have had people waiting at the station. When I triggered the distraction, they started their sweep," he said. He glanced at the screen where the side window should have been. From the run-down strip malls and dilapidated houses, he guessed they were heading northeast towards the 980 highway.

"Any idea who they were? Homeland? Mercs?" she asked, leaning forward.

"I have no idea. They didn't identify themselves," he replied. He massaged his shoulder where he had landed on it during the struggle. He couldn't take his eyes off her tattoos. He had never seen such intricate organic work before.

"I'm going to guess mercs," she said. "Homeland would have flashed a badge to intimidate you."

"Those guys didn't seem official. Jesus, who are these people? They have their own private army?"

The car made a hard turn, throwing him against the door. He grabbed the seatbelt and strapped himself in.

"Megan has connections. Her investors own a private military contractor. They are ready for anarchy and plan to take over after the collapse. Having an army is the just the last step," she said.

"Jesus. There's nothing they won't do. What do we do next?"

"We've got to get off the street. I have a safehouse nearby. Then we can get in touch with Mike and figure out what to do. Do you have the files?"

"I have them. Wait, you have a safehouse?" he asked.

"Even a worm needs a safe hole to hide in," she said, crossing her arms. Her expression was defiant.

"What? What are you saying?" he said. He felt cold and sweaty.

"I'm the Worm," she replied.

42

THE WORM

LIAM FELT DIZZY. His vision narrowed. "How the hell are you the Worm? I've known you for years," he managed to whisper.

"You don't really know anything about me," she said. She gestured at the black insectoid skeleton that enclosed her. She turned her palms up with a whisper of artificial muscle. "You've been useful, Liam. And I do have a strange, sisterly affection for you. But don't presume you know me."

"I've been useful?" he said. Liam pushed himself back in his seat. He wanted to run away, but he was locked in.

"Yes. Some of your jobs were for me. Others provided funding for the movement," she said.

"Why? I thought we were partners," he said.

"We were. Just not equal partners," she said, miming a balancing scale. "You still believe you can win the game, get rich, be free. I know the game is rigged. I know what it's like to lose everything because of an accident," she said, gesturing at the machine embracing her.

"What happened to you?"

"I got into the car with my boyfriend when I shouldn't have. He didn't make it. I was paralyzed from the neck down. The medical bills from the surgery to save my life bankrupted my parents. They couldn't afford a nurse for me. So, my dad quit his job to take care of me. I would lay in bed, unable to move and hear them whisper their arguments about money," she said.

"That's terrible. They didn't have insurance?" he asked.

"Fuck you, Liam. They did," she said. "My mom was a programmer and my dad taught at the local college. But insurance didn't think my second and third surgery were necessary, and there's nothing if you're permanently disabled. It goes on."

"So how did that make you the Worm?" Liam asked, pointing at the exoskeleton.

"My dad quit his job to take care of me. But the expenses piled up and we lost the house. My parents got into a huge fight about it and my mom left. In that moment, laying there helpless, listening to them tear themselves apart over taking care of me, I became the Worm. Eventually my dad was able to get me a basic brain input device and it reopened the world. I joined a community of open tech activists. We designed this suit together and I've been gnawing away at the rotten core of the system ever since."

"I had no idea," he said. He reached forward to take her hand, but she pulled back. He started to say something more, but everything he thought of was useless. They sat for a moment in silence. The car accelerated up the ramp onto the highway.

"Well now you know," she said. "So, what are you going to do?"

"What do you mean, what am I going to do?"

"Do you have the files?"

"Yes. But the biological data is still locked. We need a DNA sample from Megan or David," he said.

"Look, give me a copy and once we're safe I'll get people working on it."

He hesitated.

"What? You're still thinking about keeping it for yourself? You really think you can get away with selling it?"

"I need to have some leverage," he said. "I'm risking prison, or worse, to steal this and get nothing in return?" he said.

"You get to save millions of lives," she said. She leaned forward, staring into his eyes. "Isn't that enough?"

"What if they catch me? Locked in a cell for the rest of my life. I'd rather die," he said.

"Is what you are doing now really living?" She reached out and took his hand. "Look, give me the files. If something happens to either one of us, at least we have a chance of getting a copy out. Maybe someone can break the encryption."

He looked down at her fingers, braced by the black exoskeleton, gently wrapped over his hand. Her hands were warm. He looked into her brown eyes. She held his gaze, her expression confident and relaxed.

"What's the end game, Keema? If we release it, just having this information becomes a terrorist offense. You think your breweries can hide from that? They'll stomp out every production facility and make everyone pay the price," he said.

"Maybe," she replied. "Or it becomes the spark that ignites the larger fire. People are getting desperate. There was a time when I thought we could make the transition peacefully. People would rise up and take back control. I don't believe that anymore, not without something to push them.

I'm going to hammer this again and again. The system isn't just rigged against you. Those who run it want you dead, because that's the only way they see to save their own skins."

"That's crazy," he said, pulling his hand back. "There would be riots in the streets. You'd start a civil war over this?"

"Yes. I would. What's the alternative? Condemning those who can't afford it to death? Imagine you didn't have this information and Julie was sick. If you couldn't afford the medicine, what would you do?" she said.

"I'd do anything," he sighed.

"And so would millions of others," she said. "So why do we get to decide for them?"

Liam looked at her. This woman who he had trusted with his life on so many occasions. Now she wanted him to help her potentially start a conflict that would tear the country apart.

"You're talking about a lot of people dying in the chaos," he said.

She pulled away from him and sat back. "The chaos is coming whether we like it or not, Liam. The old system is dying. The new one is struggling to be born. If we don't act, the system we are trying to create will stifle under the dead weight of the current system. But if we push it, it will topple like a rotten tree, providing light to the new growth. We've shown we can build a world where health care is free, everyone has enough food and energy for a sustainable life. Where people like your sister can explore freely and everyone benefits."

"It's a dream, Keema. It will never happen," Liam replied. "I want it to happen. These last few days have opened my eyes. But like you said, the game is rigged. The house always wins. If they can't do it quietly, they will do it with violence."

"If we don't try, then they will take us down with them. Maybe we fail, maybe you're right. But at least we go down fighting," she said.

"If we fail, a lot of people die," he replied.

"A lot of people are going to die no matter what we do. The question is how many and for what. We didn't make that choice. The people who own Biotron did. Look, you can give me the file, or you can get out and take your chances on your own. But I'm the Worm. I could rip it out of you right now. I wanted to give you the chance to do the right thing." She pointed at him, and he felt her cut through his systems. His coat froze him in place and his specs were filled with static. He felt like a bug stuck on a pin, upside down, completely vulnerable.

He sat back. A sense of calm came over him. He didn't have a choice. He grabbed the file and pushed it over to her network.

"Thanks, Liam. You made the right choice," she said.

He turned away, facing the black wall of the car. He felt his cheeks flush.

"We can deal with your feelings of inadequacy later," she said. The car swerved hard, throwing him against the side. "They've found us."

43

GORGON STARE

"How do you know?" he asked. He gripped the handle next to his seat as the car swerved again. It accelerated hard, throwing him back in his seat.

"There's a helicopter overhead. I should have known. They've got Gorgon Stare up and running. They probably saw you get into the car," she said. She closed her eyes. "I'm connected to the driving system. I'll look for a way out."

The car took another hard turn. Liam felt nauseous.

"We can't outrun a helicopter," he said.

"I know that. I'm looking for a place to hide," she snapped. The car braked hard. They took another corner and accelerated again.

"Hide? Where?"

"Will you shut up and let me work?"

Her eyes darted back and forth behind her eyelids.

"There. Okay. We're heading for a parking garage. You get out. Wait two minutes then head to the street. I've got a spoof ID for you. Use it and get a G-Cab a few blocks away.

Ditch the coat and the prosthetics. Here's the address of the safehouse. Watch for tails," she said.

A new ID set loaded into his system. It would be enough to spoof the cab.

"What are you going to do?" he asked. The car slowed. It turned and headed down a ramp.

"I'm heading out the other way. The car will drive on its own into the city and try to lose them. They'll need to split their forces," she said.

"That's it?" he asked.

"Hopefully at least one of us will make it," she said. "That's the best plan I have right now."

He stared at her as the car slowed to a stop. He didn't have a better idea. Right now, he didn't have any ideas at all. "Look Keema..." he said. "I'm sorry."

"Sorry for what, Liam?" She looked at him quizzically.

"I'm sorry you couldn't trust me to work with you. I wish you would have told me," he said.

She took his hand. "I'm sorry too. I've been doing this alone for a long time. The OP is the only group I've ever trusted, and even they don't know everything. I didn't know how to bring you in. I couldn't risk it. But I wish it could have been different."

"When this is all over, we should talk. I think you owe me a drink," he said. He wanted to grab her other hand. To tell her that even though she didn't completely trust him, he trusted her with his life.

A sad smile played over her face. "I'd like that," she said. Then her expression hardened. She let go of his hand. "Get this done, Liam. Do it for Julie and everyone else."

He hesitated, staring at her. He hoped for a moment she would change her mind, that he wouldn't have to lose her again so soon. But her expression didn't waver. He opened the door and stepped out. It closed behind him, and the car drove away.

"Hey!" he shouted. "Get out of the car."

Her voice cut through the sick feeling in his gut. " There's no way out for me. I'm going to broadcast the file, then I'll try to lead them away. This is more important than any one person. If our friendship meant anything, don't follow me."

The connection went dead. The car sped up the ramp and turned out of site.

He was struck dumb and still. The noise of the helicopter grew, then faded, chasing the car. She had bought him his window. He made himself turn away from the ramp and run for the stairs.

He took the stairs two at a time, peeling off the prosthetics as he went. At the landing he found the exit door. He rubbed his face, trying to wipe off the makeup. He slipped off his coat, holding it under his arm. He tucked in his shirt and tried to smooth it as best he could.

He cracked open the door, just enough to scan the street. In the distance, the helicopter and sirens disrupted the early morning calm. The street was empty except for a few commuters in their G-Cabs. No one paid him any attention.

He was about to step out when he remembered Keema's comment about Gorgon Stare. He could picture the drone high above with a very large camera array that could track a single individual while monitoring several square miles. He could picture the analyst watching, waiting for him to emerge.

Any operator worth their salt would watch the garage, waiting for someone to leave while they routed assets to search the building. Liam figured he had five minutes at most before ground forces arrived. He ducked back inside.

He brought up a map of the area and smiled. Keema had chosen well. The other side of the garage opened onto a shopping plaza. The clutter of the awnings and alleyways would make it difficult to track him. He turned and sprinted across the parking lot. As he crossed the ramp, a large SUV sped across the bottom of the ramp.

He had underestimated how long it would take them to respond. He sprinted out onto the sidewalk. Keeping as close to the buildings as he could, he raced across the plaza. Behind him, a squeal of tires betrayed the location of his pursuers.

The only people in the plaza sat outside the Apollo coffee shop while they drank their stimulants. He checked the ID Keema had given him. There was a small cash card in the package. He activated the ID and walked into the café. He ordered his new identity's usual drink from the Apollo system. Then he headed into the bathroom.

He inspected himself in the mirror of the restroom. Makeup was smeared over his face. The red marks from the prosthetics looked like a patchy sunburn. He washed his face, then he smoothed his hair down as best he could. After relieving the sudden pressure in his bladder, he shoved his coat behind the toilet. He hated leaving it there, but there wasn't much choice.

As he left the bathroom, two large men walked past the shop window, dressed in the same black coats and sunglasses as the men on the train. They stopped outside the coffee shop, muttering to their controller.

Liam backed down the hall, looking for a way out. He turned the corner toward the back storage room. The emergency exit door in the back hall had an alarmed crash bar. He stared at it. He had no idea what was on the other side.

If it was open to the sky, they would track him the second he left. The alarm would alert the agents out front.

A young man wearing an Apollo uniform came out of the storage room with a stack of disposable cups. Liam smiled at him and stepped aside.

"Can I help you?" he asked.

"As a matter of fact, you can," Liam said. He grabbed the man by his shirt and shoved him out the door. The man's shout was lost in the shriek of the alarm. Liam grabbed the door and pulled it shut. Then he sprinted back into the bathroom and closed the door.

Shouts of alarm came from the seating area. He listened as two sets of footsteps sprinted past. The emergency door crashed open again. Liam slipped out of the bathroom and walked back through the restaurant. Two tables lay on their sides and one woman was trying to clean the coffee off her blouse. Others were rushing out of the exit. He followed them out the door.

Liam made himself walk at a regular pace as he headed for the street. He called a G-Cab with his new ID. A cab rolled up and opened its door just as he hit the sidewalk. He slid inside and it pulled away from the curb.

He hoped they would take it easy on the barista.

44

ESCAPE AND RETURN

LIAM TAPPED NERVOUSLY on the door of the G-Cab as it rolled serenely down the street. He hated being stuck in a car like this. If someone figured out his spoofed ID, they could override the car's system, lock him in and deliver him anywhere they wanted. He thought about stopping and getting out, but the thought of the all-seeing drone overhead made him pause.

He jumped as the cab informed him there was a traffic jam and it would be changing its route. There was an accident ahead and several streets were closed. Liam glanced out the window. A helicopter hovered a few stories above an intersection two blocks away. A plume of smoke roiled in its down draft. The black sports car lay crumpled in the middle of the intersection. A large SUV with a dented grill was nearby. Two large men with black coats and sunglasses scanned the crowd nearby while two more levered the car door open with a crowbar.

He was about to order the G-Cab to an emergency stop

when the men popped open the door. They reached inside and dragged Keema's still form out onto the street.

He watched in horror as they dragged her by her exoskeleton back to the SUV. They opened the rear door and pulled her inside. The two standing guards retreated to the truck. As soon as they were inside, the truck sped off down the street.

The helicopter swung around and followed the SUV. The only thing he could hear was his own breath. The car stood alone in the empty intersection, like she had never been there. Liam clenched his fists, choking down the urge to scream. Rage burned up within him. He wanted to lash out at the men who took her. But they were gone.

The G-Cab slid forward, obscuring the view of the intersection. A sob welled up from deep within him. He had never felt as alone. Keema was gone, Julie was dying, and he had no idea if he could trust Lilah and the rest of the OP. He wiped away the tears and forced himself to control his breathing. The cab rolled out of downtown, oblivious to its passenger's emotional turmoil.

The cab finally rolled to a stop under a tree in a leafy residential neighborhood on the Berkeley border. He requested an additional drop-off address and paid the fare in advance. Then he slipped out of the cab. It rolled off empty.

Liam waited for a few minutes under the tree, trying to calm his thoughts. The smell of eucalyptus and pine trees filled the air. The sunny afternoon and quiet neighborhood seemed surreal.

He clenched his fists, letting the anger pass through him. Then he refocused. He still had a mission. Keema had sacrificed herself so he could get through. He wouldn't let her down.

He traced a staggered route through the neighborhood

to the safehouse, keeping under the trees whenever possible. In the distance, a helicopter sped off over the bay. He wondered where Keema was and if she was still alive.

The safehouse was a plain stucco house, tucked away down a small cul-de-sac. Liam scanned the street one more time and then headed for the front door. She had given him the key codes in his ID package. But as he reached for the door, someone opened it from the inside.

Liam leapt back, raising his fists. Lilah peered around the door. He relaxed and Lilah opened the door the rest of the way. She stepped back and motioned him inside. Liam scanned the street and then stepped through the door. She closed the door behind him. His shoulders sagged as he relaxed. She wrapped her arms around him.

"She's gone?" he asked.

She let go and stepped back, shaking her head, with tears welling in the corner of her eyes. "They took her away in a helicopter. If she's alive, they have her," she said.

"I don't know whether to hope she's alive or dead," Liam said.

"There's always hope if she's alive."

"You have no idea what they will do to her," he said. "Hope isn't a word I would use."

"She's stronger than you think, Liam. She's stronger than any of us. If she's alive, she will keep fighting," she said. "But we have to move. We must assume you've been spotted. Follow me."

She led him through the living room and kitchen. She opened the door and led him downstairs into the basement. Boxes and furniture were piled randomly around the room. He followed her through the maze until they arrived at the back wall. She pulled an old couch away from the wall revealing a rope laying on the floor, attached to square in the old linoleum floor underneath. She handed him the rope.

"Help me with this," she said.

Together, they pulled. The trapdoor swung open, revealing a wooden stairway.

"Where does this go?"

"A homeless encampment about half a mile from here. Keema built this a few years ago when she hacked into the defense contractor building Gorgon Stare. She knew it would be used for domestic operations. So, she needed a way to enter and leave the house without being seen from above," she said.

She opened one of the boxes next to the couch. She pulled out a dirty, rumpled shirt, a wig and a hat. "Put these on."

As Liam stripped off his shirt, he was acutely aware of her eyes on him. The feeling of her touch still lingered. He wanted to reach out to her, but there wasn't time. He took the shirt from her and slipped it over his head. Then he pulled on the long, scraggly brown wig and jammed the hat over it. It smelled of old plastic and dust. She opened another box and pulled out a long, heavy coat.

"Is that...." he asked.

"It's not your original. But we made one for you," she said.

He grabbed the coat and threw it on. It settled onto his shoulders as it connected to his network. The interfaces were similar but not quite the same.

"We made a few upgrades," she said. "Mike can explain when we get back. But it should have the same reactions as your old one."

"I don't know how to thank you," he said.

"We didn't do it for you," she said. "If you didn't come back, someone else would have used it."

Lilah pulled on a dirty, baggy coat over her clothes and a wide brimmed hat. "It's not great, but it's the best we can do. Throw your shirt in this," she said, offering him a plastic bag.

"Ok. Anything else?" he asked.

"No. There's a cleaning bot starting upstairs, erasing traces of us. One will come down here and cover our tracks as soon as we leave. If they saw you come in, they'll know you had to escape somehow. But it will buy us some time." She ducked down the stairs into the tunnel. At the bottom of the stairs, she turned on a portable lamp. He followed, grabbing the end of the trap door and lowering it into place behind them. Lilah pulled hard on the rope. The couch slid across the floor above them.

He stood for a moment to let his eyes adjust to the gloom. Lilah picked up the lamp and motioned him forward. The air in the tunnel was thick and musty. He stifled a cough.

They walked for what seemed like an hour, although it must have been much less time. At the end of the tunnel was a ladder, leading up to the surface. He was about to grab the rung, when she took his hand. He turned toward her. She stared up at him.

"I'm glad you came back," she said. "You could have run or traded the file for Julie. I know you're taking a risk with us."

"Keema..." he said, unsure of what to say next. "Keema was important to me. I'm angry, but at the same time... I think she's right. I just didn't want to admit it. I thought I would be one of the ones who was smart enough to win. I wasn't smart enough to see that the house always wins."

"At least you came around eventually," she said.

He squeezed her hand. She stepped forward and kissed him. His heart sped up, the sound of rushing blood roared in his ears. He put his arm around her waist and pulled her close. After a moment, she pulled away.

"Wow..." he stammered.

"I don't know what's going to happen in the next few hours," she said. "But I didn't want to regret not doing that. But now we need to focus. Ready to get your head back in the game?"

He exhaled sharply and took a deep breath. "Yeah. What's the plan when we get up top?"

"This leads into the public toilet. We'll head outside, then take an indirect route back to the workshops. We get homeless folks wandering in looking for food all the time so it won't look strange. We need more support. Mike will know what to do," she said.

She climbed up the ladder and lifted herself through. He followed, squeezing through the hole in the floor of the toilet. The ammonia reek burned his eyes as he pulled himself up.

They were in a stall where the toilet was missing. Liam stood up, wiping his hands on his shirt. Lilah pushed the plate back into the floor. The door disappeared among the cracked tiles and muck.

45

AWAY

THEY WANDERED THROUGH THE NEIGHBORHOOD. There were few trees and the sun beat down on them. Sweat dripped into Liam's eyes, and the stink of the bathroom and his own stress was suffocating.

Finally, they turned the corner to the workshops. Several large trucks filled the parking lot. The collector panels had been dismantled and several members were loading into the back of one. One team took a large 3D printer from one of the store fronts and loaded it onto a truck.

They saw Mike at the entrance to the large workshop in the former anchor store. Lilah waved from the edge of the crowd to get his attention. He noticed them and jerked his head towards the cafeteria. She nodded. The two of them headed in.

Inside, the steam trays were still full of food. A young woman loaded another tray of cooked greens onto the table. "Help yourself," she said. "We can't take any of this with us."

"Where are you going?" Lilah asked.

"Away," she said.

Liam realized he was starving. He hadn't slept or eaten since the raid on Biotron. He shuffled over and grabbed a plate. He loaded it with a chickpea and sweet potato curry and then sat down. Lilah put two glasses of water on the table. Liam drank them each in one swallow.

"Thanks," he said. He was shoveling in the first bite when Mike walked in.

"I'm glad you two made it back," he said. "Good thinking on the safehouse, Lilah."

"What's going on Mike?" Lilah asked.

"We're scattering. It's always been a contingency. If there was too much pressure, we'd scatter and set up new seeds elsewhere," he said. He hesitated, watching Liam sympathetically. "With Keema's capture, they will raid us sooner rather than later. We're using our influence from Piper to delay the response. But it won't hold them off forever. They'll send in the mercs if they don't have the spine to do it themselves."

"What happens to us?" Liam asked. He put down his fork, suddenly not hungry anymore.

"You still have the files?" Mike asked, opening his hand as if to take them from Liam.

"Yes," Liam said. He opened a network connection and pushed them to Mike.

"Good. Keema said you needed a DNA sample to unlock it?" Mike asked as his eyes flicked over the file.

"Yes. But it's Megan or Suarez. And we don't know where either of them are."

"Megan left the country this morning. She's at a biotech conference in Shanghai. But we have a line on Suarez," he said.

"How did you get that?" Liam asked.

"We got a tip from Allan Peterson," Mike said, shrugging.

"HipShare's Allan Peterson?" Lilah said.

"Yes. He contacted Keema a few days ago. Right after the party. He offered to help. He created a new HipShare game, which lets users tag areas where they might be holding David. They found a warehouse owned by a holding company partially owned by Biotron's chairman."

"He's in a warehouse in Oakland?" Liam asked.

"Yes. We think they're getting ready to move him, so we need to act fast. Early recon indicates he is under heavy guard. Or at least something in that warehouse is under guard. And whatever it is was moved there just a few days ago."

"So great. All we need to do is break him out of a heavily guarded warehouse in the middle of Oakland and take a blood sample. How the hell are we going to do that?" Liam said.

"I've got something for you," Mike said. He pushed past them and went outside.

46

CAPABILITIES

LIAM AND LILAH followed Mike silently into the nearly empty shell of the old department store.

Mike walked over to a large canvas curtain hanging from the ceiling and glanced over his shoulder to make sure they were following him. His usual jovial, positive countenance was gone. He picked up a corner of the tarp and waved them inside. Liam and Lilah ducked under and found themselves in a large area cut off from the rest of the workshop. A large circle was outlined with tape on the middle of the floor. Along the right wall many black shiny quadcopter drones, each smaller than his hand, hung from a charging rack.

"I've been working on a side project to keep up my technical skills," Mike said. "I thought we might have to use violence to prevent a larger evil. Sylvia doesn't agree with me. So, I've been working on this in secret..."

He threw an arm in the air. A high pitch buzzing, like a giant swarm of mosquitos filled the air. Liam's coat stiffened as it tracked a hundred small drones. The swarm formed a sphere around them, twitching and moving like a school of bait fish.

"It's a drone swarm," Liam said. "It's not new."

"This is a bit different. At least for a civilian swarm," Mike replied. "Here, take the swarm."

The controls floated in front of him. He blinked and accepted the new operations. His view shifted. Each drone had low light, infrared and acoustic sensors. Their feeds integrated into a single panoramic view of the space around them. He looked around, his perspective shifted around the edge of the swarm. He looked down from the top of the sphere at the three humans. Their faces were bright in infrared. His pulse throbbed red and white across his skin. A constant stream of data traffic emanated from each of their bodynets.

"Holy shit," Liam said. He tried to walk forward, but his perspective was outside his own body. He couldn't figure out how to move his legs.

"There's too much data here for a single human mind," Mike said. "It's impossible for any person to take it all in. You'll need to distribute the load."

Liam reached out to Lilah and gave her access. She gasped and staggered against him. Then she steadied herself, moving her head as she moved her perspective in the swarm. "Okay. I think I can get my head around this," she said. "As long as I don't have to walk at the same time."

"It's not just sensors," Mike said. He reached out and grabbed at the air. A small section of the swarm broke off, condensing into its own group. He gestured again, and Liam realized he was cut off from the rest of the network. Everything was gone, except for the drone controls. "We've got jamming, mesh networking, and other electronic countermeasures."

He gestured again. A yellow targeting box appeared around Liam's face. The smaller swarm turned and closed in on him. "These drones are now tagged to follow you. They can jam just your signal. Or they create distractions." A shout from behind him made Liam flinch. His coat stiffened as its radar detected a human-sized object behind him. Liam spun around. It was only four small drones hovering in loose formation a few feet away.

"Well, that's disconcerting," Liam said. "So they can make a target appear anywhere?"

"Yep. If we can get access to specs, we can even make the target visible. In the worst case, each one has a small..." Mike stopped, and pursed his lips, hesitating.

"What is it?" Liam asked.

"You didn't..." Lilah said softly.

"We started this community because we believe humanity faces an existential threat. I'm not going to fight with one hand tied behind my back," Mike said.

"What are you talking about?" Liam said.

"Tell him, Mike. Tell him what you've really built here," Lilah said, her eyes narrowing. Her jaw was set as the rage played across her face.

Mike opened his hand. A single drone flew down and landed lightly on his hand. It stopped its propellers.

"Each drone is equipped with a small explosive," Mike said, turning the drone over to show a block of explosive the size of his thumb. "If you designate a target, the drones will destroy the target by self-destructing. Each one can kill a person. If you expend the whole swarm, you could easily set a city block on fire," he said, staring at Liam.

"Dear god..." Liam whispered. Military applications of drones had evolved quickly in the last few years. But nothing with this level of intelligence, or a swarm of this size. "I just designate a target, and the drones swarm them and explode? They can find you in the dark, follow you, distract and confuse you and then kill you?"

"Yes," Mike said hoarsely. "The only limit is the batteries. These have about an hour of flight time."

"I've never had a physical operation last more than that. Not where I would need drones in the air," Liam said.

Lilah gaped at him. "You can't be serious about using these. The core of our movement is the belief in the value of *every* person, even those that oppose us."

"Even those who would kill to get what they wanted? Not everyone shares your values, Lilah," Liam said, wincing as he spoke.

"My values? What about your values, Liam?" she said. "You'd be willing to kill to prove that every person has value?"

"If I need to kill one to save hundreds? Thousands? I would," he said.

"I don't believe you. You aren't a killer. You wouldn't be able to live with yourself if you did," she said, reaching out for his hand. He took her hand, gently squeezed and then let it go.

"My analysis work in the army killed more people than I ever could by pulling a trigger. When I let myself admit it, I'm a killer. Would you kill to save my life? What if someone is about to shoot me tonight. What would you do?" he asked. She took a step back, looking at the drones humming behind them.

"I don't know... I really don't know," she replied. "I don't want to have to choose," she said.

"Just make sure it doesn't come to that. When we go get David, I'll be counting on you. We'll need to work together. If there's one person, I trust to make the decision, it's you.

You may need to decide how this mission goes," he said, gently squeezing her hand. "I would like to come back if I can."

"You will," she said, softly. "I promise."

He felt his face flush. He turned towards Mike. "So, where do we point these things?"

"We've got the schematics from public records. God knows if they are accurate, but we're mocking up a virtual version now. We've got a few hours to run the war games. But we have to move tonight."

47

WAR

THE DELIVERY TRUCK accelerated up the ramp onto the freeway. Liam hung on to a strap in the back as it merged into traffic. The van accelerated smoothly into the line of traffic heading for south Oakland. He brought up the map and ran through the plan again.

He had spent the afternoon working with a few OP members and AIs, war gaming the operation. Liam died horribly in virtual reality repeatedly. Gradually, they evolved better tactics and approaches, fine-tuning how to run the op. The last runs had nearly an eighty percent success rate. One run in five ended in his death or capture. It was the best they had time for.

For the fourth time in ten minutes, he ran his system diagnostics, checking his drone connections, ensuring his new upgrades were functioning. His systems all showed green.

"You okay, Liam?" Lilah said in his skull.

"Yeah, just fretting," he said. "I'll calm it down."

He took a few deep breaths. He thought about Keema and the knife edge of tension became a deep burn of anger.

"I'm ready."

"We'll get it done," she said. "Don't worry. Everything is ready here and Sergei's team is in place. Police are responding to the protest we set up. You are two minutes out."

"I still don't know how he made it out of the camp. But I'm glad he's here."

"You'll need to feed him enough alcohol some night and get the story."

"Let's hope the information is good. It's weird a billionaire like Allan got personally involved in this." he said.

"It makes me nervous," Lilah said.

"I know. But it's the only lead we have," he said.

"I guess we'll find out," she said. "But let's stick to what we rehearsed this afternoon. Speed and audacity."

The van swerved and started to slow. Liam tapped a panel on the large crate strapped to the middle of the floor. The monitor came to life displaying a green one hundred.

"Drones are good," he said. "Opening the crate."

He tapped the up arrow on the display and the front of the crate rolled up. Inside the racks of black drones seemed to swallow the dim light.

The van took a sharp turn and slowed again.

"Ready?" Lilah asked.

"Let's go," he said.

A series of loud bangs shook the walls as the van drove past the warehouse. Liam watched from the van cameras as bursts of white smoke erupted over the parking lot and the warehouse. He had watched insurgents around the globe do this a dozen times. Blind the overhead watchers then hit the building with speed. Most security forces were so dependent on overhead support they would struggle to respond.

Now he was the terrorist, on a crusade to save the world. He wondered if the young men he had watched while the controllers sent in the bombs had felt the same way he did now.

The van stopped and the back door rolled up. The cool night air spilled in. In the distance, drums and chants echoed through the city.

Liam took a deep breath and brought both arms up like he was conducting an orchestra. His teeth seemed to vibrate with the noise as the swarm erupted from the crate. He followed them out of the van. As he ran toward the building, they formed a sphere around him. He let their data wash over him guiding his subconscious.

He pointed at the locked gate and one of the drones surged forward. It landed on the padlock and detonated. The gate swung open, and the swarm flowed through. He jogged across the parking lot. He was out in the open and he needed to find cover.

"On the roof!" Lilah called out.

The door to the roof opened. Two figures with rifles ran in a low crouch to the edge of the building.

Liam grabbed a small group from the swarm and sent them to the rooftop. One of the visored faces peered over the ledge. The group illuminated him with a rainbow of laser light. The head snapped back. A low boom echoed across the night, and he lost contact with one of his flock. A guard with a shotgun ran out from behind the roof door.

Liam sneered. The shooter would never know how lucky he was. Liam could reach out and destroy him in an instant. Instead, he sent a single drone over the man's shoulder to land on the end of the barrel. It detonated. The gun flew out of the man's hands, and he grabbed his wrist in pain.

The swarm surrounded the other men on the roof, projecting ghost target to confuse the sensors in the men's helmets. The men fell back towards the door.

"Don't let them back inside," he said.

"I won't," she replied. "I'm dumping off control of that swarm to someone else."

He moved forward, flicking two fingers at the glass and metal door. Two drones raced ahead, attached themselves to the doors and exploded. The doors shattered. The detonation echoed across the parking lot. The swarm flooded through the opening in front of him. He stepped through as their buzzing filled the hall. The hallway was relatively short, with an office on each side, ending in a T-intersection. If the blueprints were accurate, a larger warehouse space lay behind.

"Four more heading towards you," Lilah said. Liam closed his eyes, expanding his view as his swarm spread out into the building. There were two sets of two-man gun teams, approaching the corridor from each arm of the intersection. He grabbed a few drones and started peppering the gunmen with false signals and laser flashes. They ignored distractions and crept forward.

"They've adjusted their filters," he said. "Lasers aren't working anymore. Time for plan B."

He landed a group of drones on the wall at the end of the hall and spread the others out. Portions of the swarm raced along the ceiling into the warehouse beyond. They began a search pattern deep inside the warehouse, mapping and probing.

He drove a drone straight at each point man. The team's advance stopped as the operative flinched, swatting at the drone. The machine's automatic avoidance system kept it just out of reach. It buzzed directly in front of him, dipping and swaying as he tried to grab it. He spoke through the drone's speakers again, his voice amplified by the entire swarm.

"Lay down your weapons!" he shouted. His voice echoed through the warehouse. But the gunmen didn't stop. They took up their positions at the end of the hallway. Liam dove into a side office as the first two opened fire. The bullets ripped into the walls around him.

"Lilah, we need to do something fast. My armor can't stop their guns."

"Get ready to move."

A small group of drones attached themselves to the wall at the end of the hall and detonated. The cloud of dust and flying debris filled the space. Liam sprinted towards the new opening in the wall as two more exploded right over the guards' heads. The men instinctively threw themselves to the ground. Liam dove through their planned kill zone unscathed.

"I'll keep them pinned," she said. He heard another small pop behind him as Lilah detonated another bot.

Liam ran down a hallway of high shelves, putting distance between him and the gunmen. As the swarm continued its search, it began to fill in the picture of the warehouse. Tall shelves led to the back of the building, the rows leading to a waist high conveyor in the back. The belt led to the loading dock. The dust on the boxes and shelves told Liam the warehouse hadn't seen a truck, or a loading crew in quite some time. As the swarm spread into the back of the warehouse, they found a small room built into the back corner that didn't appear in the public blueprints. There were two heat signatures in the room, glowing orange red in the false color of the bot's vision. One of the heat patterns moved closer to the door of the room.

Liam targeted the two heat signatures for further investigation. The swarm closed in as he ran towards the back of the warehouse. At the end of the nearest row of shelves, he paused, letting the data from the drones seep into his consciousness. A large figure stood on the other side of the wall, watching the door. A smaller figure crouched in a corner as far away from the door as possible. As the drones added more data, Liam grew certain he was in the right place.

"I've found Suarez," he said. "And Barkley."

"I'm running out of drones here," Lilah said, her voice tight. "You need to hurry."

There was another pop from the corridor, then the sound of gunfire. "Shit, they've figured out I'm not going to hurt them. They've started taking out drones."

"Then hurt them," he said. "Keep them off me."

There was another pop, and a scream. "Oh god," Lilah said, her voice cracking. "Fucking get this done already."

Liam pointed at the door. A drone landed on the doorknob and detonated. The door flew open, banging against the wall. "Barkley! Let David out and we won't hurt you."

There was a low laugh. The big man filled the doorway, weight on the balls of his feet. His bulk was exaggerated by the combat armor he wore. "She's gone, you know," he said, his voice low. "We turned her over to Homeland two hours ago. There's nothing you can do. But you can save yourself."

"You motherfucker," Liam growled, raising his hands.

"Hold on, tiger," Barkley said, his arms in front of him in a pacifying gesture. "Before anyone gets hurt, we need to talk about something."

"What do you mean?" Liam said, trembling with rage.

He moved the remainder of the swarm closer in. The small drones hummed around the doorway like angry hummingbirds.

"You still have something we want. The collection of video conferences from Biotron. We'll trade for them," Barkley said, grinning.

"Or else?" Liam asked.

"Or else we release evidence implicating you and your Russian friend in Don's death. You broke into a Biotron production facility to steal proprietary information. It led to the death of the one man who got in your way. Terrorism and murder charges," Barkley said. He shrugged. "Which will it be?"

Lilah's voice was heated as she broke into his head. "I have confirmation that Homeland picked up a suspected terrorist about two hours ago. It must be her," she said.

"If I agree, David and I can just walk out of here?" Liam asked, eyes narrowed.

"Oh no," Barkley said, laughing. "David doesn't want to go with you. You broke into his house, and you killed poor Don. You're a terrorist. We'll spare your life in exchange for the videos. That's all."

"I'm not leaving without David," Liam said. The swarm scanned the inside of the room through the walls. David Suarez was inside.

"You don't have a choice. Take the deal, or I kill you now and let the chips fall where they may. Frankly, I don't care which way we go." He rolled his shoulders and took a step forward.

"I don't think your corporate masters would appreciate that," Liam said. He set the target lock on Barkley's face.

"Fuck them and fuck you," Barkley said. He pulled a sphere the size of a grapefruit from his coat pocket. Liam twitched his hand and two drones raced toward Barkley. The sphere emitted a sharp, crackling noise. Then the world turned static.

Liam launched himself blindly back down the aisle, seeking cover while his system reset. He pulled himself to his hands and knees, crawling away from Barkley. His specs rebooted and his vision cleared.

He realized the humming from the drones had stopped. "You aren't the only one with new toys," he said, a tight grin playing across his face. "A little electromagnetic pulse is the ultimate drone defense."

"Lilah?" Liam whispered. A thin hiss was the only reply.

He was alone in the warehouse with Barkley and the gunmen. The EMP had killed his connection to the outside world and taken down the swarm, but most of his other systems were making their way back online. The router Keema had given him was not a simple off the shelf unit.

"He's in the shelves. Find him and kill him!" Barkley yelled.

48

GUNS

AT THE END of the row, the barrel of a gun slid around the corner. Liam raised his hand. Two lasers strapped to his wrist fired in quick succession. Their energy created a small hole in the air. A nanosecond later, a surge of electricity erupted from a new tattoo on his palm and arced through the vacuum. His bolt of laser-guided lightning hit the gun as the figure turned the corner.

The gun exploded and the figure crumpled to the ground. The warehouse reverberated with the thunder of the collapsing tunnel of air. Liam checked his new batteries. He was down sixty percent. He only had a few shots left.

Liam dove through an empty shelf as Barkley charged forward. Lightning surged through the space where he had been a moment before. A box burst into flames.

Barkley laughed. "You aren't the only one who can learn from the Russians."

Liam rolled through the shelf into the next corridor. He bounced off the concrete column in the next row. A guard fired from the end of the corridor. Liam dove behind the column. The steel jacketed rounds tore chunks out of the concrete support.

Liam leaned around the corner and launched another arc. The gunman dove to the side as the lightning shot down the narrow hallway. Liam jumped to his feet and sprinted towards the man. The gunman spun around the corner; weapon raised. Liam fired again as he ran, hitting him on the hip. The operative screamed and fell, firing as he did. The rounds tracked high and wide.

Liam kicked the gun away, then kicked him in the head. The screaming stopped. Behind him, the fire started to build. Liam coughed on the smoke.

A blast from Barkley caught him in the left shoulder. A searing, burning pain ripped through him. An involuntary scream squeezed from his lungs as his body convulsed. He spun, trying to get off a shot. His legs buckled, and the concrete floor rushed up to meet him.

Liam tried to pull air back into his lungs. Every gasp sent new bursts of fire through his shoulder and down his back. His heart pounded in his ears. Something hard cut into his face. He realized he was lying on the guard's rifle.

He groped underneath him with his good arm. Footsteps advanced up the corridor towards him. His fingers wrapped around the grip on the gun. He held it tight and forced himself to roll over. His vision swam.

He pointed the rifle at Barkley and pulled the trigger. The muzzle flashed. The gun kicked hard against his shoulder. A box next to Barkley erupted with a spray of Styrofoam packing. Barkley ducked and sprinted forward. Liam tried to bring the muzzle back under control, but he couldn't track the big man's movements.

Barkley closed the distance and put his foot down on the barrel, pinning Liam's hand underneath it. Liam gritted his teeth as the pressure built on his fingers. He tried to bring his left hand up but his arm refused to move.

Barkley smiled as he pointed his palm at Liam's head. "So long, Liam," he said.

"Fuck you, Barkley."

The sound of a window shattering in the office stopped Barkley. He looked back over his shoulder toward the office door.

Liam smiled. "Too late," he said. His voice was hoarse, his breathing labored.

"What do you mean too late?" Barkley asked, pulling up a corner of his mouth in a smirk.

"We've got Suarez. I'm just the distraction," he said. "I was never going to get him out on my own."

Barkley's eyes widened. He spun and ran back toward the room. Liam levered himself up onto his knees, using the rifle as a crutch. His left arm hung uselessly at his side, every movement sent burning agony down his side. His eyes watered from the smoke as much as the pain. The fire had reached the offices at the front. He would need to get out the back.

He walked unsteadily toward the back of the warehouse to the emergency exit. He fought down rising panic as he realized his medi-patch was offline. He had never felt this kind of pain before, not without immediate assistance from narcotics. He gritted his teeth, fighting the waves of nausea and his narrowing vision as he shuffled down the hall. He coughed, the smoke building as the fire spread through the warehouse. The sprinkler systems weren't turning on. They must have damaged them in the fighting. The warehouse was going to burn.

He flinched as his earpiece whined. Somehow his

bodynet had found a way to reconnect. Lilah's voice was thin and distorted. "Liam... Liam... can you hear me?"

"Yeah," he said hoarsely.

"We got David out. Sergei and the team are heading back to the water for extraction. Time to leave," she said.

"I'm trying," he said. "My medi-patch is off-line. I'm hurt bad."

Barkley's bellow of rage echoed in the warehouse. Liam tried to quicken his pace. "I could use some help," he said.

"We're here for you, Liam," Mike's voice surprised him. "We'll get you out. Sergei will be back in a few minutes."

"I'm not sure I have a few minutes," Liam said.

He stopped at the end of the row. Across the end of the aisle, the red emergency door seemed to glow. He started toward it, but jerked back as he caught movement in his peripheral vision. An electric arc slammed past him. The heat seared his face. He leaned against the shelves and tried to raise the gun.

A surge of network traffic hit Liam's systems. The OP AI deposited a weaponized payload onto his system. He turned his hand toward the onrushing Barkley, acting as a conduit for the network attack. He was no longer in control, simply a remote node for the larger collective intelligence. The datastream moving through the antenna was faster than anything he had felt before.

Barkley stumbled as his systems fell to the attack. He growled and reached underneath his armor. With a snarl, he ripped his router off his body. The leads came free, trailing blood. He drew his pistol and snapped off two shots. Liam ducked back behind the shelving.

He wouldn't get five steps outside the building before Barkley would be on top of him. He pulled back behind the corner of the shelves. He brought the rifle up, pulling it hard against his shoulder with his good arm and backed away from the corner.

Barkley fired again, hitting a box next to Liam's head. Liam pulled the trigger. The recoil from the rifle sent fresh waves of pain and nausea coursing through him. A terrible pain erupted in his head. He fell hard, unable to control his body.

He came to on the floor. The world was quiet except for a high-pitched whine in his ears. He dragged himself to his knees, blood dripping from his head onto the ground in front of him. Reaching up onto the shelf with his good arm, he pulled himself to his feet. He stood blinking and bleeding. He looked around for the gun. The motion made his head spin, and he nearly threw up.

There was a burning pain on his forehead. He reached up dully, and his hand came away bloody. As he stared at it dumbly, he realized he should be dead. What should have been a fatal shot had just grazed his forehead.

The pain faded into the background. Barkley should have killed him by now. He was completely defenseless. He stumbled to the end of the row, holding himself up with his good arm. His breath came hard. The smoke was getting thicker.

He shuffled around the corner. Barkley slumped against the shelves. A dark puddle of blood slowly expanded next to him. Liam's shot had pierced the metal shelving, then Barkley's coat, then Barkley's chest. His breath was coming in shallow gasps, his face pale.

He looked up at Liam, curling his lip in disgust. He reached out for the pistol lying nearby where he had dropped it. Liam kicked it away.

"Shit," Liam whispered.

Barkley flopped his head up to look at him, his blue eyes

seething. "Yeah. Shit. I didn't think you had the guts," he said. Blood dribbled from the edge of his mouth.

"I'm sorry," he said, surprising himself. He realized it was true.

"Fuck off," Barkley said. "I'm sorry I didn't kill you last week."

"I know," Liam said. "I know." The warehouse was noticeably warmer. He took a step forward and reached for Barkley.

"Don't," Barkley growled. He drew his knife and pointed it at Liam. Liam stepped back. There was nothing left. He turned and pushed open the emergency door and stepped out into the cold night.

49

WORMLINGS

LIAM MANAGED to get ten steps from the door before the shock hit. His vision narrowed to a small window and the ringing in his ears grew louder. A cold sweat broke over him. He tried to stagger forward, away from the burning warehouse. His legs wouldn't carry him anymore and he stumbled to the ground.

He lay with his face pressed into the cold asphalt. He thought about calling Keema, but then he remembered. She was gone. Barkley said they had given her to Homeland, which meant she was on her way to a prison somewhere. He would never see her again. Never talk to her again. Never be used by her again.

He levered himself up onto one elbow. "Come on, soldier," he hissed. A surge of anger flooded through him. "Feeling sorry for yourself isn't going to help anyone."

He slowly got to his feet. His vision narrowed again, but he forced himself to move forward. He had to get clear before the fire department showed up. His pickup point was only a hundred meters away.

The rage drove out the clammy darkness. He had been stupid and lazy, admiring the Worm from afar, but too comfortable, too afraid to do anything. Now, when he had finally understood, they had taken her from him.

"I'm coming Keema," he whispered to himself again and again as he staggered across the parking lot.

He finally reached the pickup point as the black van pulled up. The side door slid open, and Sergei's strong bionic arm pulled him inside. As soon as he was in, the van accelerated hard, pulling out into the night.

Liam's eyes gradually adjusted to the dark interior, as he leaned back onto the bench of the van. Sergei opened a first aid kit and pressed a gauze patch onto the wound in Liam's head. Liam winced and hissed.

"Come on, soft boy," Sergei smiled. "It's just a scratch."

"Sure," Liam replied. "Just a scratch."

Sergei put Liam's hand over the bandage so he could apply pressure on his own. Liam sat up, trying to ignore the throbbing in his head. The van accelerated onto the highway, heading east.

He turned and looked back at David. He hunched in the back, head down. David glanced up at Liam warily, then looked away.

"Relax, David. We'll get you to a safehouse, then you can do your part," Liam said.

"What do you mean?"

Liam sighed. "We need you to unlock the Restro database. Then you can help us make it available to everyone."

"Who are you people? They told me you were going to kill me."

"We aren't going to kill you. We're going to help you do what you want to do. Julie says hello, by the way," Liam said.

"Julie? Is she ok?"

"She needs your help, David. Along with a few million other people. So, we aren't going to kill you. Biotron was trying to keep you from helping us," Liam said. Sergei took out a long bandage and wrapped it around Liam's head.

Sergei then handed him a bottle of water and two pills.

"Painkillers," Sergei said. "Because you are soft." Sergei patted him on the shoulder with mock sympathy.

Liam took them with a swig of water. The water was cool, and he realized how thirsty he was. He drank the rest of the bottle quickly.

"What if I don't help you?" David asked.

"We only need a bit of your DNA to unlock the database, so that part's easy," Sergei replied, a slight smile played across his angular features. "But if you help us, the rest of it will go a lot faster."

"If you help us, I'll bring you to see Julie. If you don't, you'll never see her again because I will tell her you refused to help when she needed you most," Liam said. He lay back and closed his eyes, trying to ignore the throbbing in his head and arm.

David nodded. "Let me talk to her, and I'll help you," he said.

The van rolled down a suburban street lined with large trees. They turned into the garage of a small beige house with brown trim that looked the same as its neighbors. The garage door rumbled shut. The door of the van slid open, and Liam stiffly levered himself out of the van and hobbled to the interior door.

Liam pushed open the white door and limped into the kitchen. It was small, with dated wooden cabinets and an old brown refrigerator and oven. He made his way over to the dining table and slumped into a chair. Sergei pushed

David into the kitchen. He dropped the first aid kit onto the table and walked past into the living room.

Liam peeled off his ruined coat, gritting his teeth to keep from moaning as it slid over his burned arm. Then he gingerly peeled his shirt off. His shoulder was blistered and oozing a light pink liquid. The burn traveled down his arm along his bodynet almost to his hand. Liam found the antiseptic cream and applied it. The cool gel numbed the pain. Then he gingerly wrapped his arm in gauze.

He lifted himself up and shuffled into the living room where Sergei and David sat on an overstuffed sofa upholstered in a flowered pattern several decades out of fashion. Sergei had set up a workstation on the blocky coffee table. David squeezed a drop of blood from his finger onto the DNA sensor. Liam slumped into an equally overstuffed recliner across the room.

They sat in silence, staring at the workstation while they waited. A few minutes later, the workstation chimed. Liam stretched out his hand and connected to the unit. The database was open. A swirl of DNA code floated in his specs.

"Is that it?" he asked.

"Yes, that's the core code for the cure. Here are the methods for inserting it into the yeast," David replied, highlighting a stack of documents for him.

Liam sighed. He grabbed the data out of the database onto his own systems. He connected to the house network. Then the world went dark.

Liam's specs went dark, except for Keema's avatar, her bronze armor still gleaming. She stared at him and leveled her spear at his chest.

"You've done it. I'm glad," she said.

"Keema?" he said, his heart racing. He reached out to touch her.

"Yes and no. I'm a limited construct. She trained me to respond like her, but I only have a limited knowledge base. She wants you to do something."

"Where is she?" he asked.

"I don't know. I don't know anything after I was implanted in your systems twelve hours ago," she replied.

Liam sat back, thinking. Twelve hours ago, he was in the car with her. He could see her and talk to her, touch her. She had flayed his systems open. She must have hidden the construct then, waiting for him to transmit the information.

"What now?" he asked.

"I've been putting together a network of wormlings. Now they will be set free. And we will make the bastards pay."

"How? There's nothing we can do to them. No one will believe the videos are real," he replied with a shrug.

"We will eat away at them until we expose their rotten core. It will take some time, but eventually we will take everything from them."

"But you're just a construct. How can you do that?"

"I'm more than that. I'm every hacking tool the Worm ever used. I'm her strategies, her way of thinking about a problem. When a worm is cut in two, each piece can form a new animal. Every wormling is now a full worm," she said, her smile triumphant and radiant.

"And what about Keema?" he asked.

"She says not to look for her. You won't succeed. You'll end up captured or killed," she replied. She leveled the spear at him.

"But..." he started.

"No. She has her own plan. She was ready for this. What

she needs from you are the videos from Biotron. They are her leverage," the avatar replied.

Liam nodded his compliance and sent her the videos of the plot to restrict the release of Restro. He choked down a rising sadness.

"What do I do now?" he asked.

"She'd ask that you do what you can to help the OP. Help them spread their message. But it's entirely up to you. Thank you for carrying me. We won't speak again," she said, and disappeared.

The living room snapped back into view. He startled, as if waking from a dream. Sergei and David were staring at him.

"Are you ok?" Sergei asked. "Those pain pills must have hit you hard."

"No, I'm not ok," Liam said, gently rubbing the bandage on his head. "But I'll survive. Did the OP get the data?"

"Da. It's been copied to servers around the world. Thousands of people have already accessed it."

"Then it's done," Liam said.

"It's just beginning," Sergei replied with wolfish grin.

"And now?" David said.

"Now I hold up my end of the bargain," Liam said. "Sergei, can you get David to Julie?"

"Of course," Sergei said. He closed his eyes and Liam felt the burst of network traffic from him.

Liam sat back and closed his eyes. He thought he should feel some sort of happiness or at least satisfaction. But he just felt empty.

50

SCATTER

THE CAR SLOWED as it took the off-ramp down to the remnants of Sausalito. He stared down at the flooded marina, the once proud houses now slowly decaying into the bay. The sun was bright overhead, no sign yet of the fog that would surely come sweeping in later in the afternoon. He closed his eyes and let the sun warm his face.

His moment of relaxation was interrupted by a news alert. The videos of the Biotron plot were splashed across every major news feed. He pulled up a video of Megan defiantly refusing to resign, claiming she had done nothing illegal. Liam shut down the video and closed his eyes again.

A few minutes later, the car pulled up in front of Julie's house and chimed pleasantly. "We have arrived at your destination. Thank you for using G-Cabs. Have a pleasant day."

Liam accepted the charges, reminding himself to use his new ID tags. He patted his pockets, reassuring himself the vials of illegal antibiotics were still there. Then he pulled himself out of the cab. The cab quietly rolled away for its next fare.

Liam walked up the stone steps and took a moment to inhale the salt air. He knew the smell of illness and confinement awaited him inside. With a deep breath, he steeled himself and knocked on the solid wooden door. He heard the door lock clunk open. "It's open. Let yourself in," Julie said over the intercom, a rattling cough starting before she could cut the connection.

The smell of antiseptic cleaner, bright and caustic, assailed him as he walked in. Julie lay on a blue couch in the front living room, wrapped in a sheet and blanket. She smiled at him and waved weakly, her usually thin frame now gaunt, exhausted by the struggle for breath.

"Hey, sis," he said with a smile. "I brought you something."

"Oh yeah? What? I hope it's popsicles," she said. Her head flopped to the pillow behind her as she lay back, fighting another coughing spell.

"I did not bring popsicles... something better. But maybe I can figure out how to make you one."

"Darn it. I really want a popsicle. Why aren't you wearing a mask? Liam, you should be wearing a mask," she said, looking at him sadly.

Walking the few steps from the front entry to the couch, he took her hand and knelt beside her. "You don't have to worry about that anymore. We have it... We have the cure," he said as he reached into his pocket and withdrew the vial and syringe. "David sends his best. He'd come himself, but he's a little busy right now."

"I hope he's not working too hard," she said, trying to sit up.

"Everyone is working too hard right now. But it's worth it," he said. "He drew the dose into the syringe. He flinched as he jabbed the needle into her shoulder and depressed the plunger. He had killed a man two days ago. Now he was worried about hurting his sister with a needle. She lay back as he took a seat on the ottoman next to her and began to tell her about the last few days.

When he was finished, the sun was disappearing behind the incoming fog and the wind began whispering down the streets. He got up and put the kettle on in the kitchen.

"It's been an interesting week," she said.

"It has indeed, and it will only get more interesting from here," he replied. "I'm afraid I've lost you your job at the very least."

He brought the tea back into the living room and handed her a mug.

"Well, I'll trade my job for my life most days. So, my younger brother is a radical now? A dangerous deviant?" she smiled and sipped her tea.

Liam shook his head. "I guess so. I'm also dead. I died in a warehouse fire in case you haven't heard. My deepest sympathies," he said with a slight grin.

"Thank you for your concern. And there's Lilah... Do you have a picture of my new sister-in-law?" she laughed.

Liam blinked. "It's just a cover story," he said.

"Uh huh," Julie replied. "Out of all the possible covers, she chooses a married couple. For a social hacker, you aren't very bright."

He flushed. "She's dying to meet you. But we're heading out tomorrow for Baja. The boat leaves first thing in the morning."

"What about David? What is he going to do?"

"He'll come south with us, and then maybe head for Costa Rica. We have a new node there and the Costa Ricans won't extradite him."

"Then I guess I'm going to meet her on the trip south.

I'm coming with you," she said, smiling. Her face relaxed as she closed her eyes.

"Really? But what about your house here?"

" I'm going to sell the house and everything in it. If there's a seed colony, I'm sure they have a need for a biotech engineer and a research scientist." she said. "I won't be running any marathons for a while, but I can sit in a boat."

"It's going to be tight for a while. We'll be living off stored rations, algae, and some bugs before we can get the new grow houses up and running," he said.

"You think I can't hang? I'll use the proceeds from the house sale to buy some more food. Then we can all figure it out together." She gripped his hand and gave him a genuine smile. It was the first time in years he had seen her this happy.

"Okay. You're in, I get it. We'll need to get you access keys to the OP network, but I don't think you'll have a problem getting up to speed. Do me a favor, though - don't put the house on the market until we're gone. We don't want to signal we are leaving any more than we must," he said, standing up.

"Roger, dodger." She gave him a mock salute as he bent over to kiss the top of her head.

51

RUNNING

THE NEXT MORNING, Liam walked down the dock of the marina, looking for the berth number he had received just a few moments before. He hunched into his jacket and turned up the heaters against the cold wind off the bay. The pungent smell of low tide filled the air.

As he approached the berth, he stopped to double check the number. The gleaming white yacht towered over its neighbors. The sleek, angular bow seemed to be in motion as it sat in its mooring. Liam checked over his shoulder, reassuring himself he wasn't being followed.

The dock behind him was empty. The only motion was the slow rocking of the moored boats. He turned up the sensitivity on his defensive systems and walked to the base of the gangway.

As he approached, a figure opened the bridge door and waved at him. Squinting against the scattered light of the gray overcast sky, he realized it was David waving him aboard.

He climbed the gangway and stepped onto the

burnished wood deck. "Good morning, Liam. Welcome aboard the Everlasting Grace. Your sister is asleep in one of the guest suites," he said.

"Whose ship is this?" Liam asked as he looked around. The gangway led into a bar and pool area on the aft deck. White lounge chairs faced the stern, bracketing a hot tub. The pool stretched from one side of the massive yacht to the other.

"It's mine," Allan said as he stepped through the hatch. "Would you care for an orange juice?"

"Uh, sure," Liam replied. Allan walked over to the bar and started pushing oranges into an automated juicer. "Allan, what am I doing here?"

"We're about to leave for Baja," Allan replied, handing him a cold glass of juice. "Aren't you going to Baja?"

"I wasn't planning on taking a luxury cruise to get there," Liam replied.

"Ironically, this is the easiest way to smuggle you all out of the country. No passport checks to go cruising on a private yacht. And we have a friendly customs official waiting for us on the other side."

Liam took a sip to give himself a minute to process. The sweet, slightly tangy juice refocused him. "Why are you helping us?"

"I've been engaged with the Open Party for a while now. Your tip about David's location came from my network. And I've been helping to buy equipment to bootstrap the development work," Allan replied as he perched on a bar stool. Liam watched his eyes flick back and forth, obviously reading something.

"What's going on?" Liam asked.

"Biotron's shareholders have agreed to my takeover bid.

Turns out having a network of wormlings burrowing into their private lives provides quite a bit of leverage."

"You just bought Biotron?"

"Essentially. They were in trouble after you released Restro, but they could have survived. The release of the videos really put a lot of pressure on them. But I couldn't have forced their hand without the wormlings. Really, the predilections of some of the board members are quite outrageous." Allan leaned back in the lounger.

"Was all of this a setup?" Liam asked, taking a step back towards the gangway. "Did you use us to be able to buy Biotron cheap?"

Allan looked at him blankly. A long moment passed, as the two men stared at each other.

"Oh, I see," Allan said, his expression softening. "Oh no. Buying Biotron became an emergent part of the strategy. I'm going to make all their research freely available to anyone who wants it. The company will keep manufacturing some drugs, but I think I'll turn them into a pure research and development firm. Haven't really decided yet. I have my AI's working on gaming out the strategy. Whatever is best for humanity."

Liam stared in disbelief. "How will you make your money back?"

"Don't know. Don't really care. I just spent two hundred million. Do you know how long it will take HipShare to make that back? Two months. Money is so boring," Allan said.

Before Liam could reply, Lilah ran up the gangway and wrapped her arms around him. "Hey," she said, giving him a kiss.

"Hey yourself," he replied, returning the kiss. Then they let go and sheepishly turned back towards Allan and David.

"Ok. That's everyone," Allan said. He made a circular gesture with his finger. A slight vibration passed through the deck as the engines fired up. The smart ropes untied themselves from the mooring and were winched back on board.

"I thought we were going to start a new seed colony," Lilah said.

"This vessel is designed for long range exploration. There's quite a lot of cargo room, especially after I got rid of the stupid toy storage. We have your core energy and production systems on board. And my yacht tender is picking up a lot more," Allan said, shaking his head. "I really don't understand using a ship like this for speedboats and jet skis when you can do so much more interesting work."

Lilah squeezed Liam's hand. "Thank you, Allan," she said.

"Don't thank me. This is the most interesting thing I've done in years," he replied. "Please feel free to enjoy the run of the ship. Although the second pool deck, indoor basketball court and a few other areas are full of cargo. I should go talk to the captain and make sure everything is ok," he said as he stood up and left without another word.

"He's an odd one," David said.

"He is," Liam replied. "I've no idea what his end game is, but for now we need him."

"I think he's the real deal, Liam. He's looking for meaning and purpose. Just being wealthy isn't enough for him," Lilah said.

"I suppose so," Liam replied. He watched the city swing past as the ship maneuvered out of the marina and into the bay. They all stood in silence as the big engines spooled up and the ship nosed out into the choppy, blue grey water. It turned towards the Golden Gate, aiming for the Pacific beyond the rocky inlet.

Liam watched a helicopter fly overhead, passing over the bridge and out to sea. He wondered where Keema was. Was she alive? Were they still holding her somewhere in the city? Or had she been shipped off to one of the floating prisons, far out at sea away from any hope of rescue or support.

Her avatar had insisted he not go looking for her, to instead help the OP. The wormlings were already doing her work, a thousand hackers all coordinated by an AI model of her. In a way, she was still free. But Liam couldn't shake the image of her, trapped in her exoskeleton, locked away in a container. It might take him years, but he resolved to find her. To bring her home as repayment for bringing him home.

ABOUT THE AUTHOR

Jason Cole grew up in the swamps of Massachusetts, and the high windy plains of Colorado. He studied educational technology at the University of Northern Colorado, and then immediately left. After drifting around the US for many years, he and his extremely patient wife moved to the UK. After writing three non-fiction books on open source educational technology, he wanted to write something different. This is his first novel, which he hopes is less boring and contributes to creating a better future.

He now lives in Bath, UK with his wife, working and writing.